INSTANT GRATIFICATION

LAUREN BLAKELY

COPYRIGHT

ABOUT

I need a fake date. She needs my late-night expertise. Now, if we can just keep our hands off each other...

As the premier best-man-for hire in all of Manhattan, I promise discretion, so when I need a plus one for a couple of "I dos," I turn to my gorgeous, clever, witty best friend's sister. She's my good friend, too, and I lust after her completely. I mean, I TRUST her completely.

After all, just look how she's kept her lips sealed about the hot, multi-O night we spent together. Yes, just look at those sexy lips.

In any case, we only fell off the wagon once, and it was months ago. I'm sure we can make it through these weddings without banging each other in the limo.

Or can we?

BE A VIP READER

To be the first to find out when all of my upcoming books go live click here!

PRO TIP: Add lauren@laurenblakely.com to your contacts before signing up to make sure the emails go to your inbox!

Did you know this book is also available in audio and paperback on all major retailers? Go to my website for links!

PROLOGUE

When you've had to tell as many "how we got together" stories as I have, you get a fair idea of the range of things a man will do to impress a woman, from thoughtful to absurd to downright unbelievable.

For starters, *bro*, did you really read *Fifty Shades of Grey*?

But that's only number one on the menu of items guys will pick and choose from in an effort to elicit flutters from a new lady.

I know men who claim to love *Pride and Prejudice*. Even go so far as to say they've read the book. And maybe we do get that desperate to see what women see in Mr. Fucking Darcy other than an English accent. Which I have, by the way, but I still don't understand the deal with Colin Firth any more than the next bloke.

I've met fellows who swear they don't like football of any variety—American or proper—to reassure a lady she'll never be a widow to the footie. Or they'll turn off a match on the TV with so much drama you'd think they were giving up a kidney.

Or a man's résumé will become suspiciously plump with female-friendly hobbies. Show me a single man in a yoga class, and I'll show you a lad who's trying to score major points with the fairer sex.

The next thing he knows, he's shaving his chest, shaving his toes, and shaving his balls. Which must mean he's serious about her because that shit hurts.

When it comes to manscaping, I think a trim here or there can go a long way, but go too far and you'll look like a porpoise. And what woman wants to roll around in the sheets with Flipper?

But by far the worst case I ever saw was a guy who swore to his sweetheart that he loved Ed Sheeran's music. Even followed Ed's Twitter feed and read reviews so he could convincingly wax on about the ginger phenom. (The fella even planned to tell his bride that he wanted "Shape Of You" to be their wedding song. I put my foot down. Go with "Castle on the Hill." "Shape of You" is too obvious, and women can see through that lie.)

As happy as I am that it worked out for these gents, especially after they pay my invoice as a specialty wedding service provider, it seems like a lot of work to keep up with all that—retweets, nether-region mainte-nance, or the pointless hell of football abstinence.

I understand why men want to show off for women. Women are like sunshine and whiskey, lilies and diamonds. They're sex and desire and everything good in the universe. They're lovelier to gaze at than a priceless work of art. Hell, women are better than football, better than pints of ale, better than the Rolling Stones and occasionally even the Beatles, though I will deny that blasphemy even under torture.

Women make a man's merry-go-round keep turning, make life worth living. And they deserve to be annoyed if a guy who swore he hated football has a drawer full of Manchester United souvenirs.

There's a fine line between putting your best foot forward and shooting yourself in it, and it's my job to help the lead-footed of the world win women without losing them.

Damn shame, then, that the one woman I'd really like to impress is off-limits.

With good reason. With a long list of good reasons, in fact.

So off-limits is how she'll have to stay, even when I learn she desperately needs my specialized knowledge to impress a new investor.

But wouldn't you know—I need something from her too.

Badly.

That can only mean it's time to impress the hell out of *myself* by resisting every single temptation to step out of the friend zone with her.

1

Her legs wrap around my waist, firm and tight. Her heels make a vise grip, tugging me closer between her thighs.

It's the perfect position for countless naughty things. The possibilities are as vast as my filthy imagination is wide, and my imagination has won blue ribbons for its width.

Its depth too.

And its length.

Yes, it's an award-winning dirty zone between my ears.

But down here? In real life? The breath rushes from my lungs as she squeezes.

Holy hell.

I. Can't. Move.

I can barely breathe.

Truly Goodman has me pinned on the mat. She's ferocious and strong, and there's literally nothing I can do to escape her clutches.

"Nice work, Truly and Jason! That's how you neutralize a bigger, stronger opponent. With a back mount combined with a choke hold." The praise comes from the instructor.

Well, Truly's definitely neutralized any chance I'll be turned on in jujitsu class again, that's for sure. The instructor gives the go-ahead for my opponent to relinquish her hold on me, and I'm both immensely saddened that the brunette unlocks her legs from my waist and also incredibly grateful I'm not about to die in the middle of this demo of a powerful grappling move.

Truly breathes hard as she heads to the water fountain in the corner of the studio and takes a long, thirsty gulp.

Water, yes. That's a brilliant idea. I follow her to the oasis. "Have you registered those hands as lethal weapons, Truly? While you're at it, license those legs too."

She turns around, eyes me up and down, then wipes her hand across her mouth. "And yet you made it out alive. No worse for the wear."

I glance down at my frame, considering her assessment. "We can have a go again if you're interested in trying to cut off all the circulation in my body. I think you achieved a ninety percent shutdown, so why not go for broke?"

She pats my chest. "I'm always happy to take you down in class if you think your pride can take it. How much ego did that cut off?"

Scoffing, I answer, "Nothing I can't spare, given its size."

"Glad to see you're not suffering from ego shrink-age." She laughs, then nudges my elbow. "Thanks for being such a good sport. I'm going to take a quick shower since I need to head to work for a meeting. Are you going that way?"

I weigh whether to leave now, or loiter a bit and join her on her walk to Gin Joint.

Who am I kidding? Those scales will always have a Truly-shaped thumb on them. "Is fifteen minutes good for you?"

"Make it ten."

True to form, she's ready quickly, looking fresh-faced and sexy as sin in a short, painted-on skirt and a black tank top. God, I fucking love summer. It's the greatest season ever invented by man. I mean God. God invented summer, obviously. Man just invented the clothes that go with it.

"So, we've established you can take any man, woman, or three-headed beast down in a dark alley," I say once we leave the studio.

"That was my goal when I started training a few years ago. But don't sell me short. Four-headed beasts are now on my takedown list too."

"How about grizzly bears? Or, say, an anaconda?"

"Been there, done that. But listen." We stop at a light, and she glances at me then takes a breath. Her tone turns more serious. "You don't go easy on me in class, do you?"

I scoff and shoot her a *you've got to be kidding* stare. "Wait. You think I was going easy on you?"

She holds up her palms. "Just making sure you're not

one of *those* guys who thinks he has to soften things for a woman."

"There's nothing *soft* about me." I take a beat. "As you well know."

She rolls her eyes. She does that to me a lot, but I won't say I don't deserve it. "That's not what I'm saying."

"But it's spot-on true. I'd never go easy just because you're a woman." I wiggle an eyebrow. "But let's talk more about how hard you want me to be. Would you like me, for instance, somewhat harder, much harder, or *oh my God, that's so hard* harder?"

"Oh yes, please. The latter."

With a straight face, I answer, "Done. Consider it done."

"And I'm glad you don't treat me any differently because I have girl parts. I want to be tough-as-nails in this martial art."

I rub my ear. "Sorry I didn't hear anything you said after 'girl parts.' Everything else sounded like *Take me home, Jason, and make me scream your name.* Did I get that right?"

"Sure. That's exactly what I said." She laughs as we turn the corner, heading down a tree-lined block in the heart of Chelsea. "You're relentless, aren't you?"

"Yes. Not a bit of relent when it comes to some things. And along those lines," I say, stroking my chin, "that position we tried in class—just wondering if it made you think of any other interesting positions."

"Hmm." She screws up the corner of her lips, as if considering. "Nope. Can't say it did."

"None at all? Wrapping your legs around me didn't trigger any memory?"

We reach Gin Joint, the speakeasy-style bar she owns, though to call it a bar would do it a disservice. It's an establishment with a full lounge, 1920s-style decor, and regular entertainment, including lounge singers. Her brother—my best friend—is one of those singers, and he helps draw crowds. Gin Joint has scored a place on more than one list of coolest theme bars in the city.

She stares at the sky, still bright even as the sun makes its trip toward the edge of the horizon. "I keep drawing a blank."

"Want me to give you more hints, or just spell it out for you? Things you said. I mean, things you screamed."

She stares at me for a beat. "We had an agreement. That all stays in the vault."

"But sometimes it's fun to revisit memories in the vault, isn't it?"

Laughing, she shakes her head. "Yes, but that's not the deal we made."

I know, but what can I say? I love the chase even if it'll never go anywhere, just for the sake of it. "So you do admit you enjoy taking a trip down dirty memory lane?"

"You do realize that can't happen again?" But a naughty glint crosses her pretty blue eyes. Ah, perhaps the memory is never far from the surface for her either.

I zip my lips, but then instantly unzip them. "I'm just saying." I drop my voice to a whisper. "Three times."

"*Jason.*"

I hold up my hands in surrender. "Fine, fine. Pretend you don't remember every detail in triplicate."

"I don't. I don't remember a single one."

"And I die yet again." I'm about to turn around when my mind snags on something she said earlier. "Who's your meeting with? A supplier?"

A grin seems to tug at her lips. "A restaurant and bar investor Charlotte hooked me up with. She's such a great bestie. Anyway, we're going to talk about expanding my brand. I pitched him on a new concept bar I want to start."

"You're going to be the queen of Manhattan nightlife. I'll say I knew you when."

"And you're the king of gentlemen," she says, a nod to the work I've done to establish myself as an expert on all the things a modern gentleman should know. "Are you writing a column tonight? Working on a new podcast?"

I look at my watch. "Actually, I'm meeting up with Nora, and I need to get going. She won't want to be kept waiting."

She stiffens, her hand freezing around the key in the lock. Her brow furrows as she turns to meet my gaze, her blue eyes inquisitive. "Nora?"

Do I detect a lovely note of jealousy in her voice? That may be one of the most glorious sounds I've ever heard coming from Truly Goodman's mouth.

"Who's Nora?" she asks before I can answer. "You've never mentioned a Nora."

She mentioned Nora's name three times. If that isn't a *third time's a charm* moment, I don't know what is. I decide to have fun with her. "She's my date to the wedding I'm working this coming weekend."

"Oh." It comes out heavily. "I thought you did those solo."

"Sometimes I do. Sometimes I don't." I drop a kiss to Truly's cheek, catching a faint whiff of her freshly scrubbed scent. I say goodbye and let her chew on the idea of me on a date.

Here's the thing: Truly has made it abundantly clear where we stand, and she's 100 percent right that we can't go there again—she's my best friend's sister, and she's also my very good friend.

Yet I can't help thinking about the other things she made abundantly clear one particular night earlier this year. Like how much she liked being underneath me, how much she liked being on top of me, and how much she liked me bending her over the bed.

I'm not going to say I haven't gotten her out of my mind, but I absolutely fucking haven't gotten her out of my mind. Trouble is, there are so many reasons this wouldn't work standing between us. Reasons that aren't going to change. Her reasons, and all of mine too.

So I flirt, and she hate-flirts back, a pretending-she-doesn't-like-it type of flirting. That's all we are, flirters and hate-flirters, and that's all we will ever be.

2

You know those movies where an Alec Baldwin or Willem Dafoe type shows up for five minutes at a pivotal moment? Blink and you'll miss him, but that actor can make or break the whole damn film.

I'm not saying a best man can make a best picture contender out of something no one should have joined together, but when it comes to the speech, if you're the best man, you'd better bring it like Willem fucking Dafoe. It's your moment to shine. Or rather, it's your moment to make the groom shine.

In a brewery in the heart of hipster Brooklyn on an evening in June, I raise a glass.

"Ladies and gentlemen, it is now time for the only five minutes of the wedding that the bride didn't plan."

The bride holds up one finger. "But I tried to. I swear, I tried so damn hard to write the speech for Gavin."

The groom jumps in, grumbling playfully. "She'd slip

me Post-its that I thought were dirty notes but were just suggestions for the toast."

I shoot a glance at the man of the hour. "I suppose now would be a bad time to tell you she did, in fact, write this? And it consists of all the yard work you're expected to do?"

"A honey-do list," someone shouts.

"Secret to a happy marriage," another chimes in.

Guests chuckle, and the blonde woman in the white dress shoots me a huge grin. That smile is like a key turning in the ignition. When the bride is happy, all systems are go.

I turn to the guests. "I promise I won't take up too much of your time, but I do have one simple request before I begin." I clear my throat, adopting a most serious tone. "If you brought your mobile phone, I highly encourage you to . . . leave it on. You might come across a great joke or a cat meme that we're all dying for. Send them on to me straight away, along with any Venmo or Square or PayPal payments. I also accept cash and credit cards."

More laughter echoes from the crowd, and that bolsters me.

I feign surprise. "Wait. That's tradition here too, right? Because back where I grew up, across the pond, it's customary to tip the best man if you enjoy his speech. And if you don't enjoy it, it's customary to tip twice as much."

Gavin makes a show of reaching into his pocket for some bills. "How many to make you stop?"

He tosses some green on the table, and I wiggle my fingers. "More. A little more. Still more."

Gavin waves a hand, laughing. "I can go all night."

"Savannah, I'll have you know, this is the only time he's thrown bills at anyone recently. Scout's honor." I make a gesture like a cross between a Vulcan salute and two fingers twined, proving that I was never a Boy Scout.

Savannah laughs and bumps him with her shoulder. "I know you didn't take him to a club, because I had a microchip implanted in my husband."

Gavin pats the back of his neck then stage-whispers, "I put one in her too. What's good for the goose is good for the gander."

Damn, they're good. They're fun, they love to rib each other, and they don't take themselves too seriously. If I didn't know differently, I'd swear we'd been best mates for ages.

About a month ago, Savannah and Gavin called me for an emergency best-man-for-hire consult. They'd already booked me as an extra groomsman for the wedding so Savannah could have an even number in the bridal party. But before we could place our order for beers at the bar, she blurted, "I went to a wedding the other week where Gavin's friend Eddie was the best man, and he told a story that involved a toilet plunger named Fred and a beer bong the size of a baseball bat. All I could think about was Eddie—what was he thinking, telling that horrifying story about the time his zipper was stuck? Love the guy, just love him, but he has zero filters and he knows it. Aunt Ellen, who's quite old-fashioned, would faint from shock, I know it. And she would never miss my wedding, especially since I'm the only daughter on my mom's side. Eddie's cool with the change, probably because he's not the speech-writing kind anyway, so can we please bump you up to the best man role?"

Could I help? Of course I could. The guidebook for the modern gentleman would advise strictly against mentioning toilet plungers in a speech, and even more so any misadventure that endangers one's ability to procreate. It dictates, too, that guys like me, trying to rise up through the ranks of New York's self-made men, not turn down the opportunity for work. Story of the last few years of my life.

"As Gavin's best man, I had many important responsibilities, first and foremost being the bachelor party. We had a long list of activities we were considering. Cupcake tasting, pottery making, and flower arranging . . . were most decidedly *not* on the list. In the end, we settled for what all the fellas in the city like to do best: we learned how to crochet."

I make eye contact with sweet Aunt Ellen, who beams at me from behind her coke-bottle glasses. She lifts up a canvas bag by her side. A crochet hook pokes out the top. Of course, I knew she loved to crochet.

"And I know you're all dying to know who was tops at a slip stitch."

Gavin lowers his face, chuckling under his breath.

Eddie chimes in. "Don't try to deny it, Gav. You were sick with the hook."

"And you were the master of the granny stitch," Gavin shouts.

But before Eddie takes over, I slide back into pole position. "But Gavin's prowess with crochet hooks aside, what stood out to me most from last night's bachelor party was not the lovely oven mitt he crafted for Aunt Ellen." I gasp in an over-the-top fashion. "Oh, dear. Was that supposed to be a secret?" I stage-whisper.

Ellen's smile spreads across her weathered face. "I can't wait to use it. Next time, we'll work on one together."

"Count on it. In any case, Ellen, I hope you enjoy it as much as I know Gavin and Savannah are enjoying this day. Because the truth is, even when we were at a pub in Williamsburg last night, enjoying a beer and a baseball game, Gav regaled us once more with tales of what a lucky man he is to have convinced this wonderful woman to be his bride."

This is the money shot—Savannah sighs happily, gazing at the groom, her eyes full of love. The rest of the crowd gives a collective *aww* too. This is why they're here: to witness one very happy couple.

"In fact, the night he met her, he rang me up, and I believe his words were 'I have to tell you something. I've met the woman I'm going to marry.'"

The bride clasps her hand to her heart as Gavin smiles goofily at the woman who took his name mere hours ago.

"I couldn't be more delighted to send Gavin off into the land of happily married men. May your love last many lifetimes."

I raise my glass once more then bring it to my lips, but that's for show. I can't drink on the job. A good understudy doesn't get pissed when he's thrust on stage in lieu of the principal actor.

Eddie lifts his glass and whispers, "Dude, you rocked that speech hard. Rocked it like you were banging a babe behind a pinball machine. Like the buzzers were going off, and the flippers were flapping."

"That's the effect I was going for," I deadpan as I sit next to Eddie while we chat.

"Achievement unlocked."

"Indeed."

Eddie downs the rest of his beverage. "I am so fucking glad they hired you. I was giving thanks last night. All I could think was how, if it were me up there, the whole joint would know about the time I ordered a policewoman stripper for Gavin's b-day. That was some night."

His eyes go hazy with the memory, or maybe it's the memory that's hazy, because Eddie suddenly slaps the table in a burst of realization.

"Hang on!" he shouts then drops his voice. "Fuck. That was my b-day I ordered a policewoman stripper for."

"It can be hard to keep track of officers of the law in thongs," I remark.

"Wait, wait—I got it! It's coming back to me. I know what happened." Laughing, he taps his skull. "I think my brain was trying to forget the whole thing. Because that night with the lady-cop stripper? That was the night my zipper got stuck." He grabs his crotch, his face

contorting as if reliving the pain. "Had to go to the ER."
He shakes his head, sighing. "Then again, it's not all bad.
I took the ER nurse home. She likes scars."

Yep, everyone is happy I was bumped up to this post,
and my bank account will be quite content too.

With the toast done, the bride and groom take a whirl
on the dance floor, and I grab the seat next to my date.

Nora has turned out to be the best plus-one an
undercover groomsman could ask for. She's upbeat, fun,
and always game for adventure. Flicking her wild
brown curls off her shoulders as John Legend's "All of
Me" hits its last note, she tips her chin to the crowd. "So
many single women here are eating you up with their
eyes. It's good that I'm here."

"Yes, please protect me from them. If too many talk
to me, they might find holes in the facade." That's why
Gavin suggested I bring a date. Not that I'd break character, but it gave me a buffer in case any prying relatives
asked too many questions.

"I'll never let them. That's my job as *Matilda* tonight,"
Nora says, using the fake name she picked for tonight,
since Nora loves fake names as much as she loves wigs.

"Then let's dance. I'm only sorry they're not playing
the alt-rock laced with the banjo. That's what your
Matilda persona loves, right? Dancing to your indie
tunes?"

"Dancing or hula hooping, and boy, do I love it when
you let me stay in character all night long."

"As if I'd do anything but support your dreams."

"And I'd never break character in front of an audience," she says.

Laughing, I offer her a hand. "Just shut up and dance with me, *Matilda*."

On the dance floor, she sets her hands on my shoulders, her pink clutch resting against me. Her warm hazel eyes sparkle as she surveys the scene. "This could be you someday."

A cough bursts from my throat. "Stranger things have happened, but it's a safe bet it won't."

She pouts. "Come now. You look so good in a tux. It'd be a shame if you were never the one up there."

"And yet it's hardly a dream of mine."

"Sounds like that's more of a nightmare to you?"

More like a thing I don't care to discuss with her, or hardly anyone. "We're talking full-on night sweats and terrors."

Laughing, she says, "Let's talk about something more pleasant. Like when the groom called you when he met Savannah. I'm dying to know how that went."

Ah, this is easier territory, since it doesn't sting. How could it? It's a fable. "I was first on his list. He had to share the news with his old pal from uni."

"Naturally. And I'm sure you had so very many things to catch up on. Stories from the quad, all-nighters in the dorm."

That's the story we cooked up when both Savannah's and Gavin's parents inevitably asked about the best man switcheroo. The groom and I met in college and kept in touch even after I returned to England. And that it was a terribly tough choice between Eddie and me, but Eddie understood and was chill with it.

In this business, that's the great thing about not being from here. It's easy to explain a friendship no one's heard of with a gent from another country. *Oh, that's my buddy from London. We met in school and then he returned to England, and so on.*

The reality is, Gavin found me the way my other clients do: word of mouth and my website.

I twirl Nora in a circle then tug her close. "That's the truth, and I'm sticking to it. And the truth has been very good to both of us this summer."

"So good. It's been the best—"

She flinches as something buzzes against my back. Yanking open her clutch, she snags her phone, and her eyes widen when she sees who's calling. "I need to take this *now*."

She scurries out of the reception like she's just learned she won an all-expenses-paid trip to Fiji.

As soon as she's gone, a redheaded bridesmaid with pouty lips and *swipe right* flashing in her eyes taps my shoulder.

"My turn, handsome," the auburn-haired woman purrs.

"Let's have a whirl, then."

"Mmm. I love whirls."

I glance around the dance floor, steering the conversation toward the event. "Having a lovely time?"

"I am, but it's better now. And I bet we could find a way to make it even more fun."

"Hmm. That would be tough when it's already beyond a barrel of monkeys."

"I bet I could find a way. I know how to make nights real fun."

I do my best to sidestep the pass. "I'm best during the day, personally."

She tries a new line of attack, gesturing to my bow tie. "You sure know how to wear a tux."

"Thank you. I'm proud of my ability to dress myself too."

"How are your undressing skills though?"

"Still working on shoe untying, but I'm pretty solid on the rest of it."

"Did you enjoy the cake? I thought it tasted like sin."

"Or maybe like heaven," I try, deflecting yet again as she makes another attempt.

"But the frosting was yummier," she says. "I'd like to take some home with me."

"They probably have doggie bags."

At the end of the song, she nibbles on the corner of her lips. "Let me be straight with you, Jay Bond. I'd really like your digits."

"Double-oh-seven." Well, she started it.

"How about the real ones, Mr. Tall, Dark, and British?"

"Thank you for your interest, but I'm involved."

"Too bad. I wouldn't mind fucking you and your accent."

"Well, we are a package deal," I deadpan.

* * *

As guests straggle out an hour later, Nora tells me she'll wait for me on the sidewalk, and she can't wait to share her news. I make the final rounds, saying good night to the deejay and the bartender; the mother of the bride; the mother of the groom; and Eddie, who wiggles his eyebrows and points to the doorway, thanking me profusely in a series of *dude, dude, dude*s. As it happens, I'm conversant in Dude. He's getting lucky tonight.

"No problem, mate. Happy to help."

"You are the best man. You are the motherfucking *best* man."

And what can I say to that but *dude*.

"Also, she likes scars, so I am in luck," he whispers as he leaves, making his way to a redhead—the same bridesmaid who danced with me. I'm glad she found someone to bang. Good on her.

"Hey, sugar," he says.

"Hey, babe. Let's get down to business, because I'm in the mood for screwing you and your scar."

Well, looks like someone has a signature pickup line.

I head into the hallway of the brewery, Gavin close behind me.

"You killed it out there. I'm almost glad Eddie has no filter." He pokes his head out the door, checking the scene in the reception room. "Coast is clear." He hands me an envelope with the rest of the rush fee in it.

"Thank you. I appreciate the prompt payment." I tuck the envelope in my inside jacket pocket. Appreciation doesn't quite cover how grateful I am for this after-hours best-man gig. It won't last forever; it *can't* last forever. But it's been a godsend now that I need the extra dough.

My undercover groomsman business started on a lark five years ago when I spotted a freelance ad for a best man speechwriter. I nabbed the gig and earned a pretty penny for that first speech. Speechwriting is still a large chunk of what I do, but I've also expanded my services to include organizing stag parties (nothing tawdry—I focus on fishing and hiking trips or nights out at the pub) and now the fill-in business when it's called for. That's rarer, but it pays the best, so I'm taking it while I can get it, reaping the rewards of wedding season and all the reasons men call on rent-a-grooms-man: they have few friends, they're from another country, the bride doesn't like the groom's true best mate, the groom doesn't want to pick between his good buds, his good bud is horrible at speeches, and so on.

"Listen, what should I say to the relatives if they start asking about you and why you're not around? They really do think you're my buddy from college and that you live in London."

"You can say I flew back to England on the next flight out of New York. Had business to tend to."

"Aunt Ellen will miss you the most, I'm sure."

"And I'll miss her and her slip stitches too. We were going to work on an afghan next."

"I can picture it now. She'd probably have crocheted your face into it too, she likes you that much. But seriously, what do I do if someone sees you wandering around the city, then asks about you?"

"Say I'm back on business, or here for a quick trip

into town. That's how I'd handle it. I can wing it if I run into your mum or dad, or even dear Aunt Ellen. Don't you worry."

I wouldn't nab referral after referral if this wasn't something I could handle. My job is to be smooth, and smooth is what I deliver.

Gavin seems to consider this. "True. You're a kick-ass wingman. A steely-eyed missile man."

I mime making a check mark. "'Steely-eyed missile man.' Be sure to leave that in your Yelp review."

"Want me to Yelp you? Because I will. I will Yelp you so hard."

I raise a brow, and Gavin laughs when he realizes why. "Okay, that did sound vaguely inappropriate."

"Only vaguely? You could enter that in Urban Dictionary. I believe you've founded a new term."

"My true calling perhaps. And thanks again, man. You were so damn believable. I was almost convinced myself that I FaceTimed you to tell you about Savannah."

"But didn't you?" I ask playfully.

Laughing, he scrubs a hand across his jaw, then his laughter fades to a kind of nervousness. And I know where this is going. I brace myself as he rocks back and forth on the balls of his feet then leaps off. "So, if you're in town and want to hang out . . . Savannah and I would love to have you and Matilda over for dinner."

Ah, this is the hard part, when the ruse seems so believable that the guy wants to stay friends.

On the one hand, what's the harm? Meet up for a

night out, a beer. But then a job becomes an unpaid job, and I need the money.

"Sure, ring me some time," I tell him, letting him down easy, knowing that when Gavin calls or texts, I'll have to be busy. I've too much on my plate, too many people to look out for. Or rather *two* people specifically —me and someone I adore who needs me, my sister.

Gavin smiles. "Awesome. I'll do that."

"I need to take off, but you are going to have one hell of a great life. You and Savannah are one of the happiest couples I've ever seen."

There. Remind him of that. Not of this momentary appearance of friendship between two bros.

I say goodbye to my client then exit the brewery, heading down the stone steps, unknotting my bow tie as I go.

Nora's waiting for me, and we head into the subway station around the corner then catch the next train as it arrives.

As soon as she grabs a seat, she bounces. "I have news."

"Spill, woman."

She sighs dramatically, but her expression is one of utter bliss as she announces: "I'm leaving you."

3

Charlotte: Soooo . . . how did the big meeting with the investor go this week? Did you wow Mr. Fancypants?

Truly: Define "wow."

Charlotte: That sounds like it didn't quite go as planned.

Truly: Does anything really ever go as planned?

Charlotte: What's the issue? Is he just not interested in the speakeasy concept? Because that is shocking. I've seen your Gin Joint numbers, you numbers-sharing whore, you.

Truly: They're like Mariano Rivera getting into the hall of fame kind of numbers. Excuse me as I pet this photo of me and the famed closer when we met once after a game.

Charlotte: Girl, I love it when you name-drop sports stars on me.

Truly: That reminds me, when are you getting us third-baseline seats to the Yankees again? I need my fix.

Charlotte: Such a greedy one. If you can tear yourself away from work for ten seconds, you can share our season tickets for the game next Sunday. Spencer has a meeting, but the kids can hang with my sister so we can go child-free.

Truly: This news delights me. Not the kid-free part, since your kids are cool. But the baseball part. The Yankees are my happy zone, and I'll work late every night to go to a Sunday game and replace your hubby.

Charlotte: We have two more tickets. You could bring Jason and Malone.

Truly: You're a goddess. I'll see if I can twist their arms. It'll be hard, but I'll do my darnedest. Anyway, thanks again for connecting me with Darren. To answer your question, he likes Gin Joint. But he wants something else first. I was kind of hoping he'd say a Parisian-style bar.

Charlotte: A Parisian-style bar would be amazing. I've wanted to do that for a long time too.

Truly: Sadly, that's not his first choice, and that's the problem. Wait! It's not a problem. I don't believe in problems. I believe in challenges. I'm simply still marinating on this one.

Charlotte: Ooh, intriguing. Tell me more. What style does he want?

Truly: Something I know little about. But I *might* have told Darren I know a helluva lot more about it than I actually do.

Charlotte: Guess it's time to come up with a whole new game plan.

Truly: That's exactly what I'll have to do.

4

"A divorce? You want a work divorce already?"

I'm shocked at Nora's declaration, and I don't want to lose my partner in crime. The groomsman-for-hire work used to be a solo gig, but lately a few men have asked me to bring a date. They figure if I have a date, there is less opportunity for guests to figure out I'm not part of the regular chummy club of guys. That's why Nora became my standing partner this summer.

"But it'll be an amicable split, I promise. This is good news, I swear. Don't you want to hear the reason why? I'm bursting. Bursting, I tell ya."

"Right. Sure. Give me the deets." As much as I want to keep working with Nora, she's a friend, and I ought to put her ahead of my own frustration over losing her. As the train chugs out of the station, I circle back to earlier. "Was it your agent who called?"

Her smile goes full Cheshire cat. "Yes! And I want to tell you every single thing." She sits straighter, doling out details with teaspoons. "First, do you remember the Steiner wedding we did the other week?"

"Sure. The bratwurst king. German guy needed a British best man."

"Yes," she squeals. "And that wedding gave me the final touch I needed."

"How so?"

"Don't you remember that wedding? I went for a German accent. And that was what I needed for my most recent audition. My agent just called to tell me I've been cast in a Chicago company. Say you're happy for me. Say you're very happy for me." Her eyes twinkle with the prospect of Tony awards and regular paychecks.

And mine, I hope, show nothing but true happiness for my friend. I yank her in for a huge hug. "That's incredible. I'm thrilled for you."

Her voice catches, and a tear rolls down her cheek. "This is what I've wanted. Thank you for the opportunity."

"The opportunity?"

"Well, you know I was always workshopping roles as your date."

Once, she was my artist lover from St. Petersburg; another time she slipped into the role of an ex-cheerleader from the heart of Texas; still another, she assumed the part of a buttoned-up banker from Berlin.

"In that case, I'm thrilled that you apprenticed at the Jason Reynolds School of Undercover Groomsmen and Their Plus-Ones. And don't forget to thank me when you nab your first Tony. Promise?"

She makes an X on her chest. "Cross my heart. Hope to die."

"Don't die. That would be bad. Or at the very least, wait till you've finished starring in *Chicago*."

She shakes her head. "It's not *Chicago the Musical*. It's a Chicago production. An out-of-town tryout for a new show. I'm going to be in the new musical adaptation of *Raiders of the Lost Ark*."

One of my eyebrows rises in question. "They're adapting that for the stage?"

"Complete with the giant boulder and everything."

"What about the snakes?"

"Those are fake. Thank God. I hate snakes."

"Yeah, everyone does. And the tunes?"

"They're fantastic. Based on many famous lines from the movie."

I break into an impromptu show tune, snapping my fingers to lyrics I make up on the fly. "Snakes. Why did it have to be snakes? Oh why, oh why, oh why did it have to be snakes?"

She dives in alongside me. "It's not the years, honey. It's the mileage."

I try to picture the rugged adventurer high-kicking it on stage with his whip and hat, and I can't quite manage it. Then, the marquees on the Great White Way read more like a cineplex of unlikely musicals: *Tootsie*, *Pretty Woman*, *Mean Girls* . . . You don't know whether to log on to Broadway.com or Fandango.

"I suppose it was only a matter of time before *Raiders* stepped up for the musical treatment. Who are you playing? Marion?"

She sighs dreamily. "I wish. That went to a big-name actor. I'm playing a German spy. And that's why the accent came in handy. I'm in the spy chorus."

"That doesn't ring a bell. Were there that many spies in the movie?"

She waves a hand airily. "No, but who cares? There will be on stage. Anyway, can you find someone else to serve as your plus-one?"

"Don't worry about me." Annoyance has no place here. "The stage is your dream, and I couldn't be happier for you."

Besides, I know a thing or two about pursuing true dreams. I chase them every damn day and into the night too, working late on the blog, seeking out media opportunities, penning guest columns, and trying to find every opportunity to be *the* expert source. But now's not the time to dwell on my goals or my needs.

"Tell me more about the songs the coolest hero ever in film sings . . ."

She rattles on about the production until the train reaches her stop. Then she says goodbye, and I'll miss having her by my side at the next wedding.

No help for it. I definitely require a shot or two tonight. Looks like a stop at Gin Joint is in order.

* * *

When I exit the subway on Eighteenth Street, I turn down the block and find a text from my buddy Malone, sent about ten minutes ago.

Malone: Just finished a set at Gin Joint. Incidentally, I killed it. I'm here with Nick and Harper for a few if you want to join.

Well, sounds like he can read my mind. I tap out a reply, then stop when I spot him walking toward me, dressed in a tailored suit, his silk tie loosened a bit. Times like this, you'd be hard-pressed to believe he wears a white coat during the day as he examines cats and dogs. After hours, he looks every bit the part of the dapper lounge singer.

"If it isn't the vet by day, Harry Connick Jr. by night."

"I am something of a superhero. But then, don't we all have our secret identities?"

"Isn't that the truth?" I check my watch. "I guess you didn't last long after you crooned your heart out to the crowd of . . . what was it, two people tonight?"

"Packed house, asshole. Packed house."

"If you say so."

He narrows his eyes. "And you wonder why I'm leaving."

"Aww, you're so sensitive. It's sweet." I gesture toward the end of the block. "I take it you're calling it a night?"

"I am. But Nick and Harper are at Gin Joint, so you can catch up with them. The place is still hopping. No surprise. My sister is a maestro of the nightlife business." He smiles, and there's pride in that grin. Malone and Truly are closer than most siblings, maybe from being twins. Now and then, though, it sends a prickle of guilt down my neck because I'm keeping a secret from him. But if he knew what happened between Truly and me one snowy night six months ago, he likely wouldn't be talking to me right now.

But since it's never going to happen with his sister again, there's nothing to worry about. "I'll go catch up with the crew."

"And I'll see you tomorrow night at softball," he says, then takes off, humming "Give My Regards to Broadway" as he goes. "*Give my regards to Broadway. Remember me to Herald Square.*"

"Stop, make it stop. It's like a chainsaw mating with a jackhammer," I shout.

"I'm sorry, did you say I'm making it rain? I thought so." He waves dismissively and continues his number down the block.

I head to the bar. Drinks, friends, people to talk to where I can be myself? A spot where I don't need to pretend I'm buddy-buddy with everyone just to make a buck? Sounds great. But the part I like best?

Sparring with Malone's sister.

I mean, with Truly.

My good friend Truly.

That's all she is. Not my best mate's sister who I screwed one Saturday night when we were out of town.

But before I reach the bar, my phone bleats. It's Chip, my client for next weekend. I answer right away, gliding into my practiced don't-ever-let-on-there-are-problems tone. I'll need it to avoid the thorny issue of whether I'm still bringing along a date as he'd requested.

5

From the pages of Truly's Drink Recipe Book

Game Plan:
Gin
Blackberry
Home-brewed ginger ale

When business throws you a curveball, what do you do? When someone surprises you and wants something a little different than you expected, do you freak out and say, "OMG! I can't do that"?

No way.

You woman up.

You figure it out.

You develop a new game plan.

If you don't have one yet, it's time for a little gin, a

little home-brewed ginger ale, and some fresh-crushed blackberries. Have a sip, savor the effervescence, and delight in the fizz. Let yourself drift off as new plans start to form.

Soon enough, you'll know what to do to get what you want.

6

"Hey, Chip, how's it going? Counting down the days till the big *I do*?"

"Hi, Jay!" I don't use my real name in the business. Jay is an easy pseudonym, and using it helps to keep my worlds separate. "Just wanted to double, triple, quadruple check everything for next weekend."

I reel off the details, hoping to avoid mentioning my now dateless state. "My groomsmen are at the ready. Troy will be with me, along with his wife. He's fantastic and has an uncanny ability to fit into any situation. And then there's Sully, also with the missus as his plus-one. He's very focused, very committed to the job, so he'll be excellent. You'll have all the groomsmen you need to pair up with the bridal party for photos and walking the aisle."

"Perfect. That's everything Ashley wants, and that's all I want—to make her happy."

"That's a great way to start a marriage." This is

perfect. He's not even thinking about whether he wants me to bring someone.

"And if anyone asks, we met in the running club and you work in advertising," he says, recapping the backstory we created.

"You've got it right. You've got everything right."

"But what's your favorite cuisine? I should probably know, right? Shoot. What if someone asks? What if someone wants to know your favorite book? What if someone wants to know your sign?"

"Of the zodiac?"

"Yes! I don't know it."

"I promise you, Chip, no one expects you to know the astrological sign of a guy friend. Also, anything by Vonnegut and nothing by Ayn Rand, and everything by Nick Offerman. And I like Thai and Japanese."

"I dig Nick Offerman too. I bet we exchanged dog-eared paperbacks. Wink, wink."

"With Offerman you really ought to get the audiobook, but sure, paperback works."

"And your favorite band? What if someone wants to know that? What if they want to know what concerts we've been to? Should I say Coldplay?"

"No!" With the fire of a thousand blazing suns, I kill that notion dead. "Never. Coldplay is what they play to torture you behind enemy lines. I'm a Beatles and Rolling Stones man."

"Oh, cool! I like them too! Almost as much as Coldplay. I'd say maybe we could go to a Stones show someday, but I'll probably be too busy. I always am. I'm sure it's the same with you."

"Absolutely."

This is what I like about Chip. Despite his puppy-dog persona, he's not poised to turn into a stage-five clinger after the wedding. He hired me because he's completely content to spend his time with his woman, his 5K runs, his work, and his dog. Friendships aren't his focus, so I don't suspect he'll be clutching my ankle and trying to follow me out the door when this is over.

"One more thing. Can you do one of those fancy accents? Ashley loves *Love Actually*, so she'd get a kick out of it. I like to pretend I'm Hugh Grant sometimes. I do the whole 'Jump' routine for her, and she digs that. *'Yeah, Betty, I'm thinking, can we move the Japanese ambassador to four o'clock tomorrow?'*"

"I'll go full Hugh Grant for the groom and bride," I say, giving him my best posh voice.

"Ahhh! Yours is so much better than mine. But hey, at least my lady likes this guy from Tallahassee. And you're bringing along your lovely lady friend. I can't wait to meet her. I love meeting new people."

I wince, slowing my pace as I reach Gin Joint, scrubbing a hand across my stubbled jaw. "About that. Turns out I'll be flying solo next weekend. But it'll be great."

I leave it at that. No need to dive into details.

"Oh, no, no." His voice zooms ten stories high. "Buddy, you can't come solo. I sold Ashley on you with the understanding that you were half of a couple. That all our men were coupled up."

"I understand, but at the end of the day, why does it matter?"

"Her youngest sister is one of the bridesmaids, and

she's only eighteen. Amelia's completely boy-obsessed. Ashley is worried her sister will throw herself at any good-looking guy in her path. And you? Well, look in the mirror. You're too hot to be single. Not my words— those are Ashley's. Actually, she said that about all of you when I showed her the pics, so you definitely need a plus-one."

"Thanks. I think. But wait a second. Do we have enough groomsmen? Don't you need one for her sister? Or is that playing into the issue?"

"Don't worry about Amelia. She'll walk with the maid of honor."

"Good to know," I say diplomatically. That's an odd situation, the bridesmaid needing a chaperone, but maybe it solves the problem of the boy obsession. "And I'll find a date."

"I bet you can find one as quickly as I can find the problem in this pipeline project I've been studying while we've been on the phone. Yup. Found it!"

"You're speedy."

"That's what she said." He laughs and says good night before I can tell him that's not really how that saying is supposed to work.

As I find myself at the door of Truly's bar, I flash back to advice I gave a reader on my blog a few weeks ago. He'd been invited to a work event on the weekend and wanted to know if he should find a date for it on Tinder.

My response?

We modern gentlemen face this "where to find my plus-one" dilemma all the time. But let me share my best advice

with you. Are you ready? Come closer. A little closer. DO
NOT FIND YOUR DATE ON TINDER.

*Tinder isn't the place for those kinds of hookups—the ones
where you need to be a gentleman. Where you want people to
remember you, not your date who drank all the free
champagne.*

No, I told this reader the best solution when we
need someone by our side for a special occasion is to
ask a friend.

It was sound advice, if I do say so myself. I suppose I
should follow it.

As a rule of thumb, I don't dwell on problems or linger over setbacks. I certainly don't wallow.

I charge forward with focus and tenacity, solving problems for myself and others.

Tonight's problem I will solve in a bar.

With my jacket slung over my arm, I head into Gin Joint, scanning the swank place for my friends. I spot Harper draped on a purple couch, chatting with her husband, Nick, and when I catch his eye, I signal that I'll join them shortly. He flips me the bird. I flip him the bird back, and all is well.

I grab a spot at the end of the bar, searching for the woman I came to see. I need to feel her out first. See what kind of mood she's in.

She's mixing a martini for a guy with hair slicked back with so much product, it looks like it's cracking. I've written a number of blogs with grooming tips that could help him out. Maybe start with *Gel—more is not your friend.*

I scan the chalkboard for the signature drinks. Among the gin specials are Game Plan, Last Word, Devil's Teeth, Hush Money, and That One Time.

A brunette with a *Great Gatsby* hairstyle—shoulder-length with one of those 1920s headbands—joins Truly behind the bar, taking over the martini.

The woman I came to see marches over to me, plunks down a napkin, then tips her chin toward the Daisy Buchanan look-alike. "Gabriella will get the next few customers, since I suspect you deserve the owner's attention."

"I like to think I always do."

"What can I get for you? Because you look like someone just told you that you can't have bacon for breakfast."

I shoot her a *have you gone mad* look. "Bacon for breakfast? I hope that's not what you think I eat."

She parks her hands on the bar. "What do you have for breakfast?"

"Eggs and soldiers."

Her brow furrows. "What is that?"

I sigh heavily, dropping my forehead to the counter. "Why, oh why, Lord, am I still explaining British references after all these years?"

"I know the basics. Chips, fish, tea, blah, blah, blah."

I look up, shaking my head sadly. "What am I going to do with you? You need a full and proper education in English food. The soldiers are pieces of toast you dip into the egg, soft-boiled and perched in a snazzy egg cup."

"Ah. Here we call that, wait for it, *toast*."

"Yes, eggs and toast. We're simply more creative across the pond. But I never have bacon."

She holds up her hand to high-five. "Welcome to the club of bacon haters."

"Wait. You have a club?" I high-five back, enjoying the contact more than I thought possible with high fives. But she does have great hands. They did wondrous things to my dick one night.

Stop.

Just stop that right now, dirty brain.

"Of course we have a club. We have meetings and bylaws too."

"Sign me up, then."

"We have much work to do, comrade. And work requires a drink. I'm getting the vibe that you're in the mood for one of my specials—a little gin, a couple cucumbers, and the best part? My homemade red-pepper laced lemonade." Her gaze sweeps to the chalk-board sign. "Otherwise known as That One Time. Can I interest you?"

"You can very much interest me in That One Time."

She spins around, grabs a glass, and starts mixing. I settle in on the black metal stool, enjoying the view.

Women like her pouring drinks—it's one of my favorite sights. Right next to women in bikinis lazing in the sun and women sliding on fishnet stockings and then slipping into heels. Wait, that's not fair to the image of women in white lace. That makes the list too.

She sets the glass in front of me, and I taste the concoction, savoring the sweet start and the fiery finish.

"Beautiful. Now, tell me, why was I in the mood for That One Time?"

She eyes me up and down, with a cool and confident gaze. "Same way I could tell my friend Presley needed one when she was here a few minutes ago. Because she clearly had had a shit day at work, and things were not going her way. And it sure looks like things didn't go your way tonight."

"And how exactly can you tell?" I ask since I'm not the kind of guy who wears his heart on his sleeve.

Truly twirls her finger in a circle at me. "I can tell because you're in your tux, Nora's not here, and you have this furrow in your brow that says all is not perfect in Jason Land."

She excuses herself to saunter to the end of the bar to help Gabriella for a moment, and I glance down at my tux then figuratively side-eye the furrow in my brow. Am I more transparent than I thought, giving off telltale signs of frustration? Well, that's unacceptable. I'm practical, I'm fun, but I'm not emotional. I've seen where emotions can lead a man, and now I'm focused and have been since Claire Wedgewood, the woman I thought I was going to marry once upon a time, decided that waiting around didn't fit in *her* schedule.

Then again, she was ridiculously good at putting herself first, so do what you know and all that.

With Truly tending to orders, I take my phone from my pocket and check my e-mail.

There's a new one from Ryder Lockhart, a relationship and advice guru superstar.

Can you do another guest appearance on my show this week?
We have a segment coming up on dos and don'ts for modern
guys in business. Good fit for you. Think of some of your best
tips and be ready to be pithy and witty.

Hell, yes. I am overflowing with pith and wit just
waiting for me to share. I write back faster than a
Bugatti, letting Ryder know I'll be there.

When Truly swings by again, I put the phone away
and answer her unasked question—what went wrong
tonight. "If you must know, the date ended terribly with
Nora."

Truly's lips curve up in the faintest of grins for a
nanosecond before flattening into a straight line. "What
happened? Did you guys split up?"

How I want to toy with her to see if she's actually
jealous. But that wouldn't help my mission. "We weren't
together."

"Oh." She sounds delighted.

"Nora has been my pretend date at a few weddings."

"I thought the best man for hire mostly rode solo?"

"For the most part, but sometimes the couple prefers a
plus-one, or it's easier in the circumstances. Nora was
quite good at it. She's an actress, and she wanted to work-
shop some characters. But she was just cast in *Raiders of
the Lost Ark the Musical*, so she's now unavailable."

Truly's eyes light up. "I want to see that when it
comes to Broadway."

"Consider it a date. I'll order tickets tonight."

For a second, a smile seems to tug at her lips, almost as if she likes the idea of a date. But it vanishes quickly. "Pick out seats in the friend zone."

I take out my sad trombone and play a few lonely notes. "You love reminding me that you cruelly friend-zoned me."

"We friend-zoned each other. It was mutual. Do I need to remind you of the morning after?"

"Only if you want me to remind you of all the things you said the night before."

She heaves a sigh. "*Jason.*"

"Yes. Like that. Only with a little more of a long, lingering moan. Kind of breathy. Sort of like *Jason, yes, right there. Harder.*"

Her eyes never waver, never break my gaze as she leans closer, dropping her voice. "*Truly, fucking hell. Yeah. That. Just like that. Your mouth on me. So fucking perfect.*"

Turn the oven off. I'm cooked. Officially roasted. I toss the figurative white flag at her. "You win."

She takes a deep bow. "Thought I might. But let's not forget the other things we both said, mainly *We can't do this again. Malone will kill us.*"

"Hmm. That does sound familiar, now that you say it. And speaking of avoiding imminent death, I have a massive boulder rolling in my direction next weekend. It's the first of a number of weddings coming up where I have been asked to bring a date."

"And how is this a problem? You can walk down the

street and pluck a date off a tree, Jason. This shouldn't be an issue."

"I can't help it if women find me incredibly charming." I flash her a grin because it *is* easier if we keep things light, friendly. "But I must inform you, women don't grow on trees. If they did, I'd be planting one in my backyard. Hell, I'd sow a whole orchard."

"If you do that, I'll go plant a field full of guys too."

"Or you can play in my field."

"I'll have to weed you out first," she says wryly.

I lean across the bar to tuck a loose strand of hair behind her ear, taking my time, making sure I get every single strand, especially since she trembles a little as I touch her. "You'd never be able to get rid of me."

"I'm feeling that's the case already."

"Seriously, here's the deal: I desperately need to take a date to the wedding next weekend and to the one after that too."

"Put an ad online. Ask one of your many female friends. How hard can it possibly be?"

I snap my fingers. "*Ask a friend.* Brilliant idea. Bloody brilliant." I bat my lashes. "We're friends, aren't we?"

She flinches, blinking. "Nooooooooo."

"We're not friends? Hmm. I distinctly remember us making a friendship pact . . . albeit after the third orgasm."

A faint blush creeps across her cheeks, and it's completely endearing. She lowers her voice and says, "Yes, we made a pact. Yes, we've been friends, even though you're five years younger," she mutters playfully. "And we are friends, we intend to stay friends. But . . ."

"We're great friends. Who else would conquer the wilds of Manhattan fitness with you? We do martial arts together. I took the obstacle course class with you. You even dragged me along to Punk Rope," I say, reminding her of one of the many exercise classes she's enlisted me to join with her.

"And how much fun did we have jumping rope and doing push-ups? Plus, the obstacle course was a blast."

"We did kick ass on the tire run." I sense an opportunity to remind her that, while we're not engaging in a repeat horizontal fitness project, we have carved out a spot in the tag-teaming department. "Come along with me to the weddings. We'll have fun, just like we do as workout buddies. You'd be a fantastic pretend date. Plus, I'm loads of fun, and you want to help a good friend."

She stares briefly across the expanse of the bar as if she's contemplating my proposition while checking out the goings-on in the lounge area. "I'm sure it would be a hoot, but there has to be someone else who'd be better."

I look her dead in the eyes, dropping all teasing and jokes. "No. There's not. I can't have this business go belly-up. It requires complete discretion, and I need somebody I trust. Somebody I know. I can't have it seeping over into the Modern Gentleman world. Potential clients might not be thrilled to know I'm an advice columnist by day and a paid best friend by night."

"You really think it'd be an issue?"

"I don't want to take the chance. How can I be the guy giving tips to other men on how to present themselves well, impress a boss with the best version of themselves, when at night I'm pretending to be Jay, who's Peter the groom's best friend from uni, only I met him a few days ago? But hey, I gave that rad toast. That's why I need somebody by my side who understands how important the gig is for me and for Abby," I say.

Truly hangs her head. "It's not fair to play the little sister card."

"But it's true. I just need to get through these jobs this summer, and I'll be nearly done with the last of the bills."

Truly's dark eyes seem to light up. "Seriously? You really have earned enough to put her through medical school?"

I straighten my shoulders, proud of this accomplishment. "For the most part, yes. She had grants and some scholarship money, and the cost in the UK isn't the same as it is here. But I've earned enough and had some well-paying gigs. I'm almost there." I rap my knuckles on the bar. "Touch wood."

"Look, I want to help. I really do. I think it's great what you're doing." She gestures wildly to the bar. "But I have a business, and it's incredibly time-consuming. Plus, I'm working next weekend. And I'm expanding now to some new concepts. I've promised to move up some employees if it all comes together. Gabriella is going to take on more work during the expansion, so I really need to focus on making sure I can win over this new investor. How about I help you find someone instead?"

But she's the one I need. "Isn't there anything I could do for you? I could be your guinea pig for new cocktail concoctions. Or what about the new concepts you're working on? I'm a bit of an expert on New York nightlife and drink culture, pubs, and whatnot. Comes with the job. So you can use me as your lab rat for that too."

She straightens her spine while lowering her voice to a whisper. "What did you just say?"

"I'll be your lab rat."

"That's brilliant." Her eyes light up like sparklers. She clasps her hand to her mouth, as if she's trying to contain her excitement, then she whispers, "That's what I need. I was going to spend all my time online, researching English pubs. I was even considering a trip. But this is just what I need: my very own pub lab rat."

I haven't connected all the dots yet, but there will be time for that. "So you'll do it? I'll be your lab rat, and you'll be my date?"

The door to the bar swings open, and a dozen or so women in slinky tops and tight jeans spill inside.

"Who's ready to have the best night ever!" one of them announces.

"We have a party of twelve in the reserve room. I need to take care of them. But can you meet me tomorrow to work out a plan? I need on-the-ground research as I work on my pitch for the investor. You help me, I'll help you. I'm free after my morning booty boot camp, and we'll go over how this will work. Deal?"

I'm not about to let her wiggle out of it, so I pounce before she can think of a better way to get what she needs. "Absolutely. Have fun working on your booty.

Wish I could be there to watch. I mean, exercise. I completely meant to do the boot camp."

Smiling, she heads to greet the pack of women while I enjoy the view of her boot camp assets.

I return to my drink, savoring every sip because . . . holy shit. She said yes.

* * *

I make my way to Nick and Harper. She shoots me a playful grin. "Let me guess—you were at the bar, flirting with Nick's cousin?"

"Let me answer—I was actually striking a business deal."

Nick cracks up. "That's a good one. What are you, angling to write speeches for her to give when she serves cocktails?"

I snap my fingers. "Not a bad idea. I better write that down in my notebook of possible new ventures."

Harper waves a hand, excitement in her eyes. "Or wait. Maybe you're going to devise names of cocktails inspired by your blog. Don't Forget to Hold the Door."

"Always Offer to Take Her Coat," Nick offers.

"A Gentleman Rises When a Lady Does," Harper adds. "Speaking of, I need to call the sitter. Be right back."

Nick rises when she stands, and I wag a finger at him. "You might think you're mocking me, but what you're really doing is proving you read my blog. Admit it—it's chock-full of the very best advice."

"It's not too bad. But seriously, what's the business deal?"

"Just a project she'll help me on."

Nick arches a brow. "Project? Is that code for something else?"

"What would it be code for?"

He scratches his jaw. "Are you forgetting who you're dealing with? You think I can't tell you're hot for her?"

"As if I'd bother to hide it from a former scoundrel such as yourself. But cool your jets—nothing is going to happen."

I tack on a silent *again*.

He lifts his glass, pausing before he drinks. "Maybe not tonight. Maybe not tomorrow. But someday."

I narrow my eyes. "Did you really just quote half of a famous line from *Casablanca* to me?"

"Yeah. Seems I did. And it seems you're going to have to sort out the feelings you have for her and what you're going to do about the fact that her brother has no idea."

"No idea what?" Harper asks when she returns. "Also, Carson and Skye are fabulous. The sitter said they already fell asleep. They get that from me. It's my superpower. Sound asleep as soon as my head hits the pillow."

"That is a pretty impressive skill. Ranks right up there with flying and invisibility."

"I'll take invisibility," Nick whispers, as if Harper can't hear him. "That way I can spy on my wife in the shower anytime."

She tilts her head. "News flash. You do that already."

Nick scratches his jaw. "True. I do that daily. It's good to have a routine."

"Anyway, what does someone have no idea about?" Harper asks. "Feed me gossip, please."

"Your husband contends I'm going to have to do something about the fact that Malone supposedly has no idea that I supposedly have a thing for Truly," I supply. "Which is a lot of supposedlys."

Harper laughs. "Sweetie, I think Malone might know."

I flinch. "How? Also, there's nothing to know."

Harper nods, still grinning. "Right. Got it."

"I mean it. There's nothing to know."

"Of course." She winks. "Sure. Nothing at all to know. And don't worry. I bet Malone doesn't have the astute power of observation that comes with ovaries."

"And yours is the most astute," Nick says to her.

But they're wrong. I don't have *feelings*. Not in the deep, emotional sense. Those don't interest me. Never have, since I've seen where they can lead.

All I truly feel is lingering lust.

And I can set that aside easily.

I may love sexy-flirting with Truly, but this new arrangement has to come first.

8

From the pages of Truly's Drink Recipe Book

That One Time:
Gin
Homemade red pepper lemonade
Cucumbers

You can still remember the way he looked that night. Cool and casual with five-o'clock shadow stubble. The way he smiled, the way he laughed—full of the connection you've shared with him for ages. Hell, for years. The connection you tried to deny, to ignore.

But then one weekend, you went away.

And that seemed to unlock all those crazy desires.

Caution fell to the wayside, and you gave in.

The next morning, you agreed it couldn't happen

again. But still, you keep lingering on that one time. That time you try and try to forget.

Doesn't always work though.

When the going gets tough, when the forgetting becomes harder, there's only one drink that'll do the trick.

Start with gin to blur the memories and add your homemade red-pepper lemonade for that sweet oblivion. You'll get there eventually.

Someday. Maybe someday soon.

9

As I tug on a pair of running shorts the next morning, I review my notes from a best man who's hired me for a speech. Committing the basics to memory, I head out, hit the park, and peel off four miles on the pavement and the skeleton draft of a toast in my head.

When I cool down, I spot a familiar figure on the path ahead of me, the spitting image of Michael B. Jordan—lucky bastard. He's power walking around the edge of the park, a knee brace hugging his leg. "Hey, tortoise! You still walking, not running?"

My friend Walker turns around and waves dismissively at his offending joint. "You try running when you've blown out a knee."

"How many times do I have to tell you? That's not the thing you want blown."

"Thanks for the reminder. I've been missing your unparalleled life advice."

I walk by his side. "What have you been up to? I

haven't seen you on the wedding circuit much recently. Used to run into you at every other ceremony, it seemed."

He raises his arms toward the sky. "As God is my witness, I've finally started cutting back."

I gesture to his limbs. "Careful there. Don't want to injure your elbow too."

He shoots me a glare. "You do know you won't always be thirty?"

"True. But I'll *always* be ten years younger than you."

"And ten times the smart-ass."

"Probably true there too. But seriously, are you finally spinning records in a club, like you wanted?"

"Landed a semi-regular gig at a place in the Meat-packing District. And they don't make me play 'Macarena' or 'I Wanna Dance with Somebody.'"

I shudder. "Least favorite wedding reception songs ever. Wait, no, that's 'Dancing Queen.'"

"And I don't have to play that either."

"You're officially the luckiest bastard. Congrats on the exodus from the wedding business. You were keen on that."

"I'm not totally out the door, but it's swinging in that direction." He scrubs a hand across his goatee, glancing thoughtfully at the sky. "Speaking of, how's your exit plan going? I bet business has been even better after that *Gentleman's Style* piece from a couple months ago."

"The one where the bloke from the UK bragged about how fast his undercover groomsman business was expanding? He's enjoying *The Wedding Ringer* effect, for sure. That film has been the best thing that ever happened to the business. Good thing I started my work well before Kevin Hart made it look cool, so I could ride the wave too."

"But you do know you can't do this forever?"

This is typical Walker. He's the wedding-circuit Buddha, and he sees it as his duty to share his wisdom.

"Thanks for the reminder. I was starting to think I was going to be making toasts in my fifties."

He shoots me a stare, holding his ground. "It's my job to remind you of the benefits of having an exit plan. The money can start to seduce you, make you think it can be your full-time lifetime gig. And I know you have other goals."

I flash an easy grin. "The whole gig is one gigantic see-you-later strategy. And I'm paving the path toward it every damn day."

"Keep paving it, man. Otherwise, someday you're going to be waxing eloquent on the radio about how to land a promotion, and when you leave, the guy down the hall will remember the toast you gave at some wedding as Jay the best man, or Jackson or Jackoff."

"Good thing I've been using the name Walker lately," I say, then wave goodbye with my middle finger.

I take off, running the last mile home, repeating Walker's reminder that this is temporary, even though the pay is quite good lately.

Quite good indeed.

* * *

When I return to my place, I down a glass of water, settle in with my laptop, and power through the speech. Next, it's shower time, where I do not think of Truly.

As the water beats down, I don't picture her jumping rope, or taking up boxing, or shaking her fantastic arse in that booty boot camp this morning.

That would make me a dirty perv.

Oh, right. I am.

Because, hell, she looks good when she sweats.

And she can screw like a woman who loves her cardio.

Dammit.

I can't let this tempt me.

Even though I *am* tempted. I have been since I met her a few years after settling into New York City. Having dual citizenship courtesy of an American-born, London-raised father gave me the flexibility to live here, one of the few decent things he managed to pass on. I connected with Malone first, thanks to the softball league we both play on, then got to know his sister soon after.

Seemed a bit like a big "piss off" from the universe to make the sister—twin sister, no less—of a good mate a right fucking fox.

But she is, and she has a fiery personality too, which is an even bigger turn-on.

I resisted for years. And soon, resistance became the norm. It was easy enough to be friends with her, to sign up for crazy, heart-pumping classes together, to run a 5K by her side.

That was how we operated. She was one of the gang.

Until that night earlier this year. She'd suggested we go snowboarding, and naturally, I'd said yes. We'd spent a Saturday shredding the white powder on the slopes a couple of hours away, tackling tough run after tougher run. That evening, still high on adrenaline and black diamonds, we wound up staying the night in her room at the ski lodge.

We didn't sleep more than an hour.

The next morning, as daylight shone its harsh light on our misdeeds, we vowed never to fall into bed again.

I knew that was for the best, especially after she explained why.

And her reasons are only a few of many that steered me back onto the well-trodden path of resisting her. Now she's going to help me with my work, which needs all my focus as I finish up these gigs.

I rinse, turn off the shower, and grab a towel. Once I'm dressed, it's time for business mode, so I put on a button-down shirt—always best to look proper—and log into Skype for a virtual coaching session. When I'm done, I see I have an hour free before I meet Truly.

I decide to give Abby a ring.

Her adorable, freckled face fills the screen. My favorite person looks exhausted, her brown eyes deeply shadowed.

Her brown hair is knotted in a messy bun. She yawns a "Hello."

"You look completely knackered."

"Gee, thanks. And you look like shit too."

"Aww, that's the sister I know and love. Always ready to sling mud at her poor, beleaguered brother."

She shakes her head, bemused. "You're so dramatic. And do you think I don't know I look like the poster child for Buzzfeed's List of Top Ten Signs You Need Sleeping Tablets? I'd be one through eleven."

I shoot her a sympathetic smile. "Few too many late nights dissecting dead bodies?" I shudder reflexively, then hold up a hand. "Wait. Don't tell me."

"Good. Because I don't think you want to know what they make us do in anatomy class."

"You're right. I don't."

"But I'm learning tons," she says with a familiar bright smile. Abby has always come to life in the classroom. Learning is her jam. She rattles off some of the topics she's studying, and it's all well over my head, but I nod and say it sounds great.

"But try to get some rest now and then."

"I will, but in the meantime, if you want to give me any suggestions for new night creams that you've found, that would be awesome."

"What makes you think I use night cream? I'm naturally handsome and glowing."

"Oh, please. I bet you have a bag full of lotions and potions."

"Hasn't anyone told you it's not nice to lie about your older brother?"

She winks. "I won't tell anyone. C'mon. I know all those face-cream companies send you samples. I read your columns on grooming tips."

"Learn anything interesting?"

She mimes stroking a beard. "Why, yes. A recent one was interesting: *Never forget that a shower always comes first. If you have time for only one grooming ritual, keep it basic—soap and water, rather than mustache or beard oil.* But are there truly men who don't realize that?"

"Abby, have you met men? Wait. Don't answer that. I know you're a celibate nun-slash-doctor-in-training. And yes. Men's advice columns are ridiculously popular because, wait for it, men need advice, even of the most basic sort."

"Can't argue with you on that. What's the latest with you? Are you still the champion of the Manhattan dating scene?"

I pretend to preen, sitting taller. "Naturally. I received an award last week to that effect." I reach behind me, out of sight of the computer's camera, and grab a trophy then thrust the cheap blue-and-gold statue in front of the screen. "Impressed now, are you?"

She laughs. "You actually have a trophy. That's adorable, but what on earth did you do to earn that? Did you join a kickball league? Nab first place in a pie-baking contest?"

I heave an aggrieved sigh. "I can't believe you're mocking my pie skills when you were the recipient of all the amazing ones I made as we were growing up."

She smiles, and it lights up the whole damn screen. "It was rather sweet, watching you help Mum bake and then test them on me."

"You ate anything."

"Could you blame me? The two of you could cook. Steak and bacon, chicken and bacon, shepherd's pie with bacon added because bacon is the best thing ever invented. My stomach is rumbling just thinking of it."

I cringe. "Bacon, so much bacon. All those years helping her turned me off it. I can barely stomach any meat these days. Fish or bust, I say."

"Not me. I plan to marry steak. And then date pork and flirt with ham on the side," Abby says with a dreamy look, as if she's floating on a whiff of something delicious.

This little turkey loved the meat pies. I'd help Mum bake them, Abby would test them, and Dad would declare them delicious. All was well for years. My parents had an idyllic marriage, or so I thought. So my mum thought, too, until seven years ago. Abby was eighteen, I was twenty-three, and Dad, the bastard, said he'd fallen madly in love with somebody else. *It's no big deal! You kids have left home, and it's time for me to follow my true heart.*

His true heart had a surprise in store for him. After he tied the knot with the other woman, he went about his new life with no regard for any of us, including his ailing mum, and finally lost all the money he'd set aside to help Abby with med school. Turned out his new wife's true heart was located in his wallet, and she knew how to pry his savings right out of him.

Love is such a ridiculous emotion. It can mess with your head and your life and your entire family.

Abby didn't ask me to pay her way through medical school. She'd planned to take out loans, but I've seen some of my friends strapped with huge debt, and I was in a position where I could likely earn what she needed faster than she could pay it back.

I pat the trophy proudly. "I'll have you know this was the jujitsu tournament I did with Truly earlier this summer. Came in first place in the men's, and she was first in the ladies.' Guess you're not the only over-achiever in the family. But speaking of medical school, I'm really interested in knowing if you've learned yet how the leg bone is connected to the ankle bone?"

She stares back at me, putting her eye to the camera lens like she's peering through a peephole. "No, but I hope to get to that in the next class."

"Study hard. Be good, don't do drugs, and don't date boys."

"I told you. I'm marrying ham."

"I thought it was pork?"

"Shh. Don't tell steak." She waves goodbye, and we sign off.

I change out of the dress shirt, pulling on a casual green polo, then grab my phone, writing a text to the woman I didn't think of naked in the shower at all.

Damn. I am impressing myself with my restraint.

I send her a non-flirty note, asking where we're meeting. She replies quickly.

Truly: I have to pop into a restaurant supply shop that's near Prospect Park. Meet me in the park after?

Jason: What? I'm not good enough to be seen in the restaurant supply shop?

Truly: Feel free to be seen there, weirdo. :) But I must warn you, it's a bit like church for me. I'll be the one genuflecting before the glasses.

Jason: Then we must meet there, weirdo. :)

Well, I do like the way she looks on her knees.

10

Truly: Good morning! It's my six-month detox check-in.

Charlotte: Has it actually been six months since THE INCIDENT, aka what you described as the best sex of your life?

Truly: Grrr. You're so not helpful.

Charlotte: Ah, but I thought good sex was one of the five great pleasures in life.

Truly: What are the other four again?

Charlotte: Sarcasm, cats riding Roombas, a well-made margarita, and high heels that feel like slippers. You know the kind—dainty and pretty on the outside and large and roomy on the inside.

Truly: I feel like those are three truths and a lie, because that last one does not exist.

Charlotte: Good sex does. But wait, we're not talking about good sex. We're talking about the fact that you're avoiding it. How hard is that?

Truly: It's awful. He's too charming, too amusing, too easy to be with. He's like a bag of popcorn. Have you ever tried to eat just one handful of popcorn?

Charlotte: That's unnatural. Who the hell can do that?

Truly: Not me, that's for sure. But here's the deal: I'm going to be spending more time with him. He asked me to go to a few weddings with him for work, like as his plus-one, and I need his help with my work stuff too.

Charlotte: You're going to be spending more time with the guy you want badly and have been secretly into forever? Sounds super wise.

Truly: Exactly. Help me.

Charlotte: I have just the thing for you. Can I show you the e-mail you sent me the morning after? Maybe you need a reminder of how you felt the next day.

* * *

From: MixologistExtraordinaire at gmail
To: LuckySpotGirl at gmail
Re: Confessions of a Bad Girl

I am the worst twin sister in the world.

The absolute worst.

How could I do this?

And by this, I mean engage in earth-shattering, toe-curling, bend-me-over-the-bed-and-take-me-hard sex with my brother's best friend. By the way, did I mention the sex was incredible?

Oh, wait. I did.

But I'm not surprised, because I've always liked his company. He's funny and clever, and he has this irreverent side that's fascinating and wildly entertaining.

But we were only supposed to go snowboarding.

WE'VE SNOWBOARDED TOGETHER BEFORE WITHOUT INCIDENT.

It all seemed innocuous, right? A day on the slopes in January.

At the end of the final run, the sun had already set, and we headed into the ski lodge and made plans to meet for dinner.

I didn't even drink at dinner. Neither did he. We just talked the whole time, and there was candlelight. Stupid candlelight. And he was flirting, and he always flirts, but this time . . . this time we weren't in New York. We were far enough away I could forget everything that went wrong years ago.

Did I ever tell you about Sarah, my closest friend growing up? She was the shoulder I leaned on when my father died, and we were the best of friends all through college. After graduation, she told me she wanted to go out with my brother and asked for my permission. Shocking, right?

But I talked to Malone about her anyway.

When I asked if he wanted to date Sarah, he said only if it was okay with me. Only if it was all out in the open. I said go for it. No one was sneaking around, so it was fine.

He went out with her for a few months, and at first, it was great. Until Sarah wanted more. She kept pushing him, and when he didn't want the same things she did, she turned into a different person. She was now Sarah, wound up and tortured edition, pining away for a man.

Malone ended it with her, and then she ended it with me.

One morning she met me for coffee to "break up" with me. She said she couldn't bear to see me anymore because I reminded her of him. When she got over him, maybe we could be friends again, she'd said. That was well over a decade— nearly thirteen years—ago. And I haven't seen or heard from her since.

Yes, I was younger, and sure, in some ways this was early-twenties relationship drama. But, Charlotte, as I'm writing this, my throat's tight and my stomach's churning. No one tells you how much it hurts to lose a friend.

But you know what hurt more?

What it did to my brother and me.

Nothing was the same between us for months. *Everything was awkward and tense, and we barely spoke to each other. When things eventually returned to normal, we made a deal—we'd never date a friend of each other's again.*

I broke my side of the bargain last night.

I slept with his best friend.

And the worst part? I want to be consumed with nothing but regret, only what's in my head is a whole lot more chaotic and crazy. It's half regret and half desire.

But here's the bottom line: it can't happen again. There are some things I can't risk losing.

Xoxo

Truly

* * *

Truly: Oomph. Nothing like having your words come back to haunt you?

Charlotte: You wanted tough love.

Truly: Yeah, that's what I needed to see. I worry what would happen to *his* friendship with Malone if I let anything go further. What if we went out and it ended badly and caused a rift?

Charlotte: That is a real risk.

Truly: That's why I can't go down that slippery slope. I need to just focus on business. Not stupid lust.

Charlotte: Lust isn't always stupid. Sometimes it's exactly the opposite. That said, can we talk about the big issue?

Truly: Funny, I thought that was the big issue.

Charlotte: The big issue of how exactly you plan to pull off going to weddings together, being his fake date, and all that. You do know what happens at weddings?

Truly: People get . . . married?

Charlotte: And other people get . . . frisky. Picture this: dancing, toasting, WITNESSING DECLARATIONS OF LOVE AND AFFECTION. I'm sure going to one with someone you're trying to keep your hands off will be as easy as resisting the seven-tiered wedding cake.

Truly: I can resist cake.

Charlotte: You're a stronger woman than I.

Truly: You're right. And you know what? I'm not that twenty-two-year-old anymore. I'm not that girl who struggled to talk to her own brother after he broke up with someone. I'm a goddamn adult, and my relationship with him is important. It's one of the most important in my life. I'm going to see if Malone is busy.

Charlotte: Go for it. That's an excellent resistance plan.

* * *

Truly: Hey, knucklehead! Want to grab coffee before I head to the restaurant supply store?

Malone: If you're buying, and if by coffee you mean coffee plus eggs and potatoes.

Truly: My, my, someone's a growing boy.

Malone: Yes, I'm having a growth spurt at age thirty-five. Are you too?

Truly: Oh no you didn't! Did you really just remind me of my age?

Malone: No, I reminded you of MY age. I can't help it if you happen to be nearly as old as your older brother.

Truly: I am and always will be younger, by an astonishing FIVE WHOLE MINUTES. And you are evil. Good thing I love you. Meet you at Wendy's Diner in twenty?

Malone: I'll be there with a glass of milk to help my bones grow faster.

Truly: Awesome. Also, I have to meet Jason after that. I'm helping him with a work thing.

Malone: Are you going into the men's advice business or the groomsman-for-hire business? Because as much as I think you can do anything, I'm not sure either is the right path for you on account of your not being a man. Just a friendly tip.

Truly: Thanks for the sage advice. So helpful. By the way, I love you. Just wanted to say it again.

Malone: You're such a goofball. I love you too.

11

I'd like to say I don't flirt, but it's too hard to resist.

When I find Truly ogling shelves of shot glasses, I point to the floor. "I believe I was told you'd be on your knees. 'Genuflecting before the glasses,' wasn't it?"

"It's called a metaphor. You use it to creatively express how you feel about something."

"Let me creatively express how much I was looking forward to seeing you on your knees—like a die-hard Yankees fan looks forward to spring training."

"Good one, since I do enjoy the arrival of spring training."

"Thought you might like that. Want to tell me the story again of how you met Mariano Rivera?"

"Are you saying I've told you that story too many times?"

"Oh, no. Never. I hardly remember it. Was it after the game one Sunday afternoon, and Charlotte snapped the photo by the third baseline?"

Truly arches a disdainful brow. "See if I ever invite you to a game again."

"Please tell it to me once more. I can hear it for the ten thousandth time."

"I'm literally never sharing someone else's season tickets with you ever."

"You will. You totally will." I shift gears, pointing to the glasses. "Have you ever collected anything? Like shot glasses or license plates or aprons?"

"Nah, I don't really like things. I suppose, technically, I collect pancake recipes. But I keep them up here." She taps her skull.

"That is worth collecting." I pause, picturing what I might amass if I had that itch. "If I were a collector, I'd go for typewriters."

"Typewriters?"

"Those things you use to write on? They have little keys with the letters of the alphabet on them."

"Ohhh. I was wondering what those were." She picks up a wineglass and runs her thumb along the stem. "Do you really write on a typewriter? That's so quaint."

"God, no. I'd have to become a registered hipster if I did, and I'm not ready to move to Brooklyn yet. Come to think of it, I don't own skinny jeans either."

"Let's keep it that way."

"All right. Stop distracting me with talk of pancakes and typewriters. Why aren't you on your knees?"

She taps me lightly on the chest with the rim of the glass. "Because you can't have everything."

"Don't I know it." I gesture to the overwhelming array of stemware lining the shelves—glasses for wine and martinis, for margaritas and champagne. "What are you shopping for?"

She shrugs happily. "Nothing and everything. By which I mean, I'll know when I see it. But if I don't check them out, how will I find that perfect new glass that tempts a customer? Gabriella's the same. She actually sent me a list of new glasses she's been coveting."

She grabs her phone and shows me a text.

Gabriella: You must get Nick and Nora glasses. I both beg you and insist on it. They are sooo cool and so trendy. Also, some V-shaped martini glasses for me? They make me happy. Pretty please!

"She's enthusiastic."

"That's why she's a keeper, and that's why I want to move her up. She might love glasses as much as I do. After all, every drink needs the right glass. I've been in love with picking glasses and making drinks since I was a kid crafting the coolest mixes for my lemonade stand."

"Seriously? You made fancy lemonades for sale?"

"Hell yeah. I hustled my ass off on the streets of the West Village, selling honey lemonade, red-pepper lemonade, cherry lemonade. But I mostly did it for fun. I made all sorts of concoctions growing up."

"What besides lemonade was in your young mixologist repertoire?"

"Started with Shirley Temple, of course. Malone loved that. I tested all my creations on him, and my parents too. My dad went crazy for my Arnold Palmer. I'd set up at the kitchen counter with all the plastic cups and mismatched mugs. I'd mix sodas with syrups, and juices with other juices, and try to figure out the perfect garnish to add."

"So you were, for all intents and purposes, always a bartender?" I ask as we wander down the next aisle, surveying sherry glasses and copper mugs.

"A businesswoman too. When I was a teenager, I made enough at my summer lemonade stand to cover my movie and lipstick budget." She smiles, her glossy red lips shining. "I do like my lipstick."

Oh, how I want to say, *And I like kissing it off*, but I'm on a flirting diet. So I focus on the non-naughty things she said. "And now you're hoping to expand your business."

"Yes. Let's dive into it." She finishes browsing the aisles, places an order with the woman who runs the shop, then we head to Prospect Park, grabbing a bench on the outskirts of the grass.

"The investor I mentioned? I pitched him on that Parisian-themed bar I want to open. He likes it, but his partners aren't ready for that yet. So he asked me to put together a concept for a new bar, modeled after Gin Joint with signature cocktails, decor, and all that . . . but with a British theme."

"And clearly I'm the only person you could possibly come to."

"You are kind of my one British friend."

"Good. Let's keep it that way. I don't want you accessible to any other Brits. They're very dangerous, what with the way they speak in that sexy accent that makes American women swoon."

She shoots me the side-eye. "You think I swoon when I hear your voice?"

"Swoon, throw your knickers at me, and want to have sex straightaway." Maybe I was supposed to behave, but hell, it's so damn hard with her. "It's quite a burden to bear."

"I thought we were trying to stay in the friend zone."

I shoot her a *you're crazy* stare. "Get your mind out of the gutter. I'm talking about the challenge of going around with this accent. Do you have any idea? Everybody wants me. Admit it. You do kind of melt a little when you hear me talk."

"I admit nothing."

"I'll take that as a good thing." I shift gears. Business now. Seriously. "Okay, so you're using me for my pub expertise. What's the plan?"

"What I thought we could do is this: I'll go with you to the weddings as your fake date, and you can go with me to visit some of the pubs I want to check out. You can be my reality check, if you will. I also want to make sure the ideas I have are authentic, so I want to test them on you. I was hoping we could even start in the next day or so? Perhaps Tuesday?"

"I'm there."

"Perfect. Now tell me about the weddings you want me to go to."

I review the details, rattling off the basics of Chip's ceremony, then the one for Enzo from Spain, who hired me since he's new to the country and doesn't know anyone yet, and another where I'm simply an extra groomsman, and I've been asked to play the part with an Aussie accent, for no other reason than the groom finds Crocodile Dundee entertaining. The groom is a superstar skateboarder in the X Games, and I tell her my friend Josh recommended me.

"Your sports agent friend?"

"Yes. Josh Summers. Reps a couple of the Yankees, some of the Rangers, and on and on. You'd like him; therefore, I will probably never introduce you to him."

Laughing softly, she gives me a curious stare. "Why would I like him?"

"All the women do."

"So all women everywhere have the same taste?"

I tap my chin. "Fair point. Your taste is finer. After all, you did enjoy the ride on my—"

Her hand covers my mouth. "Be. Good." She nudges my elbow. "So . . . when do I meet this hot sports agent friend of yours?"

I narrow my eyes, huffing. "Never. Also, I don't actually need a date for the skateboarder's wedding. It's a solo gig."

"Really? Are you sure?"

"Positive. And for that comment, you will never meet Josh."

She rubs her palms together. "And you will never get to see Presley, then. She's stunning and brilliant and hilarious. So there. I'm keeping her away from you too."

I roll my eyes. "You do know I've met her several times. She comes to jujitsu with us now and then, and yes, she's quite funny."

"Then you're not allowed to speak with her again."

"You're cute when you're jealous."

"Ha. Same to you. But enough about hot friends. About the two weddings you need me for . . . I presume we'll need backstories and fake names? A different one for each?"

I make a low whistle of appreciation. "Damn, you're good. Is there a name you've always wanted to have?"

She adopts a high, saccharine tone. "Oh, God. I love the name Truly." Her voice returns to dry and sarcastic. "It's not as if I was always made fun of for my name growing up."

"Were you made fun of for that? It's a lovely name."

"Most people don't get it. They think I'm Trudy. Or Julie. Because it's not a name; it's a freaking adverb. But it's fine. My parents loved it. What can you do? And I suppose I really don't mind it now."

"I think it's quite pretty. And it suits you."

She holds my gaze for a lingering moment, swallows, then sighs. "Listen, I saw my brother this morning. I told him I'm spending more time with you."

I flinch, unsure what to make of this admission. "He knows we hang out. Why would you feel like you had to confess something?"

"I didn't tell him what happened six months ago. I simply mentioned over breakfast that I was going to be doing this with you. I told him because this here"—she gestures from her to me—"this deal, it feels more personal than taking a class or working out together. I know we flirt and joke."

"Wait. You flirt? It's more like you tell me you don't

flirt." I hold up a stop-a-moment finger. "Oh, that's hate-flirting. My bad."

Twin spots of pink spread across her cheeks. She looks away then back at me. "Whatever. You know I'm attracted to you."

Those words. *Attracted to you.* I shouldn't let them send a charge through me. But hell, they do, an electric jolt. She's been so damn good at denying, evading, dodging.

But right now, she is confessing, and it's a turn-on exactly when it shouldn't be. And maybe because emotions are the devil but desire is angelic, I give in, brushing my fingers down her arm. "I'm wildly attracted to you."

Her breath catches. She leans closer to me, out of the friend zone and into the *more* zone. Her gaze swings down to my hand on her arm. "That's a little tempting."

"It is."

"Maybe too tempting."

"I should stop." I run my finger down her bare skin, savoring the electric sensation of touching this woman again. The air between us crackles, and all it would take is . . . well, it would take deciding to cross a line we don't want to cross.

Lines exist for a reason.

So you don't give in to lust.

So you don't let your dick or your heart control you. You don't give in to instant gratification when you have a lifetime of friendship between you.

I swallow, take a breath, find my voice again. "Are

you . . . dating anyone?" I choke out the words. They taste like last week's compost bin.

Laughing, she shakes her head. "Sounds like you'd rather I didn't?"

I shrug, affecting a relaxed pose. "You're free to date."

"And so are you. But I'm not seeing anyone. I'm too busy with the expansion plans right now. Dating is not on my agenda."

"Same here. My business, that is. Too much going on."

"So we're both in the same position. And we'll stick to the plan."

And while I'm terribly tempted to make a joke about positions, or things sticking, I resist. "I understand. I know what's at stake."

"I know you do, Jason, but sometimes you make it hard. The way you flirt. The way you touch me." Her tone is earnest, full of need. It stops me in my tracks. Normally we fire zingers at each other, we toss bouquets of flirtation. But there's something almost sad in the way she's speaking right now, like she desperately needs me to change.

"Do I touch you too much?"

"Too much for my own good."

Dear God. *Too much for my own good.* "I get that. I can stop."

"You need to know I don't want you to, but we probably should. Because I like this." She points from me to her. "I like this, but not as much as I dislike the idea of losing you or hurting Malone. I like how we are. I like seeing my brother for breakfast, like I did earlier today, and for baseball games, and when he hangs out to chat after he sings at Gin Joint. I'm at a point where things are clicking in my life. The bar, the business—*everything.* I don't want to feel the way I've felt in the past, where I'm losing the people I love."

I have to keep things on the level for her, and for me. I'm a serial monogamist for a reason—I don't want to be Claire'd again. Commitment and I have kept each other at arm's length ever since I came to the States in my early twenties to take care of my dying nan. When I left England, Claire took me to the airport, teary-eyed and looking like a Nicholas Sparks heroine, saying she'd wait as long as it took for me to return. And a month later, when I was still away, she took up with the barber down the street.

"I understand," I say. "I don't want you to lose what you care about. Not work or your closeness with Malone. And you know my deal. I'm not keen on anything more. So it's best this way."

"I do. I understand that," she says, since she's up to speed on the basics of what went wrong with Claire.

"All that said, there's something vital I want you to know."

"Sure. Tell me."

My lips curve up. "Are you aware I've been attracted to you since I met you?"

"Why are you telling me this now?"

Because I'm on an honesty kick, and I take my time, letting a wicked grin spread across my face. "So you know it's something of a miracle that we've only ever fallen into bed once."

There's that sharp stare I know so well. The *oh no, you didn't* look. "You're aware that falling into bed is exactly what we can't do?"

"Indeed. And my point is, I've been exercising restraint with you for a long time. I can keep it up."

She settles in on the bench, staring at the sun, putting on her shades, taking her time. At last she responds, a smile tugging at her lips. "I suppose you can. You do have excellent stamina."

12

That evening, I round the bases, high-fiving Nick and Malone as I cross home plate.

Nick gives me a fist bump. "Hallelujah! Miracles do happen."

"And you two tossers are the beneficiaries, seeing as I knocked you in."

Nick takes a bow. "I humbly accept your RBI, especially since it's so rare."

I stifle a laugh. "Dickhead."

"That's five years on the team, and it's your first dinger, right?" he asks.

"It's not even my first home run this season."

Malone claps me on the back but locks eyes with Nick. "Now, now, don't sell this guy short. He manages to whack a whole pair over the fences each season." He turns to me, intensely serious. "We are so proud of you for that kind of consistency."

I point to the field. "You do realize we just took the lead because of that home run?"

"That's it. I'm getting you a plaque. Best One-Homer-a-Season Hitter," Nick says.

"Don't make him feel bad that he's not at our level," Malone cuts in as we head to the dugout. "We need to keep his spirits up. After all, if we didn't have Jason on the team . . . well, we wouldn't have enough players, and we'd have to forfeit."

I groan, taking off my helmet and dragging a hand through my hair. "I just hit a home run. Or a whopper or a dinger or whatever it is you call it here."

Nick rattles off the names. "Tater. Goner. Blast. Bomb. Jack. Like, you jacked one over the fence."

"You're so classy here with your jack talk." I make the requisite offensive hand gesture.

"You could also call it a long ball," Nick retorts, gesturing to his crotch. "That better?"

"Loads." I glance at the bleachers, spotting Harper and their two kids grabbing front-row seats. "Your wife and kids just returned, so try to be a civilized bastard now. I know that'll be hard for you."

"Sooo hard. But I can do it."

When the game ends, Nick takes off with his wife and the kids, scooping up his little redheaded daughter for a piggyback ride.

"Tell your dad you want another rescue dog, Skye!" Malone calls out to the little tyke, his cousin's kid. "Vet services are on the house."

"I already told him I want one. He said yes!"

"Because he's wrapped around your little finger!"

"I'm going to work on my list of dog names tonight."

"Please consider Jason," I call out.

I sling my bag over my shoulder, making my way out of the park with Malone.

"You want a dog named after you?" he asks.

"Hell yeah. That's the ultimate compliment."

"Good point. I'll aspire to convince her to choose Malone now. Or Truly. I bet she'd like that. Speaking of, I hear my sister's going undercover with you."

My brain speeds up, spinning, as if I need to fashion an excuse. But I shut down that matchstick reaction. There's nothing wrong with her going undercover with me. Just as there's nothing wrong with me spending time with her. This exchange of favors is no different than us going to jujitsu, or for a bike ride or a hike.

I pretend our plans are a state secret, bringing my finger to my lips. I shush him. "I don't want anyone here to know." I glance around the path as if we've entered enemy territory.

"Yes, I'm sure everyone has followed you to document your whereabouts."

"You never know. I'm rather famous in this city."

"Or in your own mind."

I tap my temple. "I'm a legend up here."

"No doubt. I find it amusing it took the two of you this long to figure out she would be a perfect companion."

I snap my gaze to him, surprised at his comment. "What do you mean?"

Malone scratches his jaw, chuckling as we head toward the Columbus Circle side of the park. "It's hilarious, the idea of you two pretending to be a couple at a wedding."

Is he onto something? Trying to get under my skin and extract intel? But then I talk sense into myself because that one night was months ago, nothing more has happened, and we never let on. And since nothing has transpired in six months, isn't that proof of either a supreme lack of interest or supreme resistance?

I vote the latter and pat myself virtually on the back.

"Yeah, I suppose it's pretty amusing. Since we're obviously not a couple." I laugh for good measure, like I'm selling my case.

What the hell? I don't need to make him a pitch. Truly and I are not a couple. Maybe I should remind him that the ocean is wet and sugar is sweet.

Malone cracks up, shaking his head. "That's not what I mean."

Now I'm thoroughly confused. "What do you mean, then?"

"Seriously? You don't know?"

My skin prickles, the back of my neck growing hot. Shit. Fuck. Bugger. He does know I shagged his sister. He found out somehow, and he's going to toy with me. Malone is a clever bastard, and perhaps he's sliding the knife under my skin, ready to fillet me. I don't want to be filleted, or grilled, for that matter.

And I don't want to lose a good friend.

Especially over something that won't happen again. So I lean on my skills. I can fake this. I can pull off nothing-to-see-here. "No clue what you're on about."

"The two of you bicker so much you seem like a real couple. It's so believable that the two of you could be together."

I jerk my gaze toward him. What the hell did he say? "Your sister and me?"

"You argue enough to fool anyone into thinking you've been together forever."

He hums a tune under his breath as we turn onto Central Park West, and I chew on that observation, wondering if it means anything or nothing.

I decide it's positive. It's a damn good thing if Truly and I appear like we're a couple over the next few weekends.

But at the end of the day and the end of the night, we are only fiction.

* * *

Later that night, I head to my office, also known as the coffee shop near my apartment. But unlike half the other patrons at cafés these days, I don't FaceTime in public or conduct conference calls at top volume while sipping my mochaccino.

Like I drink mochaccinos.

With a cup of tea in hand, I settle on a leather couch in the back corner, and Troy and Sully arrive shortly.

"Gentlemen," Sully says, spreading his arms wide. "What is up?"

"This is what's up. Did you know two of Shakespeare's plays were translated into Klingon? Just learned that this evening in my playwriting class," Troy offers.

"Do you speak Klingon?" Sully asks.

"Working on it. Thinking about maybe writing my next play in half verse, half Klingon."

"Or maybe write it in all verse, wait till it blows up and Lin-Manuel Miranda partners with you, and *then* translate it into Klingon," I suggest.

"Good suggestion, boss man," Troy says.

We dive straight into wedding business. "Are you guys ready for this weekend?"

Sully rubs his palms. "I am pumped. My wife is too. She's stocking up on tissues. She loves weddings. Cries at every single one, even if she doesn't know the couple. Doesn't matter. She goes full waterworks."

"And she likes this? Crying over people she doesn't even know?" That's Troy's style—he hasn't met a question he's afraid to ask.

"She says declarations of love hit her right *here*." He taps his chest. "She likes weddings because she cries."

"That makes no sense. How does that make any sense?" Troy asks.

"I guess you've never needed a good cry," Sully says with a shrug and a sip of his coconut latte.

"If I need a good cry, I watch *Brian's Song*," Troy says.

"If I needed a good cry, and I literally never have, I think about the day The Beatles broke up," I offer.

Troy furrows his brow. "You weren't even alive then."

"That's what makes me sad. I'll never see them perform." I tap my phone and return to the details. "Here's everything you need to know about the wedding."

We review the plan. When I'm done, Sully counts off on his fingers. "Surf and turf bachelor dinner? Check.

Woman? Check. Tux? Check. But the big question is, can I wear my new Nikes?"

Troy jumps in. "Nikes as in sneakers?"

"I don't mean Nike as in a boutonniere. Unless Nike got into the boutonniere business." He grabs his phone. "Side note: look into viability of lapel decor as possible new business venture."

I don't have the heart to tell him that florists have already cornered the market on boutonnieres. Instead, I focus on the practical, even though I already know the answer to my question. "Is Nike making tuxedo-wear shoes now?"

"That would be awesome, but no." He slides his thumb across the phone screen, showing us a gorgeous set of gleaming white shelves filled with . . . sneakers. All sorts of sneakers. "My latest score is the new Air VaporMax FK. Check 'em out. They're dope."

"You actually collected all those pairs? For what? To look at?" Troy asks.

Sully scoffs. "Dude, they're like stocks. I'm going to turn around and sell these babies. Well, not the Vapor-Max, because they're too sick for words. But the others. If you buy quick and sell fast, you can make a nice profit. Always hustling, always looking for an angle."

"I completely understand where you're coming from with the hustle," I cut in. "That said, I don't think you should wear sneakers to the wedding."

"For what it's worth, I never wear sneakers when I'm working," Troy offers. "Not a wedding and not at my other job either."

Sully finishes off his latte, considers a moment, then

stares at Troy. "Hey. What's your other job? Writing plays?"

Troy glances away, his voice lowering. "That doesn't pay the bills yet."

"What does, then?"

"I do a bunch of stuff at night," he says, his cheeks reddening a bit.

"Like what?" Sully presses. "You know what I do. Manage a Foot Locker."

Troy takes a breath like this is hard for him. "I do a little construction, a little fire service, some delivery."

Sully claps his shoulder. "Don't be embarrassed, man. Nothing wrong with an honest day's work, or an honest night's labor."

Wait. Is Troy's night job what I think it might be?

"Speaking of honest work, Jason, who's the lady you're bringing with you this weekend?" Troy asks.

"She's just a good friend. That's all."

Troy snickers. "Methinks the gentleman doth protest too much."

Sully slaps his palm on the table, shouting, "*Hamlet*!"

"But can you do that line in Klingon?" I ask, successfully sending the conversation down a new rabbit hole and away from Truly.

When she texts me later to tell me the location for Tuesday's pub visit, it feels vaguely like a date. Like we're a couple.

But that's ridiculous.

This is simply a project, and that's all it'll ever be.

And that's all I want.

13

Truly: Why am I looking at my clothes early in the morning, already considering options for tonight? There aren't that many choices. My wardrobe is simple —black with a side of jeans.

Charlotte: You look foxy in black. And in jeans.

Truly: I'm not trying to look foxy! And really, what I wear this evening when I go to a pub with Jason doesn't matter much, right? I'll just dress like me.

Charlotte: The *you* look is a good look.

Truly: All right. Favorite skinny jeans it is. I'm ready for tonight and I'm planning on being a model citizen.

Charlotte: BAHAHAHAHAHAHA

Truly: You doubt me?

Charlotte: Of course not. I'm watching a Roomba cat video, not laughing at your efforts at model citizenship.

Truly: And for that, I can't wait to come back to you tomorrow and tell you I was an angel. For now, I'm off to meet Presley for a cuppa.

Charlotte: I can't wait for your report tomorrow either, you devil.

* * *

Truly: On my way to our coffee date! But question for you – have you ever gone through a million wardrobe options because you're planning to spend time with someone you're not even dating? I did that just now. I'm seeing Jason tonight, and . . . well, you know. I need to stay strong.

Presley: I'm here and I'm going to order you a coffee, black. You always order something ridiculous like a watermelon latte with a side of nutmeg when you're unsure of something, when in fact you need a coffee, black. Also, that's what you should have tonight before you see him.

Truly: Watermelon latte sounds disgusting.

Presley: And yet I'm sure somewhere in this city, some café sells it.

Truly: Let us vow to never go to that coffee shop.

Presley: I accept this suggestion wholeheartedly.

Truly: Also, black coffee sounds perfect. That'll keep me strong.

Presley: Good luck staying strong with the guy you want to bang.

Truly: I do not want to bang him.

Presley: Oh, sorry. I meant to say the guy you sooooo want to bang.

Truly: Between you and Charlotte, I've decided friends are the devil. See you in two minutes.

Presley: I'll have my best devilish smile for you.

14

Ryder meets my eye from across the booth in the studio. "And we're back for the final segment of *The Consummate Wingman*. Today, we have a special guest in the studio. You know him as the Modern Gentleman in New York, and he's dedicated to the cause of helping our listeners be the best they can be. Jason, talk to us. I need your number one new tip."

It's Tuesday morning, and I'm in the booth at the studio where Lockhart records his wildly popular radio show.

The man is a rock star in the advice business, and with good reason. He tells it like it is, and he has something to say. That's what I've learned matters most. You can have a good voice, be comfortable in front of crowds, and possess a charming grin that warms people to you. But if you want to be an "expert," you must have a point of view.

I move closer to the mic. "I've been thinking about how we can help our fellow men out there, and I have just the tidbit to share with your listeners. Ryder, tell me something. Do you think there's ever a need to manspread?"

He chuckles. "No. Never."

"Exactly. I propose an end to manspreading. In the ongoing quest to make manners the next cool trend, can we please keep our knees inside our own personal space?"

Ryder hoots. "I'm down with that."

"Am I right? But if you don't believe me, gentlemen of the city, put yourself in the place of someone who must share space with you. Let's say you're sitting on the train, heading into work, and you spread your legs. Do you really need a foot of space or more between your knees? Is that essential to your comfort and well-being? Your mating posture?"

Ryder smiles broadly. He's clearly amused with today's advice. "Nor is it necessary for your junk."

"Exactly. And when you do manspread, do you know what the other person across from you is thinking? They're thinking, 'I can't believe that's somebody's son, husband, brother, or what have you.' Because spread legs are tacky and virtually always uncalled for."

Ryder raises a fist. "Down with manspreading. Let's bring an end to it."

"Precisely. One of the reasons I say don't do this in public is if you keep doing it in public, you're going to do it in business. You're going to do it when you sit down for a job interview. You're going to do it when you sit across from somebody you want to hire you.

And I tell you this: it's highly unlikely anyone is interested in hiring a manspreader."

"I think it's safe to say that employers of the world are thanking you right now."

"And I'm thanking your listeners who I know are going to change their habits today."

"Well, you heard it here," Ryder says, shifting to a wrap-it-up tone, "from the Modern Gentlemen in New York. Today's tip? Just cut that nasty habit, dudes, and we'll be heading toward a classier society."

When the segment finishes, Ryder walks out of the studio with me. "The listeners dig you. It doesn't hurt that they think you're speaking from a position of authority simply because of that accent."

"It's true. The accent proves I'm always correct," I joke.

"Let's get you back in the studio in another week. Next Monday good for you?"

A smile threatens to take over my face, but I do my best to appear grateful and professional and not out of my mind with glee. Don't want to scare him away. "Sounds great to me."

"And listen, I'm really impressed that you've built a reputation as an expert on your own over the years. It's amazing to meet somebody your age who's gone through Toastmasters and done all sorts of public speaking. We may have an opening soon. I'm going to advocate for you."

"Thank you. I appreciate that."

When I leave the building, I want to pump a fist, to jump up and down. It's an odd job I've cobbled together, but it's one I love. Talking. Sharing. Giving advice. And really, trying to save the world one man or woman at a time by keeping them from being disgusting pigs.

Later that night, I do something else I enjoy.

I meet up with Truly.

15

From the pages of Truly's Drink Recipe Book

Gentleman Friend:
Coffee
Just Coffee

Some guys are just . . . hard to categorize. They don't want to stay in that neat drawer you've selected for them.

There's the friend drawer, the date drawer, the colleague drawer, the lover drawer, and the boyfriend-material drawer.

But some men don't fit in your bureau.

Take that guy who's a friend, but not the average friend. You rely on him, you turn to him, and you laugh with him.

He has interesting things to say. He has a point of view. And you like that. Damn it, you like that more than you should. You find him . . . intriguing. You think you know him, but you're also keenly aware that you haven't unearthed everything that makes him tick. And you want to.

Because there's more going on.

You're not talking about looks, but he has all that. You're talking about who he is. His brains, his heart, his smarts.

His charisma.

Damn, his charisma.

He has that by the gallon.

But you made a deal. You have a plan. There is a road map. He's your friend, he's simply your gentleman friend.

And sometimes when you're heading out to see your gentleman friend, you need a shot of courage.

No liquor this time, ladies.

You need to be in complete control.

If you want to make it through a night with your gentleman friend, you need something strong. We're talking the stiffest, toughest drink possible to gird yourself.

Garlic juice.

.

.

.

.

.

.

.

.

Kidding! Garlic is like bacon. It's a no-go.

But coffee? A strong pot of coffee? Yes. Come to mama. None of that French roast crap for the Gentleman Friend drink. The Gentleman Friend is single origin Ethiopian, natural wash, handcrafted, organic with a bright, juicy taste. Never more than 202 degrees. Keeps the brain on high alert. Keeps your attention on anything other than the way your gentleman friend looks when he walks down the street in those dark jeans and that pullover shirt that hugs his pecs, wearing that five-o'clock shadow you want to run your hands over. Coffee will hold your focus when he gets that twinkle in his amber eyes—damn that twinkle. Damn it to hell and back for the way it makes your stomach flip.

Coffee. God bless coffee.

Coffee keeps you strong.

16

She waits for me outside the pub in Tribeca she picked.

Dressed in dark jeans that hug her legs and a clingy top that slopes off one shoulder, she's the woman in black. She hardly ever wears anything colorful, except her lipstick. It's a wine red and shiny, like there's a layer of gloss over it.

Somehow it's fitting that she's the color of night, because there's a toughness to Truly. An edge. She's no-nonsense, all business, and naturally, I want to take all those black clothes off her.

But I remind myself I need to maintain balance and exist peacefully in this state of wanting but not having. This is a normal feeling for me to have around her, and I've learned to live with it.

She waves, smiles, then when I reach her, she throws her arms around me. I'm taken aback, nearly knocked over by the unexpectedness of her embrace. But I'm not nimble for nothing. I seize the opportunity and sniff her hair. Fresh, clean, so very her—and do I detect the faintest scent of coffee beans? I do, and hell, now coffee reminds me of sex. "I'll take this, and gladly. But I'm not sure what the returning hero greeting is for."

She grasps me tighter, her arms looping around me, and yes, that's quite nice too. "Thank you for spreading the gospel of no more manspreading." She breaks the embrace and clasps my shoulder. "Manspreading is the bane of my existence, and you're a superhero for doing your part to eliminate the virus that it is."

"That's what I'm here for. To make the world a little more civilized, one bloke at a time."

"I see it all night long at the bar. Men have no idea how much it turns off women. I swear, I see groups of women walk away from packs of manspreaders."

"*Packs.* Seems apropos for men with such wild and unruly behavior."

"It's almost as bad as mansplaining. That's a touch worse, since it's an insult to intelligence. Down with mansplainers, I say!"

"You're on fire tonight."

"I might have had a cup of coffee a few minutes ago."

"So if you're normally at a ten when it comes to energy, vim and vigor, you're at about one hundred now?"

"Something like that. Also, coffee keeps me strong."

"News flash—you're already strong."

She shoots me a look, one I can't quite read, but it seems to fall squarely on the side of I-know-what-you-look-like-naked. "I need to be strong."

"Okay, then."

She gestures to the door. "Ready for pub lesson number one?"

"As ready as I'll ever be."

We head inside and grab two stools at the bar, surveying the decor: leather chairs, round tables, high-backed booths, and the darkest of dark wood everywhere.

I nod appreciatively. "Looks pretty solid." My gaze drifts to the bar itself. Beer tankards hang above it. "Very authentic."

"Filing that tidbit away," she says. "I picked this one because it was on my list as having promise. It has that local pub feel, right?"

"Yes, so you can check that off the list." I peer toward the back room, cataloging the pool table, and the table football one too, then I make a note to stroll back there later for a proper survey.

"Good. Because I did a lot of research online. I don't want you to think I'm simply going to expect you to do all the work."

"Like when I fucked you from behind?"

Her jaw drops, and for the first time in my life, I think I might get slapped. I probably deserve it.

I definitely deserve it.

She doesn't speak at first, just stares. "Did you really just say that?"

"Did I? Seems that might have been the little devil who sometimes takes over my mouth."

"Gentleman, my ass."

I shrug a little sheepishly, hoping I haven't gone too far. "Even the best gentlemen have devils in them."

"You and your devil are terrible."

"Are you sure that's what you meant? I feel like *incredible* was the first line in the review you gave me after."

She shakes her head, huffing. "You're the worst."

"Or am I really the best?"

She leans in close. "Just a little reminder, since you seem to have forgotten some details. I did all the work when I rode you. I seem to remember you saying, *Yeah, ride me like that, Truly. Let me watch you fuck me hard.*"

Hallelujah! It worked. "You do realize it's still hot as fuck when you talk dirty, even if you're imitating me talking dirty to you? And for the record, that was my favorite view." My brain has the courtesy to slide that image front and center. "Picturing it again right now."

She covers my eyes. "Stop. Just stop."

"Nice try, but it's here in my head with me."

She drops her hand. "The worst."

"Also, a gentleman always apologizes, so please allow me. I'm sorry for saying you didn't do any of the work. Now that I think about it, I recall you were fantastic at rocking against me when I bent you over the bed."

Her eyes bug out. "You won't ever stop, will you?"

I gaze at the ceiling, considering. "Probably not." I return my focus to her, lowering my voice. "Do you really want me to? To stop?"

She locks her pretty blue eyes with mine. "Do I? I suppose that's the question, isn't it?"

And she doesn't technically answer it.

Perhaps that's the answer. *Don't stop.*

* * *

The bartender swings by, setting down coasters and looking far too much like Liam Hemsworth for my taste. He better not speak like him.

"Cheers! Welcome to Fox and Frog's Finest, serving the most authentic pints this side of the pond."

Great, really great. He's Daniel Fucking Craig, with his now-I'm-from-London-and-all-the-ladies-throw-knickers-at-me accent. Why can't he just sound like a stuffy, rich uncle from *Downton Abbey*?

"We are indeed here for the authenticity," Truly remarks.

"You have come to the right place, then. I'm Marcus, and I'm here for you tonight."

Fantastic. His personality is a combination of a tour conductor on a double-decker red bus and Frasier, with the whole "I'm listening" routine.

"Nice to meet you, Marcus. Great pub you have," Truly says.

"I appreciate you saying that. I'm the manager. Newly promoted. Pretty excited for the new role."

"As you should be. Congrats," Truly says.

"Thank you very much. But enough about me. Can I interest you in a pint?"

"Pale ale for me, and a porter for my . . ." She casts her gaze at me, mischief in her eyes. "My friend."

Friend. A reminder of who we are. This is our zone, no matter how many times I might call up scenes from that night.

But *friends* is what I want, I remind myself.

"Would you like to hear about the pale ale?" Daniel—I mean, Marcus—asks.

"I would," Truly replies, sounding captivated. "Go on. I'm all ears."

Marcus clears his throat and rolls up his shirtsleeves. Fantastic. He has arms like a Hemsworth too, and dresses like, well, like he listens to my advice on how a man should dress. "Let me tell you about the pale ale. Because you picked well. You are going to get the finest hops this side of the Hudson."

Truly scoots closer, listening intently. "Tell me all about it."

He chuckles, rubs his palms together. "You'll find this East Coast IPA is sweeter and juicier than a West Coast IPA. Personally, I'd say the flaked oats provide just the right sweet touch."

Truly nods excitedly, her lips curving into a grin, and a sharp pang of awareness hits me. She's fascinated with flaked oats. She's mesmerized by his fucking beer.

"I love a little hint of sweetness in an IPA," she says.

Marcus Hemsworth beams from here to London, then all the way back. "You'll adore it, then. There's almost no bittering hops, and in addition to that, we layered in loads of aroma hops in the whirlpool. Who doesn't love a whirlpool?"

"Whirlpools rock."

"That they do."

"And what kind of aroma hops were rocking out in the whirlpool?"

Fucking hell. Could she be any more excited about

the beer? It's a pint, for fuck's sake. You drink it; it tastes good. End of story.

"The best kind. The brewer uses the Citra hop, which brings the most tantalizing orange, grapefruit, and lime flavors. It takes the beer to a whole new level. A heavenly level. Do you know what I mean?"

"There is nothing I want more in a beer than for it to be heavenly."

"But then, that's what good beer is. Like angels concocted it on high."

Have I slipped into an alternate world? One where barmen look like matinee idols and talk like Daniel Craig and captivate my woman?

I mean, my friend.

She's just a friend, and she's allowed to be interested in hops.

I remind myself that emotions like envy are unbecoming to my entire worldview.

"Let me pour that for you." Marcus spins around and crosses the bar to the taps.

I shoot her a curious stare. "Want me to leave you alone to chat with Daniel Craig-Hemsworth?"

"Aww, you're jealous."

"No. Please. Not at all."

"I'm just interested in how the beer is made. You don't have to be so green."

"Not jealous. Not in the least."

She holds up her thumb and forefinger. "Maybe a little? I mean, he does have a nice accent, you have to admit. Not that yours isn't ever so lovely too," she says, slipping a posh accent onto the last few words.

I jerk back. "I don't sound like that."

"You don't think you sound like Hugh Bonneville?" she asks, continuing in that high-class tone.

"Like a rich, stuffy uncle? Are you kidding me?"

"He's delightful to listen to. Like Jim Dale. Don't you like the Harry Potter voice? *Astonishing things were happening*, and all that."

"One, Jim Dale is a national treasure, so naturally, I think he's the cat's whiskers. Two, I do not sound like Jim Dale or Hugh Bonneville."

"Maybe Hugh Grant, then?"

"Daniel Craig," I say, standing my ground.

With utter amusement in her eyes, she sets her hand on my arm. "You're completely jealous that you're not the only Brit in the room, aren't you?"

"Please. As if."

"Jealous. Calling it."

"Not an ounce of it in me."

"Liar."

"Woman, you are relentless."

She shimmies her shoulders in a little victory dance. "I am indeed."

A few seconds later, Marcus turns around, sets down the pints, and issues a declaration. "I promise you this pale ale will coat your palate, and you'll love every second of it going down your throat." He blinks, realization hitting him clearly. "Er, sorry. That sounded . . .well, sometimes I get carried away."

Truly regards the glass with a smile. "We all get carried away sometimes, Marcus."

I groan. The innuendo. Dear God, the innuendo. I can't take it anymore.

Another customer walks in, and Marcus gestures to the man in a cap who's surveying the beer board. Yes, go away, Marcus. Go away, this instant.

"Now, I'll be right over there. If you need anything at all, just shout. I'll be here for you." He's Frasier again, and he takes off, possibly to begin a history lesson with a new customer.

Truly lifts her glass. "I like him."

I flinch and try to blink back my shock. "You like him?"

That wasn't what I wanted her to say.

17

I point to Hemsworth. "Him? You like him?"

"Yeah, he's a character. I like to call that type . . . the soapbox bartender." She taps her chest. "Personally, I'm a mixologist. But the mixologist gets along well with the soapboxer because we're both kind of obsessed with what goes into drinks."

"And you like him?" I ask again, still incredulous.

"I like him professionally," she says, then presses the back of her hand against my forehead. "You really ought to see if your temperature has risen from this fit of jealousy."

"I'm cool as ice."

"Then, since you're so unaffected by him, take a drink and give an honest opinion."

I down some of the IPA, and it's pretty damn tasty. "It's okay," I admit grudgingly. "Maybe you and Soapbox want to discuss it."

She laughs and drinks her beer. "I've never seen you so wound up. It's adorable."

"I'm not wound up, and I'm not adorable."

She pokes my side. "Totally adorable."

Laughing, I blurt out, "That tickles."

"You're ticklish?" This seems to delight her to the ends of the earth.

"It's my curse."

She darts her fingers out again, prodding my sides. I squirm away, trying not to laugh. "That's too cute."

"Not cute," I mutter. "Not cute at all."

She takes another swallow, then sets down the glass, her nose crinkling. "This beer is tickling me, but I do love a little beer tickle."

Damn, she's cute with her nose crinkling and her talk of tickling and her calling me adorable. And none of this, none of it whatsoever, ought to be appealing. But it is, so I reroute the conversation to where it started. Me. Us. Not that guy or his beer. "So, you listen to me? When I'm on Ryder's show?"

"Maybe I do a little."

"Or perhaps a lot?"

She licks her lips, smiling. "I like hearing what you have to say. You have interesting observations. On life, on men, on relationships. On business. It's kind of fascinating."

A smile tugs at my lips, coming from deep inside. "Thank you. That means a lot."

"I read your blog too." It doesn't come out like a confession, more like she's pleased to share this news.

"You really do?"

"And I really enjoy it."

And I'm lit up, beaming with pride. This is even

better than flirting. The fact that she likes reading my columns and listening to my advice warms me up. Hell, maybe it's similar to how I enjoy listening when she tells stories of her love of mixology and how she names cocktails. "I'm stoked to hear that."

"You always have something to say. And I like your opinions. They fascinate me. What made you this way? Why did you want to become the"—she stops to sketch air quotes—"'Modern Gentleman of New York'?"

I sigh, wishing I had a lighter answer for her. But I don't. "Let's just say I've seen people behave in ways that aren't exactly the best. So I try to offer suggestions on how we can be better."

"What sort of things? Is it related to your dad? I know you're not close with him."

The mere mention of him sends a jolt of tension down my spine. "That's true, and also a complete understatement."

"Did something else happen? Beyond the obvious—him leaving your mom?"

I take another drink, finishing the glass, then bite off the bitter truth. "After he left her and ran away with the other woman, his own mum was sick. She lived here in the States, since he was born here."

She nods. "Yes, he's why you have dual citizenship."

"One good thing I got from him, I reckon. The ability to live on either side of the ocean, no questions asked. In any case, my nan was quite ill, yet he couldn't be bothered to come over and look after her. I came instead, cared for her, stayed with her till the end." I take time with each word. Those are days I don't want to revisit but want to give their proper weight.

"That's terrible he wouldn't take care of his own mom," Truly says softly, placing her hand over mine. I stare at her hand for a second, and it feels good. Like it belongs there. "Do you ever speak to him?"

"No. I don't want to. Don't care to. There's really no point. I have nothing to say to the man."

"Did you want to return to London? After she passed? Or did your ex turn you completely off going home?"

"Good question. I did want to return at the time, but when Claire took off with the barber, it made me rethink everything."

"Like what?"

"Where I wanted to live, what I wanted to do. I mean, for life. Not just cobbling together a little bit of this, a little bit of that. It was my second time in the States, since I'd been here for college. So I had to decide if I wanted to go home and chase gigs in London at *The Guardian* and whatnot, or stay here. When I landed some assignments at a New York-based website, the decision seemed made for me."

"Any regrets?"

I flash back on the last six years here, the times I've had, the friends I've made, and the work I've done. "Not a one."

"To no regrets." She raises her glass with a smile, and I clink mine against hers.

"Enough about my soap-operatic family. Let's talk

about pubs. Have you figured out if this place is the model for a perfect pub or not?"

"I think it's pretty close, but I can't shake the sense that there's something slightly off." She whips her gaze around the place. She stands, paces like an archaeologist, studying all the nooks and crannies at Fox and Frog's Finest. She heads to the back room, with the pool table, table football, and trivia machine. "I think something's missing from here."

I flash her a smile. "You're getting warmer."

She spins the poles on the table football then lets it go. It clatters as it circles and stops. "Okay, guinea pig, what is it?"

I smile at her nickname. "You were heading in the right direction. It's missing . . ." I mime tossing a small arrow at the wall.

"Oh my God. There are no darts. No dartboard."

"You can't have a proper traditional pub without a proper dartboard."

"Yes! Exactly! I saw dartboards in all the pubs I was researching. I can't believe I missed it."

"This is your first in-person lesson in pubs. Don't be hard on yourself."

She lifts an eyebrow. "I'll leave that part to you. Being hard on me."

A wicked grin crosses my lips. "Who's relentless now?"

She bumps shoulders with me. "Too bad there's no dartboard. Darts would have been fun."

I tuck a strand of hair over her ear. "I'd have enjoyed watching you play."

"I'd have enjoyed beating you." She tips her forehead to the bar. "Also, thanks for sharing back there."

I mime ripping my chest open. "It pained me, woman."

"I could tell, but I appreciate you telling me. I like knowing what motivates you, especially since I know you're not big on"—she gasps—"emotions."

"You're not exactly an open book either."

She tilts her head to the side. "I'm not?"

"You're pretty much a full-speed-ahead kind of woman. You don't linger on . . . *feelings*."

A crease forms in her brow. "I'm not sure that's true. But maybe it seems that way because you know my story already. I don't hold back. I've told you about Sarah. You know I'm close to my family and my brother. You know I still miss my dad, even though he's been gone eighteen years. And you know I'm a workaholic. You know me. Maybe that's why it's easy for us to be friends?"

Her question is entirely earnest, but my answer isn't, even though I try to make it seem that way. "Right. It's incredibly easy."

But the truth is, it's not at all simple being her friend.

It's becoming one of the hardest things I've done.

* * *

Soon it's time to leave, and as Truly gathers her purse, Marcus gives us a goodbye salute. "Cheers. Come back sometime. I want to share a new type of malt we're bringing in. I'd love to tell you about it. It tastes like grapeseed oil and sunflowers."

"That sounds fantastic." Truly hums then taps the bar. "Also, I had an idea for you. It's all about beer."

My fists clench. Please, God, can she stop talking to him?

"I'd love to hear it."

"I think you should write a blog about beer. You have a lot of insight. You ought to share it with the world. That is, if you don't blog about it already."

He strokes his chin. "Actually, I do. But it's been kind of a hard slog. I want to share my love of beer with the world, but I'd much rather talk about it than write about it."

"Start a beer podcast, then."

He snaps his fingers, his eyes lighting up. "That's a damn good idea. I've been looking into ways to expand."

"Always hustling," she says, then gestures to me. "That's what he says."

"That's good advice, mate."

"Thanks. Happy to give it," I say grudgingly.

I check the time, clearing my throat as if to remind her she has someplace to be.

"One more second," she says to me, and fantastic, now I'm the annoying dick who's trying to herd her out of here.

"If you want to talk about it, I'm Truly Goodman. I run Gin Joint in Chelsea."

He gasps. "I love that place. I was there the other weekend. Heard that guy sing and had a Hush Money. Best gin cocktail I've had in ages."

Truly's smile hits new levels on the Richter scale of delight, and I want to shove a sock in this guy's mouth. "That's my brother. He's a lounge singer and a veterinarian. Or, I should say, he's a vet and a lounge singer. And Hush Money is mine."

"It was delicious. Like heaven in a glass."

I scrub a hand across the back of my neck, wishing this exchange would stop.

"Thank you. I appreciate that. And the beer was great."

"No, thank you. Your idea is fantastic. You're amazing. I could kiss you."

Every territorial instinct in me snaps to attention, calling up the caveman that lurks within. Draping an arm around Truly, I tug her close. I can't *not*. "Sorry, mate. I've got dibs on that."

His eyes pop out like they're attached to springs. He raises his hands like stop signs, and his voice brims with contrition. "Sorry, sorry. I didn't mean anything by that."

"No worries." I flash him a grin, even as I bring her closer to me because she fits fucking perfectly there. She fits against me like she belongs.

We leave, and when we reach the street, I let go of her. She swivels to face me, a challenge written across her eyes. "And what if I wanted him to kiss me?"

"Did you? Did you want to kiss Marcus?"

She parks her hands on her hips. "Well, if I did, you just ruined it."

"I thought you weren't interested in dating. That was what you said on Sunday."

"And I meant it. I wasn't trying to date Marcus, for God's sake. I was not picking him up. We were talking about work."

"You two were pretty damn chatty."

"It was business. I was learning from him. Stop being such a jealous ass."

"Ass? Now I'm an ass?"

"You are kind of acting like one."

"Well, pardon me, then. I'll just leave so you can return to Marcus the soapbox bartender, who looks like he sprang from Central Casting for Movie Stars."

She raises an eyebrow. "Are you serious?"

I wave a hand in his direction. "Oh, come on now."

"I didn't even notice."

"You didn't notice he looks like . . . like . . ." Well, I'm not going to point it out to her.

"I told you. I was only interested in talking to him about beer. I was only interested in learning more about the business. This is business for me." She stabs at her chest with one finger. "Hello? Workaholic here. Just like you."

I huff sullenly and mutter an apology. "Sorry." Then, because that's not how apologies work and I should know better, I man up and meet her gaze. "I'm sorry I acted like a jealous ass. But I still don't think Marcus is your type."

She raises her chin. "How do you know?"

Adrenaline courses through me. It's this argument, Marcus, the whole damned night. I step closer, lift a hand, and run my thumb over her jawline. "Because you are the kind of woman who needs a particular kind of kiss, and he's not the man who can give it to you."

"What type of kiss do I need?" she asks, and it comes out breathy. I want to hear that sound again. I want to be the reason she makes it.

I move closer, and she doesn't back away. I need to get other men out of her head. I need to erase them, so I say, "Hot, hard, deep, and completely consuming."

She swallows, her voice a little wobbly but still fierce. "How do you know that's what I need?"

"Because when I kissed you that night, you melted. You turned boneless. You said no one had ever kissed you that way before."

Her words are some kind of invitation. "Maybe I like it soft and slow now."

"Do you?"

"Perhaps." It lasts for five syllables, and with the vibration of each one, I move closer. I run a hand down her arm. Goosebumps trail in my wake, and she doesn't pull away.

"Perhaps you do," I repeat. She's inches from me. Her eyes lock with mine and heat flashes across hers. "Only one way to find out."

I slide a hand into her hair, then brush my lips over hers, barely kissing her, hardly touching. It's enough to drive me wild, to make me want more. To make me want her again, want her more than I already do. This woman taunts me, tempts me.

And I want her to feel tempted too.

Her soft lips seal against mine, and even though I've kissed her hard and hot and heavy, even though I've kissed her like I'm going to fuck her, tonight isn't for devouring.

I give her exactly what she asked for—soft and slow.

How much I enjoy it takes me by surprise. It's like we're discovering a new way to kiss. I bring her closer. She parts her lips, and the second she does, my mind goes haywire, wild with images of what might come next. Here on the streets of Tribeca, I can barely contain the desire that rockets through me.

Especially when she slinks her hands around my waist, dipping them into the back pockets of my jeans. Grabbing my ass. Driving me crazy as I yank her closer for a final hot, searing kiss.

When we break apart, my mind has traveled to another country. My logic and reason have packed up and left too, no forwarding address.

She drags her fingertips down the front of my shirt. "What do you know? Turns out soft and slow is nice too."

I run a hand through my hair, trying to reconnect thoughts to reality. "Yeah, works for me as well."

She drops her forehead to my chest, and damn, that feels nice. But when she lifts her face, it's like she's reset herself, cleared her thoughts. "But that was simply a test. You know that, right?"

I need to reset too, so I nod automatically. "Sure. Just testing a theory. Won't happen again."

"It can't happen again." She takes a deep breath. "Also, there's something I've been meaning to refresh your memory about." She moves closer once more, so there's barely any space between us. "I don't know where this idea of three times comes from. Maybe you ought to have your brain checked."

"What are you talking about?"

She dips her face near me and whispers against my neck, her fresh scent drifting into my nose. "It was four."

She lets go and leaves.

I stand there, wishing it were Chip's wedding right now because I can't wait to see her again.

And that's a big fucking problem.

18

From the pages of Truly's Drink Recipe Book

Slippery Slope:
Wasabi powder
Sake
Lime juice
Splash of gin

So maybe you took a step down a slippery slope the other night. Maybe you tumbled a little farther than you thought. No worries. We can get you back up with a certain cocktail. Mix wasabi powder, sake, lime juice and a splash of gin. Strain it into a Collins glass, and take a hearty swallow.

That fire in your nose?

That kick?

It'll knock you right back up to where you started.

Top of the hill with your feet firmly planted.

You're good.

No slippery slope for you, no matter how pretty you feel when you slide into that blue dress he sent over to your place for you to wear tomorrow. It fits perfectly, like he knows all the curves and dips of your body.

No matter how sharp the drop seems when you read the note he included: *I'd say try not to look too tempting, but that's a lost cause. See you tomorrow night.*

Slippery slope indeed.

19

On the way to Chip's bachelor party, my phone pings with a message. I unlock the screen, laughing when I find a cartoonish image of a leg bone connected to the ankle bone, and a text from my sister.

Abby: At last! Now we know how they're connected.

As I turn the corner toward the restaurant, I hunt for a GIF, find one I like, and send it to her. It's a shot of the board game Operation.

Jason: Well done! For your next assignment, I'd like you to master Operation. It'll be tough, but I believe in you.

Abby: Jason, don't be silly. That's the fourth year.

Jason: I know that. Why don't you tell me something I don't know? I mean that literally. Go on. Try and find something that impresses me.

Abby: Sure, let's talk about the anatomy of the brachial plexus.

A quick Google search tells me that's the network of nerves extending from the spinal cord over the first rib and into the armpit.

   I reply.

Jason: Now you're talking!

Abby: Impressed? I told you that you'd get a strong return on your investment. Just wanted you to know your money is going to good use.

Jason: I never thought anything different.

I say goodbye fondly and head into the restaurant.

* * *

The clatter of forks and the clink of glasses echo across the dark restaurant in the heart of the Upper East Side.

Chip picked this surf and turf spot for his last single night, and the man seems pleased.

He stretches his arms wide across the back of the booth, sighing contentedly as he regards the remains of his sea creature. "Guys, this was the best night ever. Thank you so much for being in my wedding party. I'm so dang busy running the firm that I don't have time for friends. This though? This kind of night out? It's the perfect solution for a guy like me."

There's something refreshing about Chip. He's entirely forthright about his situation and his need for a best man. He's not cloying or clingy. He's simply having a blast and paying for it.

Perhaps that makes me a hooker.

Well, at least I don't put out.

I raise a glass. "Happy to be a part of it." But Walker's advice rings in my ears. *You do know you can't do this forever.*

"It's an honor," Sully says, playing the part of Chip's good friend to the T.

Chip points to the meal. "And this lobster? This was the best lobster ever. I'm going to write an ode to this shellfish."

That sparks Troy's interest. "What will you say?"

Troy and I worked a few weddings together this summer, and he's a suave cat. His inquisitive nature makes him a good fit for the gig.

Chip regards the lobster, screwing up his brow as he thinks. "All right. I've been working on this for a while. I'm not there yet, but work with me." He clears his throat and adopts an old English accent, sliding into a riff on Shakespeare's Sonnet 18 and its opening lines about a summer's day.

"Shall I compare thee to my dream fillet? Thou art more buttery and more succulent." He grins at us. "What do you think?"

"Nice!" Troy jumps in.

"Well done," I second, using my best Hugh Grant tone, as requested.

"But I kind of get stuck there. I've been reworking the first few lines for a while now, and I can't seem to move past it. I bet you can help, being English."

I laugh and turn to Troy, who's nearly bursting to take on the challenge. "You don't need me when you have our resident Shakespeare scholar and aspiring playwright."

Troy, seeming energized by the opportunity, snaps his fingers, muttering under his breath the actual lines from the bard's most famous sonnet. *Shall I compare thee to a summer's day? Thou art more lovely and more temperate. Rough winds do shake the darling buds of May, and summer's lease hath all too short a date.* A long sigh, then he pumps a fist. "Got it. Ready?"

"I'm ready," Chip says. "Lay it on us."

"Shall I compare thee to my dream fillet? Thou art more buttery and more succulent. Other fish will storm your plate, try to claim your place . . . But none will win, all are but a supplement."

Chip's jaw drops. "Are you kidding me? I've been stuck on rhyming 'succulent' forever."

Troy gestures broadly, amped up by the creative exercise. "My first thought was 'truculent,' but that means aggressive and doesn't really fit that well. So, 'supplement' it is."

Sully's eyes bounce back and forth like he's watching ping-pong in the Olympics, then he bows *Wayne's World*–style. "You just rhymed on the spot. We are not worthy."

Troy blows on his fingers. "When you got it, you got it. I can rap the entire sonnet actually."

"You can? That's an awesome party trick. Can you do it right now?" Chip asks, sounding awestruck.

Troy glances to me as if asking for permission, and holy hell, he has it. "Dying to hear this." I cross my arms and listen as Troy makes a beatbox of his mouth and proceeds to hip-hop his way through "Sonnet Eighteen," starting with *Shall I compare thee to a summer's day? Thou art more lovely and more temperate.*

I clap when he's done. We all do.

The word *idea* seems to flash in neon above Chip's head. "Can you do that at the wedding tomorrow? Maybe with 'Sonnet One Hundred Sixteen'?"

"*If music be the food of love, play on,*" Troy says. "Though that's from *Twelfth Night*. But it's my way of saying yes, I'd be honored."

"What do you do when you're not . . ." Chip lowers his voice. "You know, doing this . . .?"

Ah, the question of the hour. In addition to the groomsman work, how exactly does he support his playwriting habit? Lately, I've begun to suspect he works the pole. How else would he know all the words to 50 Cent's "Candy Shop" and Ginuwine's "Pony"?

"He does a little of everything," Sully interjects

proudly. "A real man of the people. Jack-of-all-trades. Isn't that right?"

"Yeah, sometimes I work as a cop. Sometimes I'm the maître d'. Other times, I'm just the pool guy."

"Those are a lot of . . . odd jobs." Chip's eyebrow rises, like none of that computes.

Troy lifts his water glass and takes a drink. "Just to support the wife and me before the plays take off."

Everything makes perfect sense now. He's a stripper. Magic Mike meets Eugene O'Neill is my rent-a-groomsman.

Chip smiles like he has a secret. "I love Shakespeare. I quoted a sonnet when Pugalicious and I asked Ashley to marry me."

I snap my gaze to him. "Pugalicious?"

"Pugalicious is my dog. Ashley and I met at a dog park. She has a pug too. It was love at first pug."

"That is . . . thoroughly sweet," I say.

"Hooked her with the pug, won her with a sonnet. Hopefully, she'll stay for me."

"I'll drink to that," I say, raising a glass.

"What about you? Who's your date? Is she sonnet-worthy?" Chip asks.

"Julie," I say quickly.

"What's she like?"

I don't answer Chip at first. Not aloud.

She's like . . . the bottle of scotch you want to open but can't because it's on your father's shelf. She's like the car you long for when you spot the red Ferrari cruising around the bend. She's the sexiest, wittiest, most clever woman—no, person—you've ever known, and you want her so fucking much, it's a persistent ache.

I turn to Chip. "She's just a great girl. That's all."

When dinner ends, capped with loads of selfies that Chip sends to his family and his bride, Troy pulls me aside.

"I need to take off. I have a . . . thing."

"Good luck with the *thing*. See you tomorrow at the ceremony."

After I say good night to Chip and head out into the Manhattan evening, it occurs to me that all of these guys, this random collection of men, are heading home to their various ladies. Chip to his soon-to-be bride, Sully to Jana (and his sneakers), and Troy to his woman, Irene. Well, after he shakes it all night long.

As for me, I wander downtown, happily single, loving the night breeze and enjoying my solitude.

Though what is Truly up to right now, on a Friday night in the summer? Is she out with friends too? At home? Or behind the bar at Gin Joint?

A tug pulls me toward Chelsea, telling me to casually pop into her bar. Chat with her. Flirt with her.

Steal a moment alone with her and kiss her so damn senseless she melts completely in my arms.

I blink the far-too-tempting thoughts away. Another kiss would be dangerous. It could make the next few gigs with her rockier than they need to be. Not to mention the potential strain it would put on my friendship with her brother.

I clench my fists, holding tight to those thoughts as I head home instead. No need to catch a few extra moments with a woman I'm not involved with, not seeing, and not going home to.

My phone bleats.

It's Nora.

"Hallo, German spy," I say.

"*Guten Abend*. I'm calling because I want to go out on a high note, and I won't take no for an answer."

20

The next morning, Nora spins her replacement around to face the mirror hanging on Truly's bedroom door, presenting her like she's in a pageant. Granted, Truly looks stunning in the simple blue dress I sent to her.

"You look *amazing*." Nora sings the last word. "Now, have you thought about what name you're going to use?"

Nora's here because . . . well, she insisted. She leaves tonight for Chicago, and she wanted to send us out on a high note, she told me when she rang last night. She also wanted to ride in style to the airport, and I can't blame her. Chip is sending a swank limo for me, and I'm taking off soon and will drop Nora off at the airport on the way to the photo shoot. Truly will join me later.

"She's Julie. That's the name I told Chip," I say from my spot on Truly's couch.

Nora shoots death rays at me with her hazel eyes. "She can't be a Julie. Why did you give her that name?"

"Why can't she be a Julie?"

"Julie's pretty easy for me not to fuck up," Truly says dryly. "I have to agree with Jason on this one."

Nora grabs Truly's shoulders. "Because this is your opportunity. This is your chance. You could have been Ramona, a naughty librarian who wears fishnet stockings under her pencil skirts. You could have been Svetlana, a Russian orphan finally finding her way in America. Or, even better, Francesca, the Brazilian heir to an oil conglomerate, who escaped from . . . a cartel. Personally, I liked to use names like Zosa and Marta."

It's a wonder no one saw through the ruse. But then again, Nora *can* act. She's not always over-the-top. Just with friends.

"But then I'd have to do an accent, wouldn't I?" Truly reminds us. "I'm not really an accent person. Though I can do a good Midwestern one. *And then when Damien Grey the Third bent me over the piano, he spanked me and slid inside me, and it felt oh so good.*"

My jaw disengages from my skull and falls to the floor. Even in her Midwestern good-girl accent, she sounds fucking hot. "Yes, just do that all night."

Nora laughs. "It's very convincing. Maybe for the next one?" Nora's hope is like an extra exuberant person in the room. "Or maybe you could be a delightful Southern belle. Perhaps you could be Abigail Anna from Savannah."

"Why would I want to draw more attention to myself? I'm only there as a shield for him." Truly flaps her arm at me.

"You're both a shield and a lubricant," Nora says,

amused. "It's what my agent says. Use me as your shield or your lubricant."

I raise a hand. "If you're choosing, I'd really like to be the lube."

"Darling," Truly says, trying on Southern Belle after all, "I'm the lube. Try to remember."

Nora claps. "See? It's so much more fun."

Truly twirls her hair and smacks her lips, as if she's chewing gum. "Like, I don't know. I totally don't know if it's more fun. Does it, like, feel more fun to you?"

I crack up at her ditz routine. "Look at all your hidden talents."

Truly takes a bow then says in her own voice, "Listen, I'm only going as Jason's date. I don't need to do a whole song and dance."

Nora scoffs for a full minute. "Oh no, no, no, *no*. He's not Jason tonight. You can't call him by his real name."

"Right, I nearly forgot." Truly meets my gaze. "What am I calling you? Can you be Cornelius?"

I wiggle an eyebrow. "Depends when you want to call me that."

Nora fluffs Truly's hair and offers more names. "How about Mortimer? Or better yet, Wilbur? Hold on. Let me grab a comb." She scurries to the other side of the room where she left her purse.

Truly walks closer to me, a smile tugging at her lips. "Can I call you Wilbur tonight?"

"Only if I'm deep inside you," I mouth.

Truly's eyes simmer. "You're not going to be inside me."

"Then you're not going to call me Wilbur."

Nora returns with a silver hair clip. "Let me just do this. If you like it, I'll show you how, and you can do it tonight, okay? Personally, I like wigs, but the idea is the same. A new hairstyle can make you feel like a whole different person. It'll help you get into character."

She threads her hands through Truly's hair, fashioning it into a French twist, and . . . wow. Truly looks . . . just *wow*. Her neck is divine and begging me to kiss it.

Be good. She's your best friend's sister. She's your friend. And you need this job badly to help Abby.

But that neck. I want to get my mouth all over it. I want to inhale her. Devour her.

Truly gestures to her new 'do. "What do you think?"

I think my mouth is dry. I think I can't form words without gravel in them. But I find my voice, answering her as nonchalantly as I possibly can, given the hard matters south of the border. "I think down works fine."

Nora gives a dismissive grunt. "Fine? Fine is for peanut butter sandwiches. You look delicious like this. Like a strawberry cupcake. Ooh, one more thing. What's your job, if someone asks? You could be a banker, all buttoned up. Or even a belly dancer. That's exotic but believable. No one can call you on that."

"I took a belly-dancing class once." Truly wiggles her hips, then she snaps her fingers. "I know! I know what I want to do."

She heads for her bedroom and returns wearing a pair of black glasses. "Costume glasses. You approve?"

"Of everything," I say, picturing how all the pieces— dress, hair, hot-for-teacher glasses—will come together.

If I didn't have a sexy librarian fetish before, I do now.

No, that's not it. If I'm honest, I just have a Truly fetish, and it's getting so damn strong I'd even be willing to let her call me Wilbur.

21

I see blue.

Gorgeous sapphire blue.

How is it possible that outfit looks even better now? Perhaps it's the sunset, that golden hue that makes everyone and everything a little softer, a little closer to perfect. Or maybe it's because I've been thinking of her all day. Thinking of her since I saw her try on that dress. Thinking of her taking it off.

Truly arrives before the ceremony as I'm waiting on the lawn at the inn in Connecticut.

Her chestnut hair is in a twist, black glasses frame her face, and that dress hugs her fantastic body. What was I thinking? I should have bought her sweatpants, and I mean *real* sweatpants, the elastic ankles kind, not those yoga pants that radiate sex. Or a sweatshirt, all bulky and frumpy.

Then again, I've seen her in a sweatshirt, and I still found her alluring, so it's on me to keep my lust in check.

She reaches me, rises on her tiptoes, and dusts a soft kiss to my cheek. "Hi, Jay."

That's not helping. I go up in flames. The temperature in me shoots up like I'm a space capsule reentering the atmosphere, radio signal lost, heat shield threatening to melt. This woman has my number. She is so fucking sexy, but I can't let it distract me . . . because it's expensive to teach Abby about the brachial plexus and solar plexus and whatever—screw all those bundles of neurons. All my nerves are unraveling for her.

"Hi, Julie."

She shoots me a naughty grin. "Or should I call you Wilbur?"

"You know my conditions on that." And maybe because she called me Wilbur, maybe because she looks good enough to undress, eat, and worship all night long, and maybe because resisting her is exhausting, I give myself a little leeway.

She's my date, after all. Might as well enjoy the perks. I slide my arm around her waist.

Her reaction? Priceless. She trembles as I touch her. "Nice glasses. So glad you could make it, Julie."

"Good to be here, Jay." She sounds breathless, and for a split second, it feels like we're the only people here, especially with our role-play.

With my arm still around her waist, I return the favor from the other night when she slipped her hands into my jean pockets. I let my palm slide down to her ass. I give the slightest of squeezes, enough to elicit a hitch in her breath.

"Behave," she warns, shooting a stern stare over her

lenses. But she wriggles against my hand, seeking out the curve of my palm.

I groan. "I'd tell you to behave too . . . but I don't want you to."

"We're supposed to be good." Wriggle, wriggle. "We're in the friend zone." She presses a little harder, a little more firmly into my hand, and the heat shield burns through, melting away.

I slide my fingers lower, teasing at the line—that absolutely delicious line—where her ass meets her leg. Ah, yes. I do enjoy where the tailbone is connected to the leg bone.

"If this is the friend zone, I'd like to live here." I squeeze her ass, and a gust of a sigh rushes from her lips.

Too bad we're surrounded by people.

Those people include my client, who's rushing across the grass, looking dapper in his tuxedo. He pumps Truly's hand. "You must be Julie."

"And you must be Chip. I've heard so much about you. It's a pleasure."

"And you as well. Thank you for being here." He turns to me. "And you. Without you, I wouldn't be able to give Ashley the wedding she's always dreamed of. Though, in all fairness, I should thank my ex-girlfriend. If she hadn't dumped me for some other guy, I wouldn't be here. I should send her a thank-you note."

His genuine smile loosens some of the bricks in my facade. Because in his story, I hear echoes of mine, reminders of Claire. If she *had* held up her end of the bargain, where would I even be right now? With her?

Without her? Back in London, trying to cobble together a living as . . . what? A meat-pie baking apprentice? A business reporter? I shudder at the thought of either. And honestly, I don't know that I'd be doing the Modern Gentleman work in the UK. The cachet of *not* being from here seems to elevate my station when it comes to landing work in New York—speaking gigs and radio bits.

And I like my other job at the moment too. *This* one.

For the first time in a long time, I'm really enjoying this after-hours gig, and I suspect that's not only because of the companion next to me. But because Chip's a decent guy.

I clap his shoulder. "It's her loss, isn't it, mate?"

"Abso-flipping-lutely," he says, the picture of happiness. "Speaking of, I just got word from Ashley that everyone's here. We're good to go." He glances at the sun, slipping toward the horizon. His photographer is taking photos before the ceremony, so the light is ideal. "We can get the bridesmaid and maid of honor."

"Right. Bring out the ladies." When he darts off, I bring my face closer to Truly's and whisper, "Remember, I'm too hot to be single. So feel free to put your hands all over me."

"I feel like you can fend off any advances without me mauling you."

"No, I can't. I really can't. You're going to have to manhandle me. Just pat me down like you're a TSA agent." I widen my stance, raising my arms in the air. "Go ahead. I'm ready."

"You're ready? Is that so?"

"Completely. One hundred percent."

She lifts her hands, draws a breath, then darts out her fingers and tickles me.

I muffle a shout, barely, squirming away from her on the lawn. "You're vicious. Totally vicious." But it comes out in a peal of laughter.

She grabs me, looping an arm around my shoulder. "Want me to put you in a back mount?" But the flirting stops when seconds later, a wrinkly, panting pug rushes across the lawn.

"Pugalove!" a young voice calls out, and I follow the sound, finding the bridesmaid shouting to her dog. "Pugalove! You come right back to me, you rapscallion."

The rapscallion in question seems well-trained, since she spins around and rushes back to the bridesmaid, who bends and scratches the dog's chin. "You are such a good girl. So good. But you're supposed to have your maid-of-honor dress on, you nutty pug."

I jerk my gaze toward her.

Maid of honor?

The young woman scoops up the dog. "Let's get you dolled up, my lovebug." The bridesmaid stands and brushes a hand down her dress, switching from dog baby-talk to something a little more seductive. "Oh, hi, Jay."

"Hi, Amelia."

She nibbles on the corner of her lip. "Pugalove was going to . . . well, I think she wanted to come over and meet you." Her words come out all breathy.

Truly drapes an arm possessively around me. "Who doesn't want to meet Jay? Get in line, Pugalove."

The bridesmaid laughs. "I know. I'll take tickets for that line."

"You're telling me," Truly adds, squeezing my shoulder and snuggling a little closer. Well, there. Maybe I can get Amelia to hang around a little longer.

"Ah, you ladies are too kind," I say.

Amelia slides me a dreamy look. "I promise, it's not kindness that makes Pugalove and me want to wait in line."

Truly chuckles. "Soul sisters. Am I right?" Then she brushes a quick kiss to my cheek, marking her territory.

Amelia sighs dreamily. "You're so lucky."

"I know," Truly says.

"I want to be like you someday." On that note, Amelia smiles sadly, spins around, and disappears back into the inn.

"Seems she brings out the jealous side of you."

"You think so?"

"You were pretty handsy, Julie."

"Just doing my job, Jay." But the way she touches my arm—sensuously, seductively—doesn't feel like she's thinking about work at all.

Seconds later, the bride strides over to me, extending a hand. "I'm Ashley. So great to meet you . . . *Jay.*" In her soft North Carolina twang, she overemphasizes my name because, of course, she knows Chip hired me. Ashley turns to Truly. "You must be Julie. So glad you could come too. And I saw you met my little bestie. Isn't she a doll? Pugalove's the reason I'm here today."

"Is Pugalove a matchmaker?" Truly asks with a smile.

"You bet she is." With a knowing grin, Ashley stage-whispers, "She served as my guy magnet. Helped locate the *right* man for me."

"She has some top-notch man radar, then?" Truly looks just shy of smiling at the bride's candid good humor.

"She absolutely does. And boy, was it tough out there before then. Finding a good man is harder than finding a bra that fits you just right."

"Well, that's a level-five challenge right there."

"I know. I spent years looking for just the right fit. But dating these days? That's a level ten."

"You're telling me. It's rough out there in those waters."

I grit my teeth at Truly even alluding to the cruel world of modern dating.

"Exactly. But when you have a dog like Pugalove, friendly and with excellent radar, you have an icebreaker with the handsome fellas."

"So how exactly does her radar work? Did she find Chip for you or grease the wheels?"

"Well, in my defense, I did spot him myself. I'd seen him heading into the dog park a few times, and I had a hunch about him because he was so sweet with his dog. I thought, *He's got to be a good one*, and all I wanted was to finally meet a real nice guy like that. So I timed my visit one day. I brought Pugalove when I knew he'd be there, and once I let her off-leash, she ran right up to him and Pugalicious. Two seconds later, she wagged her tail, asked for a little ear scratch, and that was all she wrote. Boom. Done."

"Wow. She opened the door and gave you her seal of approval at the same time."

"Exactly. Like she knew what I needed, and I definitely needed him. Chip and I talked for an hour, and he asked me out that night, and the rest is history, all thanks to her."

"She's the perfect wingwoman."

"She's a rescue pup, but really, she rescued me from the misery of dating jerks. I *love* her."

I flash back to Chip's words from last night. Yep, this woman is staying for him. Absolutely.

Truly gestures toward the inn. "She earned the maid-of-honor job, then. I'd say she deserves a slice of steak-flavored wedding cake for helping you find true love."

"I know, right? Don't we all want that? And listen, sweetie, if you ever need any tips on dating, let me know. I can give you the number of the pug rescue or the address of some dog parks." Ashley points from Truly to me. "Unless y'all decide to level up. And if you do, you'd make a hella cute couple."

She waves and spins around, and I'm left holding a bowl full of dating advice from the newlyweds. I suppose it's fitting they're trying to tell us how it all works. Simply being married doesn't qualify one to give advice, but being happily in love makes you dole it out with abandon, because everyone should be so lucky.

I let go of Truly's hand and join the ridiculously happy couple for photos, feeling strangely empty.

* * *

When she reaches the end of the aisle, Ashley's gaze finds Chip's, and her smile is wildly happy and a bit wicked. She gives a tiny little wave and whispers, "Hey, you handsome man."

"Hey, beautiful bride."

"Are you ready?" she whispers.

"So ready," he whispers back.

"I've been waiting a long time for someone like you."

"I've been waiting longer."

"No, I have."

"No, I have."

I bet this is how they were in the dog park, lovey and sweet.

They take their vows, and it suits everything I've seen of them, from that private exchange to when the justice of the peace pronounces them man and wife and tells Chip he may kiss the bride.

But she's faster on the draw. Ashley grabs her husband's face and plants a massive smooch on his lips. Yes, she's keeping him.

Truly shoots me a smile that's neither naughty nor droll. It's simply . . . sweet.

And it does something to my cold heart.

Something that feels a bit like a thaw.

And that's a whole lot of a problem.

* * *

Chip and Ashley's plan to keep Amelia at bay seems to have worked. Jana keeps Sully occupied, Irene keeps

Troy busy, and Amelia seems to have gotten the message that we're all partnered up.

She's ceased the flirting and instead is making besties with Truly at the head table later that night. "So there's the guy at school . . . I can't decide if I hate him or maybe love him . . . or if he loves me or hates me. It's all so confusing, and I don't know what to do."

"What makes it so confusing? Can you give me an example?" Truly asks, in that helpful tone she has with people she hardly knows. Must be another reason why she's so good at her job. She's great with people. She can talk to anyone, and find common ground with them.

"Well, he did listen to Ariana Grande with me. That's a good sign that he likes me, isn't it?"

"I'd say it's a great sign."

"But he also didn't invite me to the dance next weekend, and it would be awesome if he asked me."

"Well, does he know you like him? Sometimes men need a little reassurance before they put themselves out there."

"True. He did Snapchat me earlier today and I never wrote back. Maybe I should Snapchat him back."

"I think you should go for it. Snapchat him tonight."

"I will. He's so adorbs. Like you and your guy."

Truly loops an arm around me. "Jay is totes adorbs."

I slide a hand along her wrist. "So are you."

"Awww, you guys are the most adorbs," Amelia says with a sigh. "I want this kind of thing for myself. You guys have to stay like this. It's sooo sweet."

I meet Truly's gaze, thinking Amelia has some damn good ideas. Staying like this sounds brilliant.

I lean closer to Truly, whispering, "Thanks for coming tonight."

"Thanks for inviting me."

She leaves her arm around me, and it hardly feels like it's for Amelia's benefit anymore.

Soon enough, it's time for the best man's speech, and I keep it short and simple per Chip's request, but I talk him up, waxing on about all the ways he's a good, fun, and caring man. The funny thing is, it's all true. Chip is a good guy. That's patently obvious.

When I'm through, I turn the reins over to Troy who clears his throat. "I'm here to celebrate this union with a little Shakespeare. Is everyone ready for Sonnet One Hundred Sixteen?"

"Go for it!" Chip shouts.

Troy then proceeds to rap the hell out of the Bard, starting with: *"Let me not to the marriage of true minds... Admit impediments."*

When he finishes, Chip turns to his bride. "Surprise, sweetie! I had him do that for you."

Ashley throws her arms around him. "I am never ever letting you go."

Chip's smile can power a rocket launch. "That's the goal."

When Ashley drops a kiss to his lips, that pang in my chest returns, like a drumbeat, persistent and a little annoying.

Or maybe it's simply that Ed Sheeran is playing, and the dancing has begun.

Truly sets down her champagne and grabs my hand. "Let's dance."

"To Ed Sheeran?"

"Yes. I know you hate him, and I don't care."

Funny, I don't care right now that I hate him either. The chance to have her in my arms is worth the assault on my eardrums.

I take her hand, guide her to the dance floor, and loop my hands around her waist.

I'd like to say we're good. I'd like to say I feel nothing.

But that'd be a bigger lie than pretending the groom isn't paying me to be here.

22

From the pages of Truly's Drink Recipe Book

A Little Hanky Panky:
Champagne, Straight Up

You tell yourself you'll stick to the plan.

You know you can do it.

Hell, you've done it for a while now. For years, even. For as long as you've known that guy, the one you can't stop thinking about.

You go over the reasons. You list them, highlight them, stick them to a Post-it, and slap it on the fridge.

But then there are the things he says, dirty and sweet, entertaining and thoughtful. The way he listens —the way he talks. How he holds the door, pulls out your chair, takes your coat.

He's a man in a city that is teeming with boys.

Or maybe it's simpler. Maybe it's how he touches your hand, your waist, your hair. Perhaps it's the tender way he meets your gaze when you demand a dance, or the hint of vulnerability that flashes across his amber eyes.

Or it could be that, once again, you're away from the city.

You're not in that five-mile radius of your regular life, your regular job, and your regular people.

This is an escape, and you know when you indulge in that first sip of champagne it's going straight to your head. Not just the drink, but the night, the dress, the tux, and the talking.

When you take that sip, it tastes like a getaway, like a delicious secret, like a treasure to grab tight.

Times like this, when the man you want takes your hand at a wedding, you're already in a champagne state of mind.

23

Dancing with her is not at all like dancing with Nora or anyone else in the world.

My pulse beats faster, my blood runs hotter. She slides against me, fitting perfectly in my arms. My gaze swings down to the neckline of her dress. It's classy but shows a hint of creamy skin, just the way I like it. I brush my fingertips across the tops of her breasts, and she shivers as I touch her. "This dress looks stunning. Have I told you that?"

She licks her lips. "I'm not really sure. It's hard for me to remember what I had for breakfast. But you can tell me again." Her tone is so damn inviting.

I inch a little closer, my hands tightening on her hips as her arms loop around my neck. "You look good enough to eat."

She offers me a smile, like my words have unlocked her. "You always look good enough to eat."

This woman. Her appetite. Her naughty mouth. "And you say I'm relentless."

"I guess it takes one to know one."

"I like this mood you're in tonight," I tell her as I finger a strand of her hair.

She tilts her head. "What mood do you think I'm in?"

I whisper in her ear. "The same one I'm in."

She shudders against me, and my bones crackle. My mind floods with filthy images of her. I'm dangerously close to overheating. I pull back slightly, trying to clear the haze so I don't take her, toss her over my shoulder, and stalk into the inn to fuck her, forgetting my client, forgetting the job I've been paid to do.

I glance around the reception, tipping my chin toward the guests swaying under the lights, others laughing and chatting at the tables and the deejay swaying in place as he plays pop songs I despise, but I can't find the energy to loathe anything right now. "What do you think of the wedding?"

"It feels like it's real." She lowers her voice to a whisper. "Like we're not here as fake friends of the groom."

"I know what you mean. It's not like I think I'm going to hang out with Chip when this is done, but there's something about him I like."

"He's authentic," she says.

"He is. All he wants is to make her happy."

"I think he's succeeded." The couple is on the dance floor too, practically sealed together. You'd need a butter knife to wedge them apart, but who would want to? The way they hang on to each other, the way they maul each other's mouth, says they both chose well.

I turn my full attention back to Truly, cataloging her face, her midnight-blue eyes, the sweep of her hair off her neck, and those glasses. She fits perfectly in my arms, and I let myself imagine what it would be like to have more of her.

She doesn't feel like a fake date. "I'm glad you're here."

She lifts her chin, meeting my gaze. "How glad?"

I laugh, pressing against her. "Incredibly glad. Isn't that obvious?"

"Maybe it is now," she says, sliding against the outline of my length.

I groan appreciatively. "Are you trying to send me a message?"

She shrugs, her eyes a little glossy, her voice a little rough. "I don't know what I'm doing, Jason."

I curl my fingers around her hip, squeezing, loving her frankness. "Really? It seems like you know exactly."

She plays with the ends of my hair, sending sparks down my spine. "Do I?"

My entire body is lit up, charged by her touch. "I think we both know what we're doing."

She tangos her fingers across my shoulders, playing with the lapels on my jacket. "But we said it was a bad idea. You and me. We said it made no sense."

"I know. And yet here we are." My gaze drifts down to her fingers, now toying with my bow tie. "And you're trying to undress me in front of everyone."

"I'm finding it a little hard to keep my hands off you."

"I know that feeling well. It's always that way with you. It's a constant battle not to touch you, kiss you, or steal you away to a dark corner."

"And how's the battle going tonight?"

"Let's see. I'm dancing with you. Pretending you're mine. Yeah, I think I'm losing the battle for control." I slide my palm over the top of her ass, and she gasps then sucks in a breath. "All I can think about is how to get this dress off you."

"And have you figured it out?"

"Oh, I absolutely have. I've mapped out the fastest way to undress you. In my head, you're already naked."

She smiles naughtily. "And how is it with me naked in your head?"

I meet her gaze, holding it as electricity radiates down my skin. "Dirty. Wild. Sweaty. Carnal."

She shudders, pressing her breasts against my chest. "Sounds about right."

I dip my face close to her, brushing my jaw across her cheek, letting her feel my stubble. "Wet. I left that out. You're so fucking wet in my head."

She trembles, her voice barely a whisper. "It's not only in your head, Jason."

I can barely contain my desire for her. I drag a finger down her spine. "You mean I could take off this dress, strip you down to nothing, and find out how much you want me?"

"Yes, and that's why you need to stop."

"Why?"

"Because we're not ready to leave yet, and I don't want to walk around the rest of this wedding a hot, wet mess."

I glance toward the inn, then back at her. "I could

take you inside, find a room, and fuck you right now up against the door. Would you like that?"

"You know I'd like it, but you can't do that. You're on the job."

"Look at you, being so thoughtful and considering when I can and can't fuck you," I say.

"I think about you a lot. I think about you fucking me a lot."

A groan rips from my throat. I'm on fire for her. Every square inch of me is sizzling. "Do you have any idea how much I want to make you call out my name right now?"

"Wilbur?"

I laugh, then the laughter fades when I give her my answer. "Like I said, you can call me anything while I'm fucking you hard."

She seems to let my last words roll around her tongue like she's tasting them, biting the juice from them. "*Fucking me hard.* Is that what you're going to do to me tonight?"

"You and I both know how this night is ending."

But when the song finishes a second later and turns into a faster one, we stop the dirty talk, the flirting. If we don't, it's going to be perfectly obvious to everyone that we want this wedding to end right now, and there are two more hours on the clock.

Instead, we dance, fast and hot, moving and grooving. We dance together, we dance with others, and we toast again to the couple. I knock fists with the groomsmen, I listen as Chip tells a joke, we talk to Ashley, we pet the pugs, and then finally, mercifully, it's over.

Even though it's been wonderful in its own way, I'm desperate for it to end.

I take her to the limo that Chip reserved for me and open the door for her, this woman I want.

Once inside, we lunge at each other.

24

From the pages of Truly's Drink Recipe Book

Water, Ice Cold

When you're parched, when you're so damn thirsty, when your mouth is a desert of longing, you grab a glass of ice water and down it. That is your true liquid courage. You don't need any liquor. You don't need to be buzzed. Hell, you're not even tipsy. That last champagne you had was hours ago. You have a clear head and a crystal-clear mind. You know exactly what you're doing.

What you want.

You want one thing, one person, and you're going to get him. Get in the car and go.

25

Our lips crash together. Hands dive into hair. Our bodies collide in lust and dirty desire as the car pulls away, the partition separating us from the driver and the tinted windows separating us from the world.

I unclip her hair, slide my hand through it, pulling hard. She groans into my mouth but never lets go. So fierce. So hungry.

Just like me.

We stop for a brief second as she removes her glasses and tucks them into her purse.

I pull her onto my lap, and she straddles me, grinding as she kisses. I kiss her back just as hard, just as greedily. We were soft and slow outside the pub the other night, and now we're frenzied. Two animals unleashed, devouring each other's mouth. She tastes spectacular, smells divine, and I need to be inside her right the fuck now.

Grabbing her ass, I make her grind faster. My brain goes haywire, my senses amped all the way up. She rocks against my length, her hips going wild, her pace frantic.

I grab at the hem of her dress. "As good as this looks on, I bet it looks even better gone."

"Take it off."

I do as instructed, pulling up her dress to her waist as she reaches for my zipper.

She slides it down. "I need you inside me. Need you to fuck me hard. Now, please, now."

"As if I can wait any longer."

I unzip my trousers the rest of the way, reach into my pocket for my wallet, and fish around for a condom. As I find it, I groan. Because holy hell. She has my dick in her hands, and she feels spectacular. Her soft fingers wrap around my hard length, and she squeezes and tugs, stroking up, running her thumb over the head, then back down.

"Your dick is prettier than I remembered."

I raise an eyebrow. "You think my dick is pretty? Not macho? Or hot? Or handsome?"

She shakes her head and licks her lips. "'Pretty' is good. I want this pretty cock inside me. I want this hot, hard, fantastic, pretty cock inside me. Does that work for you?"

My dick twitches against her hand, answering for me.

"Seems your dick agrees, Wilbur."

"'Pretty' works, it turns out. Hell, you can even call me cute if it means you're coming on my cock." I slide the condom on as she wriggles out of her knickers. "I've missed this sight. You, hot, wet, and bothered."

"Aching. Don't forget aching."

"Let me ease it for you," I tell her, sliding my fingers between her legs. My head falls back, and I groan my appreciation for all this fantastic slippery wetness. "Look at you. So fucking turned on. So aroused."

"Told you I was."

"I feel so awful that you were walking around all night like this," I say, teasing her, stroking her, feeling her rub against my fingers.

"So awful you'll get your cock inside me now?"

"Sure. That awful."

She positions herself over me and sinks down. This must be what a Beatles concert was like—magnificent. All my synapses fire at once and nearly fry. Because this is sensational. Pleasure ricochets through my every cell, runs over every bit of my skin.

She gasps, and I groan, and then we fuck.

There is no prelude. No moment to adjust or slow down. This is pure pent-up screwing. Desperate and determined, she rises up and slides down, using my hard-on for her pleasure, finding just the right speed, just the right friction. I grip her ass tighter, squeezing the firm flesh as she rides me.

Her hands curl over my shoulders, digging in. Her jaw tightens, and she lets her head fall in the crook of my neck.

"I have to tell you something." Her voice is filthy and seductive.

"Tell me. Tell me as you ride my cock."

"I thought about you naked all night too."

"Did it drive you crazy? Because I've wanted to fuck

you so badly tonight, I thought I'd go insane." I punch up my hips, thrusting deeper to prove my point.

"I'm already there."

"Good, now go crazy on me, my naughty minx, because I know how you like it. I know you want to fuck hard and be fucked even harder."

She likes it hard, she likes it rough, and she likes it fast and frenzied. So I give it to her that way, fucking her from beneath, thrusting up into her, bringing her down hard on my cock. Threading my hand into her hair, I tug her head back, and the sound she makes is carnal and so fucking passionate. It sends shock waves of white-hot desire through me.

My breath comes faster. Her hips move at a wild pace. We are raw nerve endings, lust, and crackling electricity. She grips me tighter, her moans stuttering with her ragged breath.

Her mouth falls open, and she lets out the longest, most delicious moan as she starts to lose control. "Yes, like that, just like that."

I slide a hand between her legs, where she wants me most. And she detonates. She cries out, loud and tortured and exquisitely erotic, as she comes undone on me.

And that's all I need. Her pleasure, her noises, her desire—they flip the switch in me. Pleasure barrels down my spine like a tsunami careening toward the shore, washing away everything—common sense, loyalty, goals.

None of that matters as I give in to the utter oblivion of release in this woman.

This woman I want again and again.

Hell, she can even call me Wilbur out of bed if I can just have her one more time.

But when she opens her eyes and sighs deeply, contentedly, it's not my name she says.

It's someone else's.

26

The music comes from within her purse.

It sounds like a cartoon's about to start, as the opening music for *Looney Tunes* blares loudly.

"Darren." She snaps to attention, slides off me, scoots next to me, and grapples for her purse. "That's the investor." Furiously, she rips the zipper open, snags her phone, and slams it to her ear. "Hi, Darren, how are you?"

She rearranges her voice as if she's stripped the post-coital glow off it with paint thinner. It's impressive the way she can go from minx to mogul in seconds flat.

There's a pause as he chats, then she answers.

"Yes, it's great. I've been running through some options, testing various concepts."

Another beat.

"Definitely. Sure. Yeah. I can check out that place." She scrambles for a pen in her purse, and I spot a box of tissues on the console. I reach for one, remove the condom, and put it in the rubbish bag hidden on the side of the door. A good limo driver truly thinks of everything. Maybe I'll even mention that in my next blog: be sure to tip handsomely any driver who accommodates discreet disposal of prophylactics.

Truly cradles the phone against her head as she tugs down her dress. "Absolutely. When are you leaving? Sure, let's get it done sooner."

I zip my trousers and straighten my clothes, then find her knickers on the leather seat. I hand them to her as a small knot of frustration in me tightens. But I'm not sure why the knot is here, so I ignore it.

"Don't think twice about it. You can call anytime. It's not late at all. I work all hours." One more beat. "Yes, the crowd is great tonight, as always. Thanks, Darren."

She ends the call, heaving a relieved breath, as if she escaped from the boulder in the nick of time, grabbing her trusty hat before it was too late. "Glad I was able to answer that."

"Why? Does he need you straightaway?"

She slides the lacy fabric back up her long, toned legs. "No, but still . . . I want to impress him, and I need to get my presentation and pitch ready a little sooner."

"Is that why you told him you were at work? To impress him?"

She gestures from me to her, indicating our rumpled appearance. "He doesn't need to know where I am or what I'm doing."

"Well, of course. I wasn't suggesting you tell him you just had the best sex of your life," I say, a little more sharply than I intended, and then I understand my own annoyance—I wish the best sex of her life had rattled her so thoroughly that she'd ignored the call. I wanted her to be so blissed out she couldn't remember her name, let alone that of the caller or the ringtone she'd assigned him.

Her eyes twinkle at my remark, and there—that look. It's hard to be annoyed when she's looking at me like she wants another round or three. "Is that so?" she asks. "Is that what it was?"

"Uh, yeah."

She laughs, smooths a hand down her skirt, then looks at me from beneath her bangs, too seductive for words. Her voice is all soft and breathy. "Yeah, it was, Jason."

No more annoyance.

This'll do. This will do just fine, since I'm instantly drunk on pure masculine pride, courtesy of the injection she just gave me.

But there's no time to indulge, since she zips right back to the topic. "Also, I said it because it's better if he thinks I'm obsessed with work. He's obsessed with work. He'll be more inclined to sign off if he feels I'm the same way."

"But you are obsessed with work," I point out, since it's clear she wants to talk about it. And that's fine. It has to be fine.

"True." Her acknowledgment sounds a little sad.

"It's not a bad thing. I mean, no judgment. I'm the same. Business is what I need to survive, it seems."

"Same here," she says. "I get a little crazy when I don't work. Like I'm a junkie who needs a fix."

"I know exactly how you feel. I love the rush of

hustling for new clients and new options. It's like you're coming down from a high when you've been away from it. Strange in a way, isn't it?"

"It is. It becomes a need. A deep and powerful one. You know that saying? *Work to live, don't live to work*? I don't entirely see why that's such a bad thing. Sometimes work is the thing that makes me happiest. It gives me a rush. That's what I need it for. Do you know what I mean?"

Do I ever. She's talking my language. "Like the thrill you get when you see your numbers grow, or you hear from someone who changed his behavior or attitude because of one of your columns, or when you get another chance to appear on a show you like being on," I say with a wink, dropping that little nugget of good news into the conversational stew.

Her eyes widen with admiration. "That's awesome. I'll have to tune in. You'll let me know when?"

"Absolutely. And thanks, I was pretty psyched when Ryder asked me to come back. So yes, I do get what you're saying. It fulfills you."

"Exactly. Work makes me happy. It's gratifying to build a business, to nurture it, to see it grow. It's reliable too. But I know that my mind-set isn't something that usually meshes with other people's."

"Meshes? What do you mean?"

She shoots me a look like it ought to be obvious. "I'm thirty-five and single. I'm married to work at this point."

"Is that how you see it? You're single because you love work?"

"Pretty much, but that's okay. I'm sure it's different for you, being younger and, well, being a man."

I nod thoughtfully. "I suppose you're right. Society doesn't seem to think it's such an issue if a man is obsessed with work."

"But when a woman is, that must mean she'll never have anything else. Then again, maybe it's true—I am somewhat obsessive. At least, that's what my last boyfriend said when he ended things."

I grit my teeth, thinking of Elias, a guy she was involved with a year or so ago. I used to see him at Gin Joint when he stopped by, always sidling up to the counter, making eyes at the sexy brunette. I hated him on principle.

"He said you were obsessed with work?"

"Yes. And he said he wanted to be with someone who had more of herself to give. He asked for me to cut back my hours, to work less. I said thanks, but no thanks. Work is good to me, so I'm good to work."

"But you can't be entirely obsessed. You're not working tonight, after all. You were with me."

"News flash—I worked all day. I worked for six hours before I caught the train to Connecticut for the wedding."

"That surprises me, but of course, it shouldn't, since you are, by your own admission, a workaholic."

"And you're the same. We're wired the same way—to want, to chase, to go after things."

I run my fingertips along the bare skin of her thigh, returning to my favorite topic. "Like I did with you tonight?"

She inches closer, her voice turning sultry. "You did go after me."

"I wanted you. You wanted me. We both needed it."

"That's not in dispute."

But it feels like something is. Like maybe we're not entirely on the same page. Maybe I'm reading something into nothing, but I also feel like she's reminding me we are only a fuck.

But what the hell?

I know that.

Sure, there's a small part of me that wants to say, *Let's do it again next weekend. Let's make a deal. Let's screw each other's brains out till we're through.* But I'm intensely aware of the many reasons it would be a bad idea to keep this going.

I have jobs to do. She has a business to expand. We have her brother, and that's a big fucking deal. There is no time or space for anything more than this—a tryst in a limo after a wedding—and I need to stand firm on this hill, not die on a nagging desire for a little more.

I shove that desire out the door, speeding past it.

And speeding down Ninth Avenue too, since we're back in the city, close to Truly's home.

I rub my palms together and pretend to roll up my sleeves like we're getting to work, since that's what she loves. "All right, Mr. Investor wants your report sooner, so that means we need to hop to it with our pub crawl. Every day, every night, we need to finish your homework, and you need to use me as your lab rat."

The smile that spreads across her face is magic. Now I'm really talking her language. "That would be great."

She rattles off the places she wants to check out and suggests a timeline.

"Yes, yes, yes," I say since she said yes to helping me.

That's us—two friends helping each other. Nothing more.

She gives me a soft smile. "We're still friends, right?"

She might be reading my mind. I shoot her a look that says she's bananas for asking. "Of course." But inside I'm wishing she felt the same desire for more. Even though I know *friends* is what makes sense.

As we near her block, she glances out the window then tucks her phone in her purse.

"By the way, if he gets *Looney Tunes* as his ringtone, what's mine?"

"Why don't you call me and find out?"

I grab my mobile from my pocket and ring her number.

"Bond. Jay Bond," her phone says.

"And I thought you weren't affected by British accents."

She shrugs coquettishly. "Perhaps I am, after all."

"Good, then you can continue to enjoy mine from the friend zone," I say, reminding myself of the score.

I mean *her*. I need to remind *her* of the score.

She smiles. "Yes, we're good in the friend zone. Aren't we?"

"We're great."

"I think so too."

When we turn on her block, I get out of the car and walk her to her door, since that's what a gentleman should do. "Thank you for coming with me tonight."

"I say this with all sincerity and in every sense of the word . . . coming with you was *my* pleasure."

The way she ends that sentence, so sultry, so inviting, I want to slide out of the zone once again, rope my fingers through her hair, and haul her in for a kiss. But I don't leave her with a hot, possessive kiss that makes her arch her back and drag her nails through my hair.

Because that's not what we agreed to. We agreed that tonight was a blip. So we'll put it behind us.

"See you tomorrow, Truly."

"Good night, Jason."

See? That was so friendly.

I head to the car. As the limo pulls away, she's already inside the lobby, walking to the elevator.

Ready to dive into work.

As we make our way across town, there's that annoying twinge in my chest again. That nagging little ache. Only this time, it's filled with longing.

Which is unacceptable.

There's no room here for wanting more.

There is no space in my life for more, if I could have it.

Besides, when I check my phone, the message on it reminds me of one of the biggest reasons this won't work.

Malone: On a scale of one to ten, how easy was it tonight to fool everyone into thinking you and Truly were a thing?

. . .

Ten, I want to say, but not for the reasons he thinks.

Ten, because one of the things men will do to impress a woman is listen to her.

Only, I didn't just talk to Truly. I didn't just listen to Truly. I didn't ask questions about her work just to impress her.

I didn't do any of those things to woo her or win her.

I did it because I want to understand her deeply, inside and out.

And that's getting to be a problem.

I don't reply to Malone. I don't know what to say.

27

Truly: I suppose this is where I say you were right.

Charlotte: But what was I right about? Was it that a wedding would make you relapse? About the number of days it took? Or how hard it would be to resist him?

Truly: All of the above. And it was out of this world. We're talking mind-bending Os.

Charlotte: Mmm. Best kind to have. Also, I'm shocked. So shocked. Here's my shocked face. *sends selfie of shocked face*

Truly: Yes, I can see from the blank expression that it's a HUGE surprise to you.

Charlotte: You're into him, you went to a wedding, you were in a limo. Doesn't take a world-class detective to add up the clues. But I suppose it's sorta maybe kinda cool to know that the second time was excellent? Yay to good sex and all. :)

Truly: I love that you're trying to see the positive in me breaking a promise a second time.

Charlotte: I'm upbeat like that. Also, stop beating yourself up. You're still a good person underneath that horny-for-Jason exterior.

Truly: Shut up!

Charlotte: I'm just saying. I still love you.

Truly: And I still love you . . . but it would have been nice if the sex was terrible.

Charlotte: Really? Would it really have been nice to have awful sex?

Truly: YES! Because if it had been terrible, I wouldn't be thinking about him all the time. I wouldn't want to do it again or have wanted to invite him over to my house last night. If it were terrible, I wouldn't be wide awake at seven in the morning wishing that things were different.

Charlotte: What exactly do you wish were different?

Truly: That's what I'm trying to figure out.

28

"How do I look? As good as, say, when I did the Gigante ad?"

I draw a blank as I consider Enzo's reflection in the mirror at the tuxedo shop. Gigante—what the hell is that? A Spanish brand of tequila? Some new make of cigarettes from Barcelona? Or perhaps condoms for the fellas for whom jumbo is a tight squeeze?

I finesse my answer. After all, he is a supermodel, so I'm sure there's only one answer to his question. "Better. You look even better."

He arches a brow, giving me a come-hither look that I don't think contains any emotion but is, rather, one of his cache of expressions. *Open a bureau, pick a look from a drawer.* "Excellent. Then I'd say I look pretty fucking fabulous. At least, that's what they all said when I posed in my underwear for Gigante. You should have seen the billboards. But the traffic accidents. I still feel terrible for all the accidents caused when people stopped to stare."

Ah, Gigante is underwear. I should have known that. I'll berate myself later for not prepping with a complete list of underwear brands worn by supermodels.

"That's a shame," I say. "But hey, hazard of the job, right?"

"My God, yes. One time when I was crossing Fifth Avenue, a woman tripped and nearly fell into a manhole from ogling me."

"Who knew the risk to society you could be as a superstar model?"

"I caught her just in time though. I didn't want to have that on my conscience."

"I bet you made her swoon when you caught her."

He flashes his ten-million-dollar grin. "I did. But I'd already met Valerie, so I was a taken man. Valerie and I met on my undies shoot. She'll be here in a few minutes."

"Yeah, about that. Can I give you a tip about undies?"

"Of course." His brown eyes go wide and earnest. Enzo contains an interesting mix of Royal Caribbean cruise ship–size confidence and a doe-eyed desire to learn. Then again, anyone who looks like this man really ought to have universe-level stores of bravado. I don't care for lads, not one bit, and I never have. But I can tell he's not made like the rest of us. He's not even in the top one percent. He's the one percent of the one percent of the one percent, with cheekbones carved by a hundred vestal virgins and eyes that would Svengali anyone into anything. I bet he could even charm a lion into becoming a vegetarian with a single smoldering look.

Or convince men to buy skin-tight briefs. Come to think of it, the way his backside looks in those trousers, I bet his ass was sculpted by the same crew who did his cheeks. But there's still one thing about this man that is not going to make women swoon, no matter the firmness of those abs.

"Here's my tip: don't call them undies. You're in America now, and clearly you're a rock star at the language. But sometimes we need to master the lingo too. Even I've had to adapt. All I want to do is call them pants, but no one would understand me. It's either boxers or briefs here."

"Ah, boxers or briefs. But what about when I wear nothing? What do you call that?"

I go stock-still for a second. But of course. It makes perfect sense. Naturally Enzo, the six-foot-two, twenty-six-year-old Spanish model who recently moved from Madrid to New York City to marry Valerie Wu, the nearly-twice-his-age CEO of a media and advertising conglomerate, walks around in the buff. "We call that commando. But please tell me you're not wearing nothing right now as you try on the tux?"

He gives me an eyebrow wriggle. "Wouldn't you like to see?"

"No, I actually wouldn't."

He laughs then clasps my shoulder, doubling over. "Oh, the look on your face. I wound you up. Don't worry. I have on pants too. Right?"

I wag a finger at him. "You took the piss out of me. Also, I'd say you're ready for the wedding next weekend."

He regards himself one final time in the mirror, shooting approving looks at his reflection. And those must be from the give-them-sex-eyes drawer. "Valerie will probably want to jump me the second she sees me. But she always wants to jump me. That's a nice thing about women of a certain age. In fact," he says, picking up his phone and checking the screen, "she'll be here in a minute."

"To jump you?"

"Please. She'd never do that in a store. Probably in her town car, though, and I'll look forward to that. But she's on her way, since I sent her a selfie after I tried it on and she wants to see me in this in the flesh. Selfies of me make her happy, and I want a happy bride."

A few minutes later, a statuesque woman with striking cheekbones sweeps into the tux shop, red Jackie O shades perched atop her waterfall of silky black hair, flashing smiles at the sales associates.

"Hello. Good morning, Delia. Don't you look dashing, Simon? That suit fits perfectly. And that tie! Do you sell it here? I'll take one of each. Thank you so very much. Add it to my account."

She arrives at the dressing room area, brown eyes taking a leisurely stroll up and down her fiancé's body. "Yes. Just as I suspected. Even better than the photo."

"I had a feeling you might think so."

"And I've already added the photo to my private collection."

"Of course you have. I knew you would. I know you so well," he says, his tone laced with affection, his gaze only for her.

"You know I love to look at them when you're away in Bali, in Paris, in Milan, and I'm left behind all by my lonesome," she pouts playfully, her eyes only on him.

He chuckles. "You make it seem like you're left behind to make casseroles."

"As if I'd even touch an oven. How do they work? You use them to cook food?"

He laughs, clearly delighted with her. "I believe so. But the phone and all the wonderful apps on it do that just the same. So you can run your empire while I am away from you."

"And that's why I love when you indulge me with my favorite photos." Valerie and Enzo share a secret smile, then she spins around. "Where are my manners? It's a pleasure to meet you in person at last . . ."

She extends a hand, waiting for me to supply my fake name.

"Jay," I tell her.

"Jay. How lovely to finally meet the best man." She winks at me, since she's in on it. After all, she's the one who found me. She's the one who hired me—well, her assistant did. But, point being, she knows the score. The only thing she doesn't know is my real name, since I don't generally give it.

I take her hand to shake. "And a pleasure to meet the bride."

"I'm dying to hear all about you. I love meeting new people. I love learning about what makes them tick. I want to know everything. But right now, I have some business to attend to. I have a call with my COO over a new partnership. I must return to my office on wheels. So we'll talk more at the cocktail party?"

"I'm looking forward to it."

She looks to her fiancé. "I'll be waiting for you right outside. Then we'll go to that gallery opening of the painter you love."

"Ahhh. You got the tickets!"

"Of course I did. I know how much you love his work."

"Now who's indulging who?"

"What can I say? You know what I like. I know what you like," she says with a smile.

He raises a hand, runs his thumb along her jawline. "You're too good to me, my love." He drops a kiss to her lips, a proper store kiss, nothing inappropriate, but clearly the kind that seems to say something about their union. They're not even randy. They're simply tender and, it seems, truly in love. On the surface he might appear to be her boy toy, but he's a multi-millionaire model who indulges her whims, and she's the billionaire who indulges his.

Funny, in a good way, how all these couples might be hiring me for appearance's sake, but their connections with each other seem genuine. From Chip and Ashley and their delight in finding someone truly nice, to Enzo and Valerie and their surprisingly mutual romance, and even to Gavin and Savannah and the way they finished each other's sentences.

They might have needed me for the ceremonies, but they don't need me to be happy.

But I shove all thoughts of love, shagging, and deep

connections out of my head when I meet Truly at the pub for lunch and a little recon.

When I see her lounging in a dark booth in a dingy corner, her head bent, tapping away on her phone, I'm not stealing the chance to stare at her privately before she notices me. I'm not cataloging those pouty red lips, that lush chestnut hair, that tight, toned body.

No, deliberately I'm thinking of Gigante ads, and that wipes any vestiges of lust and longing straight from my brain.

29

I'm ready for my blue ribbon in resistance. Consider what I've accomplished so far today, and it's only one thirty in the afternoon.

For starters, we've had an entire flight of beer samples, and I haven't made a single flirty remark. Not one.

Nor did I utter a naughty word when Truly played a round at the pool table. Not when I caught a peek at the tops of her tits as she bent over to send the purple ball screaming into the corner pocket, and not when I watched the rear view as she whacked the next ball somewhere.

Where, I don't know. Because I was enjoying the rear view.

And when she peeked under the table to run her hand along the leather material of the booth, I suggested not one filthy thing she could do while she was under there.

This is the new me.

Back in the friend zone. After all, we're seeing Malone later today at a Yankees game. It'll be the perfect chance to prove to myself, and to her, that I can stay right here, no problem.

I take a final drink of the beer. "So how are we doing? In the friend zone, that is?"

"And the you-scratch-my-back-I'll-scratch-yours zone," she adds, and just like that, I slide out of one zone and into another.

"Why did you have to say that?"

"The back-scratching zone?"

"Yes. I've been completely Zen today. I've been totally in the I-don't-want-to-fuck-you-senseless zone, then you say that, and it reminds me of how you dug your nails into my back last night."

"I did?"

"Do you want me to take off my shirt and show you?" I ask, because when I slide, I don't half-ass it. I don't tiptoe into flirt-infested waters. I do it all the way. Fins up.

She peers over my shoulder as if she can actually see the marks. "Did I really scratch your back?"

"Yes. And I loved it. Also, thanks a fucking lot. I was going to nominate myself for the Men's Buddha Mastery Award for Not Thinking about Sex around a Woman You Want."

She pats my arm. "I can still nominate you. I'm so impressed that you haven't once said any filthy words. Like *cock*. Or *pussy*. Or *fuck you senseless*. Wait, my bad. You said those last ones."

I toss my hands up. "You're kicking a man when he's

down, woman. You can't say 'pussy' and expect me to handle it with any sort of dignity or aplomb."

"Dignity's overrated when it comes to pussies. So's aplomb. Also, *pussy, pussy, pussy*."

"That's it. I'm going to have to give you like twenty innuendos for saying that word."

"Twenty? So that's a normal hour for you and me."

I scratch my jaw as if considering. "Sounds about right."

She arches a brow with a quizzical look. "Have you ever thought about the word *pussy?*"

"Have I? Literally all the time. Well, I was behaving for an hour, and you ruined it. Now all I can think about is that word."

"No, I mean the way it sounds. It's kind of harsh."

I slide closer to her in the booth. "There is nothing harsh about pussies."

"But the word is harsh. Clearly, a man thought of the word. There's no reason 'pussy' should be the slang term for a vagina."

I cringe.

"Oh, please. Vagina, vagina, vagina."

"No, that wasn't why I made that face. I simply don't see pussy as anything less than the most wonderful thing ever created."

"Exactly. Therefore, it should have a better nickname. Think about 'cock.' That's a fantastic nickname for the penis. It says what it is. It's strong, it's phallic— it's a proud word. 'Pussy'? Eh. It's a little crude-sounding, a little dismissive."

"What would you call that wonderful treasure between your legs?"

"If it were up to me, I'd have coined a much better nickname. Like silver. Or lily. Or summer. And then I could say, *Oh, please touch my lily. Please finger my silver. Or go down on my summer. Go down on my summer now.*"

My skin is sizzling, and I'm officially toastier than a forest fire. "Yes, I'd very much like to eat your summer, lick your lily, and kiss your silver. Also, I'd like to bury my face in your pussy."

She lets out a shuddering breath as if this is hard for her too.

"And on that, want to go to Yankee Stadium and see your brother?" I ask.

"Thanks for the buzzkill."

"You started it."

30

It's not football. And by football, I mean proper football. But baseball will definitely do.

Truth is, I rather like this American pastime, and that is unrelated to having an American-born dad and entirely down to how utterly cool his mother—my nan —was.

Nan, a born-and-bred New Yorker, was loyal to the Bronx Bombers till her dying day. She made me read her the box scores from the newspaper—the actual ink and print thing, not even online—during her last few days. She had season tickets before it was cool to have season tickets. She sat in the upper deck, hunched over in her blue-and-white windbreaker, keeping score and teaching me.

Yes, that's one of my party tricks. I can record errors, strikeouts, fielder's choice, double plays, and line drives.

I do it this afternoon, recording the first play while enjoying peanuts and more beer as the sun shines brightly overhead.

"Your little scorekeeping notebook is so cute. Don't forget to record *all the balls*," Malone says as I write down the count on which the pitcher walked the guy.

"Classy, Malone. Mock me for my hobby. Do I mock you for singing?"

He scoff-laughs. "Every. Single. Time."

"No," I say, affecting seriousness. "I sing along." I slide into the tune I heard him singing the other week. *"Tell all the gang at Forty-Second Street, that I will soon be there. Give my regards to old Broadway . . . See? I'm a much more supportive friend than you, being all respectful of your hobby."

I write down the flyout that comes next on the field. But as my words make landfall, I wince. I'm not entirely the better friend, not even close. I'm the worst friend, given what I did in a limo last night. But I'm on the straight and narrow today. Turning over a new leaf.

Malone takes a drink of his beer. "Like I said, you mock me every time, and if you didn't, I'd take you to the hospital for a psychological evaluation. You told me that once. That's how I'd know you were an impostor."

I stroke my chin. "True, true. Your insults are proof that it's you and not a doppelgänger, pod-person, or robot."

"Hey, I have an idea," Charlotte says as the pitcher winds up. "We could actually, I dunno, watch the action on the field?"

Truly pats Charlotte's shoulder. "It always falls on us women to make sure the men know why they're actually at a game. Everything is a trash-talk fiesta for them."

Malone shoots the woman I screwed last night a curious look.

I mean, his sister. He gives his sister a look.

"But I thought you came here because you liked the way the shortstop looked in his uniform," Malone remarks.

"Ah, the plot thickens. Is that so?" I ask Truly. "Don't deny it. You do come here to perv on Lorenzo Marquez."

Truly shrugs like she has a naughty little secret she's not giving up. "Truth. Preach it."

Charlotte nods. "Amen. Shortstops are the hottest. I think that's why my husband decided to play shortstop on your softball team."

"Because they're hot?" Malone asks incredulously. "That's why Spencer is the shortstop? I thought it was because, call me crazy, he was actually good at fielding the ball."

"That too. But also because shortstops are traditionally the hottest players. If you don't believe me, just look it up."

"And you're complaining that we sit in the stands and do things other than watch the game and only the game? I believe that makes you the pot calling the kettle black, ladies," Malone says.

Truly squeezes his arm. "Dear brother, at some point, you're going to have to accept that baseball history is incredibly inclusive and now encompasses everything from not only the greatest ballparks, players, and plays of all time, but also the best parks for craft beer as well as the cutest butts in uniform. Also, I know you're a historian of athletic physique too. You had a poster of Brandi Chastain above your desk in high school."

"Whoa," Charlotte cuts in. "I'm just hearing this story now? I've known you two clowns for years, and I'm just now learning your brother had a crush on Brandi Chastain?"

Truly wiggles her eyebrows. "The one and only. He has good taste."

I tap Malone's shoulder. "It was *the* picture, right?"

"Of course."

"I had that picture too. She was tops when she won the World Cup with the fifth kick in the penalty shootout. Have you ever seen any game that fantastic before?"

Truly cracks up. "Jason, you're so adorable. He did not have the photo because of the absolutely incredible play she made. He had it because of the sports bra."

Malone cuts in. "Just like you had posters of Derek Jeter all over your room because of his five Gold Gloves or his World Series victories?"

Truly gasps indignantly. "I totally had his picture because of his World Series wins. He's the man in the post season."

"Oh, right," I say, winking. "Of course. That's why you hung up his shot. Just like everyone who read a certain magazine for, ahem, the articles."

Truly crosses her arms, straightens her shoulders. "I admired him."

"Admired his backside," Malone coughs under his breath.

"I admired his gamesmanship."

Malone chuckles, raising a finger to make a point. "So much that you also used to draw hearts in your notebook and write TG and DJ."

She slaps his thigh. "I did not."

Charlotte holds up a hand in admission. "I'll confess. I did that. I also liked to add TLF for *True Love Forever*. But in my defense, I was fourteen."

"Same, same," Truly says quickly. "And just to be clear, I liked him because of his talent. Because of his skills."

Malone clears his throat. "She liked his ass. It's that simple."

I pop a peanut into my mouth, making a mental note that some things never change. Truly Goodman is an ass woman. She squeezed mine the other night on the street, after all. And I have to say, my derriere is just as good as Jeter's. Maybe not on par with Enzo's, but Jeter's will do.

Wait. I can't be thinking about her interest in my ass. I'm at a game with her brother.

I direct my thoughts to baseball and only baseball for the next several innings as Malone and Truly trade stories, poking each other in places only a sibling can reach, with Charlotte and I chiming in from time to time.

But as we slide into the seventh-inning stretch, something I've been sidestepping is becoming unside-steppable. These two are so connected. They love each other madly, and they support each other savagely.

As it should be.

I love my little sister like crazy. I'd do anything for her, and I do—running a second business to finance her education. And I have zero regrets about it.

I understand the deep and abiding love between siblings.

But guilt is a splinter under my skin. Guilt over the lie I'm telling Malone. The lie of omission.

For the second time, I slept with my best mate's sister.

Once can be a mistake, can be forgivable, even.

But twice is deliberate.

And if I do it again, it'll feel like an affair.

Though nothing about last night felt illicit. Everything felt all too right, all too true. Was it that way for her? Did she feel the same *something more* too?

The loudspeaker crackles, interrupting my thoughts as the announcer tells us it's time for "Take Me Out to the Ballgame."

We stand and sing a rousing rendition.

When it ends, Truly smiles at her brother. "Remember how we used to duet that song when we were kids and Dad took us to the games?"

Malone's smile is genuine and a little wistful, like he's remembering those times with their father. "We duetted everything. We had a blast, especially with Dad."

"We did." Truly drapes an arm around him. "You have the pipes, but I can hold my own. We killed it at Christmas."

"Jingle Bells, jingle bells, jingle all the way," Malone croons.

"*Oh what fun it is to ride in a one-horse open sleigh,*" she sings.

Malone returns to his speaking voice. "But that was nothing compared to the time you came home from college, and whipped up some pancakes for breakfast and a song about them too. Right on the spot, with your spatula as a microphone. I was all kinds of impressed."

"Hello? I love pancakes. They deserve all the odes." Truly shimmies her shoulders, and with a bluesy tone, she and Malone sing to the tune of "On a Bicycle Built for Two."

"*Pancakes, pancakes, give me your answer true . . . I'm half-crazy over the love of you . . . it won't be a stylish affair . . . we can't afford flatware, but I'll gobble you down, till you're all around . . . in my huge belly!*"

I lean back in the seat, watching them. It's completely endearing. It tugs on my heart and makes it ache at the same damn time. When they're done, I slow-clap along with Charlotte.

"And this is why I'm so damn grateful you sing at my bar too," Charlotte says, patting Malone on the arm.

"It was nice of me to share my brother with you, wasn't it?" Truly says.

"Ladies, ladies. There's enough of me to go around," Malone says, then looks at Truly. "But that's your family-friendly pancake number, sis. Don't hold back on the naughtier one you sang when Mom left the kitchen. As a matter of fact, I sang it to Sloane the other morning."

"You sang my pancake seduction number to your

fiancée? The woman who swoons every time you sing? I'm shocked."

He shrugs with a smirk. "It worked."

I chime in. "I want to hear the pancake seduction tune."

Truly huffs, the kind of sound you make when you're not really irritated. "Really? You want my not-safe-for-work pancake song?"

Charlotte's hand shoots up. "Hello! How did I not know about this? Sing it, girl. Sing it now."

Truly straightens her shoulders, purses her lips, and makes a sexy little humming sound in the back of her throat. *"Come get some pancakes. I know you want 'em. I got some pancakes. Hot off the griddle. Come get some pancakes."*

I tug on my collar because it's too hot for words here. I'd like to come get her pancakes. I'd like to pour syrup all over her and lick it off.

And yet, here I am at a ballgame, having a blast with my friends. Am I willing to risk moments like this too?

There are my stakes, there are hers, and then there are *these*. This deep familial bond.

Truly and Malone are so close they can sing Christmas songs together at Yankee Stadium. They can harmonize about fluffy carbs, they can talk about missing their dad, and it's all part of who they are.

I can't ruin that. I can't take a chance I might damage this precious connection.

I have to stay out of the horizontal zone with Truly. No matter how hard it is.

31

Truly: That went well, I'd say.

Charlotte: They won. Of course it went well. Oh, did you mean how you and Jason should be nominated for Oscars for acting like you're friends?

Truly: It's not an act!

Charlotte: I know. You really are good friends. Like Spencer and I were. And obviously we still are.

Truly: And now you're husband and wife, and mommy and daddy too. :)

Charlotte: Seems we did okay. :) Point being, I didn't smell anything fishy. Well, except for the floor of Yankee Stadium, but that's up there with the ten surfaces on which you never want to place a purse.

Truly: Alongside the Port Authority?

Charlotte: Yes, and any men's restroom. Including those in the Four Seasons.

Truly: Don't forget the Ritz too.

Charlotte: Anyway, just keep on this falling-out-of-bed path and you'll be fine. As long as you don't slip onto his dick again, you can totally be friends forever!

Truly: Thanks for the tip. I'll try to avoid falling onto his cock.

Charlotte: Well, you do have a history of accidentally landing on it.

Truly: Purposefully. It was a purposeful landing.

Charlotte: Own it.

32

The next morning as I run in the park, I call my sister, who's usually between classes at this time of day in London. Talking to her is always a good reminder of why I do what I do—why I bust my ass, work hard, and keep things on the level.

Or rather, why I'm going to stay on the good-boy side forever.

"Hey, you! What's going on?" she asks when she answers.

"What would you do if you really wanted something but couldn't have it?"

"Like strawberries? Because you know I break out in a rash when I eat them."

"Sure. Yeah. Good analogy."

She laughs, a little surprise in her tone. "I don't eat them."

"It's that simple?"

"Jason. Of course it's that simple. But I don't think you're asking me about strawberries."

"Hell, was it that obvious?"

"As obvious as the fact that all cats ignore humans. So, who is the girl you can't have?"

I heave a sigh, slowing my pace so I can share this. "Best friend's sister. But it's okay. I have it under control. I'm fine. I'm not even thinking about her."

"Are you sure? Because you called me to talk about her. Well, strawberries. But I suspect she's the strawberries."

"Fine. You can see right through me. She's definitely the strawberries, and I will just pretend I have a strawberry allergy. It works for you."

"Mine's real, you twit."

"Sure, right. And it works for you too. It's exactly what you need to resist strawberries. Therefore, I now have a strawberry allergy."

"But you don't have a strawberry allergy," she insists.

"Of course not. And I'd never make light of one either. But perhaps I've just recently developed a dire reaction to . . ." I imagine the woman I want, the way she smells, her breezy scent. "Fresh air."

When Truly and I go to jujitsu the next night, I keep my fresh-air allergy at the top of my mind. I'm not rude to fresh air. I don't ignore fresh air. I might even praise fresh air for how excellently she executes all sorts of moves, especially when she and Presley go at it during a demo on the mat. Not going to lie. A cat fight is fun as hell to watch, even when it's staged.

"Grab her hair!" I call out. See, that's friendly.

"I'll grab your hair next time," Presley says to me in a huff.

I grin and throw out, "Scratch her back!"

"I'm not going to scratch your back, Jason," Presley shouts.

"You're a terrible sport."

"I'm not scratching your back either," Truly says.

Well, I can't resist that. "You mean . . . *again*. You're not scratching it *again*."

When they finish the demo, Truly's look says I'm in trouble, and she challenges, "Back-scratching?"

"I meant it in a friendly way."

"Then please note I mean this in a friendly way: you make a terrible cheerleader. Your peanut gallery comments are the worst," Truly says.

"It's because I don't have pom-poms," I say.

Truly tries to rein in a laugh, and so does Presley. There. See. All is well.

When it's my turn to demo with Truly, we work on grappling on the floor and I'm all business. A total pro all through class and as we finish.

And I valiantly resist catching a whiff of the delicious fresh air when we leave class, say goodbye to Presley, and visit another pub that night.

I am the master of this zone.

When Truly spins efficiently on her heel, regarding the surroundings and rattling off all the elements of the pub that work (dark wood, types of beers, tankards) and those that don't (the TV is too close to the pool table, and when a match is on, you can't hear your friends—

plus, pubs are supposed to be warm, homey environments that enable conversations), I tell her I'm giving her an A-plus.

"You have mastered all things pub."

"I'll take my pub master badge, thank you very much. And I'm ready. I'm going to nail this presentation like a sixteen-year-old gymnast going for Olympic gold."

"Or as Eddie the erstwhile best man would say, you're going to nail it like a showgirl being banged behind a pinball machine."

Truly arches a brow. "Hmm. That does sound like a promising way to bang, but I'll stick with the gymnast analogy. Or how about this? Like a hammer on the head?"

"That's a good one too." I congratulate myself for resisting hammering innuendos, abstaining from nailing, and sidestepping all banging double entendres. Not even tempted, because they'd make me break out in hives due to my sudden onset fresh-air sensitivity. "And let me know how it goes tomorrow. I want a full report."

"You'll get one." She takes a breath, seems to study my face. Her voice lowers to that tender volume that tries to hook into a part of me I don't want hooked. "Jason?"

"Yes?"

"Thanks for everything. I feel ready . . . because of you. I appreciate everything you've done. And we have your final wedding this weekend. I hope this exchange has been helpful for you too."

"It's been great. And we'll nail the wedding. Speaking of nailing it, how good are we at nailing this friend-zone thing?"

She smiles softly. "We're the best. We're definitely nailing the friend zone."

"Like you wanted," I say, a slight question in my voice that I immediately wish I could strip out. But maybe she won't notice.

"And like *you* wanted as well." She noticed, but so it goes.

I stuff my hands into my pockets, holding tightly to resistance. "Yeah. We both did. We both agreed it made sense." I swallow my desire to kiss her, to thread a hand through her hair, to tell her I want to be so much more than friends. I shove all those nagging feelings aside, along with the wish to spend more time with her, to help each other on other projects, on every project, to be her support in business and life and vice versa.

After I put Truly in a Lyft home, I walk across town to my place, needing the city air, the fumes, the scent of garbage to erase all my unwise wants.

Once upon a time, I wrote a column on how a man can reinvent himself. Make changes to his mindset, his style, his attitude.

It remains one of my most popular for one reason. It's a column about Kara's Flowers. But it's the name I gave to my philosophy of reinvention that really shines: *Adam Levine-ing.*

For the record, I do not listen to his music. I don't even think I could live with the shame if anyone found Maroon 5 piping into my earbuds. And yet, Kara's Flowers is the model for reinvention, and I say as much when Ryder has me back on his show that week.

"And what do we need to know about Kara's Flowers?"

"Everything. It's literally the model to follow if you feel like you want to make changes in your life. If you want a new career, a new approach to dating, whether you like men, women, or some combination thereof, look no further than a little pop band named Kara's

Flowers. They totally bombed in the mid-90s and were dropped by their label about a month after their first record. But you know what they did?"

"Tell us. Don't hold back."

"They took one of their guys and made him their front man. Changed their type of music and became a band that has sold more than twenty-seven million albums. Adam Levine is their lead singer."

Ryder brings his fingers to his forehead, mimes an explosion, adding in the requisite sound effects. "I'd say they did just fine indeed with this reinvention trick."

"Not too shabby, right? It's a reminder, and frankly, an inspiration, even if you don't like their music. Sometimes you need to shake things up. Rejigger who you are, how you present, and what type of music you make."

"All right, let's apply this to our audience. Let's say one of our listeners wants a whole new career. How does he do it? How does he *Adam Levine* himself?"

"He does it step by step," I say, detailing my tips for prioritizing, changing, and communicating. "And don't forget one of the most important aspects of Adam Levine-ing."

"Serve it up. Give us your best hot tip."

"Dress better. That's what I always tell the men of the world. I don't know what's happened to society and this whole *wear basketball shorts for everything* trend or the *athletic wear is now street wear* thing. Even jeans, for that matter, should be worn judiciously."

Ryder stands in his chair, leaning over the soundboard, checking out my garb. "Guys, this man walks the walk. He's wearing slacks."

"Of course I am. Even if the listeners can't see it, you need to dress well. No one was ever sent home early from work or school for dressing well. Do that, and it'll help your cause."

When the show is over, Ryder shakes my hand. "You're killing it, man. Making me look too damn good."

"You do that on your own."

"See you next week. Make sure to pop by Marie's office on the way out. She's cutting checks today for contractors, and she always loves seeing you. I think she's hoping for your soccer tips."

"Football, Ryder. Football."

"Never. Not even on pain of torture will I ever say football."

That's a sign, if I ever needed one, that this is becoming a regular gig. I say goodbye and head down the hall, feeling pretty damn good about how things are looking.

"Oh, yes, he's so charming."

I hear a drawling feminine voice coming from the breakroom down the hall, her intonation a mix of Dallas and, well, more Dallas.

Then another voice joins in, sounding like she's from Brooklyn—as in, a lifelong Brooklynite. "And he knows everything on the topic. He's a total delight to listen to with that accent."

I square my shoulders, smiling to myself. I am indeed a delight.

The first voice goes again. "I'm not even into that stuff, Betty, but I find myself trying new things because of him."

Well, how about that. My work is reaching women too.

"I love his attitude, love his style. I told Ryder to hire him for the job. We sooo need someone like that," says the woman named Betty.

I pump a fist, slowing my pace because eavesdropping is so not acceptable, but these are extenuating circumstances. I need to hear this.

"What did he say?" the Dallas woman asks.

"He thought it was a great idea. He's bringing him in to finalize it," Betty from Brooklyn says.

Yes!

"He's the breath of fresh air we need on that show," Betty adds.

"Don't I know it. It's about time. It's also about time for our meeting. We better skedaddle," the Texan replies, and I take that as my cue to nip into Marie's office and retrieve my check.

"Looking lovely as always, Miss Marie." I always enjoy seeing her when it's paycheck time, and that's not simply because she's terrific at handing over money. She's from the homeland too, so we've bonded.

She pats her blonde hair. "I have a very good hairdresser. She deserves all the credit. Somehow she makes me look like my two teens haven't made me go gray."

"Teenagers? I would have thought toddlers."

"Flattery will get you everywhere, Mr. Reynolds. Now, take this check and take your girl out for a nice meal."

"I don't have a girl, but if I did, I'd take her someplace fantastic."

"I can't believe you don't have a lady. If you let me, I could set you up with some of my friends. I have a few divorced ladies who would just scoop you up like an ice cream cone."

"I do enjoy ice cream. What flavor exactly?"

"Does that mean I can play matchmaker?" she leans in to whisper.

Maybe it's because our relationship exists on this simple level, or maybe it's because I'm in a damn fine mood. I glance around as if to make sure the coast is clear, then whisper back. "Not yet. Truth be told, there's someone I fancy. But we're just friends."

"Friends make the best lovers."

"Mrs. Williams!" I say, like she's shocked me in a Henry James novel.

"Oh please. Don't act so astonished. Mr. Williams and I were friends first. And let me tell you, that made all the difference." She drops her voice. "Why do you think my kids were born one year after I said *I do*?"

"I didn't actually realize they were."

"And now you do. Because we were good friends first. So, what's she like? Your prospective lady?"

"She's just a friend. I swear. We are only friends."

She rolls her eyes. "Come back in a few weeks and tell me how that's working out for you. Fifty dollars says you're more than friends."

"One hundred says we're only friends."

We shake on it.

"Now," she asks, "who are we betting on this week-end? Chelsea or Manchester United?"

We debate the merits of each, then decide where to place our bets.

"Now keep me posted on your *friend*."

"Just a friend."

"Right. I believe you. I totally believe you."

I blow her a kiss. "Of course," I say, then tell her I'll see her next week.

When I look at the check, I see it'll cover many nice meals. I breathe a sigh of relief. I don't love money so much as its ability to pay for things I need.

As I make my way out of the building, I tune in to a podcast on restaurant reviews, since it's always good to have food recommendations at the ready.

"The soufflés at Cloud Nine are the very definition of pillowy. Soft, fluffy, and bursting with flavor, they wooed me the entire evening. In fact, I seriously considered spending the rest of the night with my cheese soufflé."

I chuckle at the reviewer's passion. Coco even speaks in a kind of seductive voice that fits her reviews, since food seems to be the ultimate passion for her.

"In fact, I'm tempted to leave my boyfriend for this . . ."

I bump into Marcus as I turn into the lobby. He's out of context here, so it takes a moment for the brain cells to link up.

Marcus Daniel Craig-Hemsworth?

"Hey!" He waves to me as he walks over.

I take out my earbuds. "Hello."

"I know you! I mean, I didn't know you were *you* when I saw you at my pub."

"What do you mean?" I ask, unsure why the bartender is here.

"The Modern Gentleman in New York! I read all your columns. I listen to your podcast. It didn't click till you left, but then I remembered where I'd heard your voice. On your podcast, and now here. I'm like a Modern Gentleman acolyte."

Inside, I'm thinking Walker was dead wrong. I'm not running into wedding guests at my Modern Gentleman gigs. I'm running into fans. Bona fide fans. Could this day be any better? "Thrilled to hear that."

"You're Jason Reynolds, and you have been an inspiration. You're the reason I'm here today. Well, and your girl too. Let me back up and explain. I can do it in a word, actually. A brilliant term you coined." He takes a deep, fueling breath. "*Adam Levine-ing.*"

"Oh, you heard me on Ryder's show just now?" I ask, figuring perhaps it's piped into the lobby or he'd tuned in on his phone.

"No. I listen to you all the time. I read you every day. Your idea of reinvention is my gospel. I was basically working two jobs, waiting tables, piecing together a living to pay some bills, and I came across your column. It was everything I needed to prioritize, communicate, and dress for the part." He tugs at his blue button-down. "I learned everything I could about beer. Became a top bartender, and now I make substantially more money. And I took my blog and turned it into a podcast, like your girl suggested. Always hustling."

I don't correct the possessive pronoun before *girl*. "That was fast."

"You're telling me."

I clap him on the shoulder. "Good on you, mate. Good on you."

Maybe I need to revise my stance on how I feel about Marcus with his *I know everything about beer* and *I could kiss you* attitude. After all, the man recognized me. The real me. Not the best man, pretend-friend me.

He points his thumb back down the hallway. "And now I'm here to talk to Ryder about this new job I've been hired for."

I blink in surprise. "He hired you?"

"Sure did. My friend Betty told him about me and my new podcast. He called me straightaway and told me he had something for me. And I have you to thank."

And Truly.

He has Truly to thank.

For that terrible, awful, horrid suggestion.

I grit my teeth to within a millimeter of cracking their enamel, then slap on my best practiced smile as I shake his hand and wish him well. After all, that's the gentlemanly thing to do.

But inside, the reality lashes me harshly.

I was wrong. I heard the women wrong. Marcus is the guy they were talking about. Marcus is the one they find charming. And Marcus has come here to take the job.

Because he fucking *Adam Levine'd* himself, thanks to my advice.

To mine and to my good friend Truly's.

34

Charlotte: I tossed a whole silver dollar in the fountain at Lincoln Center today, making a wish for your meeting.

Truly: Whoa. Big spender.

Charlotte: Dreams are more likely to come true if you pony up for wishes, right?

Truly: Absolutely. Imma go toss my gold bars into the fountain right now. Be right back.

Charlotte: Anyway, just texting to wish you luck. You don't need it, but I'm required to wish it anyway. It's going to be fabulous. Will you let me know how it goes?

Truly: Of course. And thanks for the intro in the first place. I wouldn't have this shot if it weren't for you. Dinner is on me, well, basically forever.

Charlotte: Nah, that's crazy. I was happy to hook you up.

Truly: Hey, I wanted to tell you something.

Charlotte: *perks up * *presses ear to phone* *waits with bated breath*

Truly: *deep breath* Jason and I made it back to the friend zone. We've been helping each other all week, and it's worked really well. No more slips.

Charlotte: Ohhh. Congrats, I think.

Truly: Yeah, congrats, I think too.

Charlotte: And is that what you really want?

Truly: What I really want is irrelevant. This is what makes sense. And I'm fine with it. I mean it. I'm totally fine with everything.

Charlotte: Well, I'm here in case you're ever not.

35

He stole my idea. He stole my show. He stole my spot.

It's that simple and that shitty.

Normally, I'd go to Gin Joint right about now.

Okay, well, not exactly right about now because it's five in the evening and that's workout time, and a workout is precisely what I need. An hour at the gym, some time on the exercise bike, some Beatles and Rolling Stones, and maybe, hey, maybe some Eric Clapton too, since my countrymen always reset me properly.

But after a shower, I can still smell fumes of annoyance wafting off me. I hate being annoyed. I hate feeling like I'm spinning on a hamster wheel.

And I wish I could go to Gin Joint, catch Malone singing, grab a beer with Nick if he's there, then chat with Truly. I want to sort out this epic ball of frustration inside me by talking to friends. But I can't separate this knot from her right now, as much as I want to.

Rationally, I know it's not her fault. She made an

offhand suggestion to a barman. A smart idea too. The same suggestion I'd give the guy. Hell, it's the advice I spew out all the bloody time.

And yet, it's bitten me in the arse.

* * *

I head to a club in the Meatpacking District where Walker is deejaying, figuring a stiff drink certainly can't hurt matters. That's exactly what I get when I arrive, ordering whiskey amid the haze of cosmopolitan-this and martini-that going out to the young twenty-some-things in leather pants and tight tops that slouch off the shoulders. I grab my drink, knock it back, and check my watch. Walker told me he usually puts on a longer mix and takes a short break at nine.

As I turn around to make my way to a booth, I spot my buddy Josh, who looks as out of place as a man in dress pants, a crisp white shirt, and a silk tie can look at a dance club. I stop when I see him, eyeing him up and down derisively, practically shouting, "Didn't you get the memo to dress for the occasion?"

"Yeah. This is my occasion. Business. That's why I dress like I'm wheeling and dealing millions of dollars in pro athlete contracts."

I break out my imaginary violin. "I feel so bad for you, what with all those rich athletes you have to represent."

"Hey, I have to be a virtuoso, because there's this new basketball player in town that everyone's trying to get a piece of. Including Haven."

"Ah, Haven. The one, the only."

He shoots me a look, like he can't believe I'd refer to her that way. "No, Haven is not the one, the only. She's this . . . this . . . She's a total ballbuster. She's a pain in the ass. She's a double serving of *I can't even*."

"Sounds as if you fancy her."

He shoots me a searing look. "No. Just no."

I clap him on the shoulder. "Have it your way. Why don't I treat you to a glass of whiskey, Mr. Monopoly?"

We head to a quieter bar in a corner of the club. When I see Walker making his way through the crowd, I motion for him to join us.

He claps us both on the back. "What brings you cats to my club? You can't resist the skills I share with the night owls, right?"

"It's barely nine. It's hardly night-owl hour. More like Wall Street and Madison Avenue hour."

Walker rubs his thumb and forefinger together. "And they bring the greenbacks to hear me spin."

We catch up for a few minutes about business, and I order another drink while Walker asks for a water. As we talk, Josh jerks his gaze toward the dance floor occasionally, then Walker narrows his eyes at me. "What's with you tonight, Reynolds? You're not your usual chipper self."

I drag a hand through my hair, slumping against the bar. "It's that obvious?"

Walker points his thumb at Josh. "As obvious as his interest in Leather Pants Woman."

Josh snaps to attention. "What are you talking about?"

"The woman in the tight leather pants and silver-sequined top. The one who looks like she'd have your balls for breakfast along with a kale smoothie, all before she goes to her Zumba class. C'mon. You think I didn't notice you were staring at her? You forget who you're dealing with. I see everything." He points to his eyes.

"She's not having my balls for breakfast."

"But is she having the kale smoothie before Zumba?" I ask.

"Whatever. That's Haven. She's . . ."

"She's the ballbuster?" I supply.

Walker pats Josh's shoulder. "Maybe you need your balls busted. Ever consider that?"

"No. But maybe you need yours waxed. Ever consider that?"

"Who's to say I don't wax them already?"

Josh cracks a rare smile, then signals a time-out. "TMI."

"We'll put a pin in the ball convo for now." Walker turns to me. "All right. Serve it up, man."

I heave a sigh as the bartender brings my drink, and I thank him then answer Walker. "I'm just annoyed. I was on Ryder's show this morning, and everything seemed to be going well. He asked me to come back—there's an opening there, and I felt like I was primed to nab it. On my way out, though, I ran into this other guy —who's bloody fucking British too—who might as well have been carrying the job around like a wrapped present, playing with the bow so everyone looks at it."

Walker sighs sympathetically. "Happens to the best

of us, man. Somebody's always taking jobs. That's just the way it goes."

"Not really what I wanted to hear." I knock back some whiskey.

Josh shoots me a look. "Why is that not what you wanted to hear? That's the truth. That's the truth of business. I lose business to Leigh Jensen, to Scott Borehead, to CAA and that guy who looks like Dwayne Johnson. And they lose business to me. We're all reeling our lines off the same boat, angling for the same fish. Right now, the shortstop on the Yankees is up for grabs. And Haven wants Lorenzo too, I'm sure."

"The shortstop. Always the shortstop," I say with a groan.

Walker simply shrugs. "If I were a shortstop, I'd literally want for nothing in life."

"Yeah, no kidding," I say.

Josh barely notices our exchange. He just picks up where he left off. "I'm not going to let Haven win him though. Not after I lost two clients to her in the last month." He growls in her general direction. "Haven Fucking Delilah."

Walker rolls his eyes. "Hey, Josh. Why don't you tell us how you really feel?"

"You want to hear what happened? Because she poached my clients, man."

"Yeah, I'm dying to hear all about the poaching. Tell us about Leather-Pants Poacher," Walker says dryly.

Josh huffs, dismissing it with a wave. "I'm not talking about her. I'm done talking about her. She pisses me off too much. Plus, look at her." Our eyes drift toward the aforementioned Haven. The poacher. The evil one.

The complete and absolute babe.

"Seems you can't stop looking at her," I remark, and he snaps his gaze back to us.

"Anyway, let's help our sorry-ass friend," Walker says, meaning me, and downs his water quickly. "I have five minutes." Walker turns to me. "Here's the deal. You had an opportunity. It looks like it went to someone else. You just move on."

"I know. I know. It's just that some days I feel like I make progress, then I'm back to square one."

Josh lifts a glass. "Welcome to the grind, man. That's how it is. You have to get used to it, and don't stop moving."

"I'm used to it. Don't you see? It's what I've been doing for the last six or seven years."

Josh shoots me a look. "Dude, I'm in my mid-thirties. I've been hustling since I was twenty-one. Wait, no. I've been hustling since I was six and watched Montana win back-to-back Superbowls, and decided I wanted to rep superstars like him. It never ends."

Walker points to himself. "I've been a hardcore music fan since, well, since I was in the womb, I think."

Josh nudges him, a smirk on his face. "Please, tell us about the music you listened to in the womb. That sounds really fascinating. Was Mozart playing when you were in mommy's tummy?"

I laugh. "Or did your mum get you addicted to Cyndi Lauper?"

Walker scoffs. "My mom played Mozart for me, and

I'm damn proud of it. Made me smart. I graduated early from college. But the point is, this is how it goes. You take the awesome highs with the messy, muddy middles and the dreary lows, and we'll be here to support you. That's what good friends are for. To stop you from wallowing in your own misery. You have friends because you're not always going to get what you want at work. Work is a fickle mistress. But friends?" He gestures from himself to Josh to me. "Friends are the glue."

Josh nods, holding up a fist. "Bro code."

"Man code," Walker corrects as he knocks back. I join in, though a voice in the back of my head tells me I'm the worst violator of the code, in spite of my fresh-air sabbatical.

"Friends make it all more bearable. You see your friends, you have a drink, you listen to a tune, and you kick back. You reflect on the state of the world. You realize that there's all sorts of shit going on that's way worse than a gig not going your way. You donate a little money to a charity. You move on, and then you pull yourself up. When you get home tonight, give money to the homeless or to rescue dogs or to kids living in poverty, okay?"

A bit of shame coats my throat as I finish my drink. I have been wallowing, and I'm not a wallower. "You're right. I can't feel sorry for myself. What the fuck is that? One hundred percent unacceptable is what."

Josh lifts his glass. "Amen, brother. To never feeling sorry for yourself."

I clink my glass to his. "I'll drink to that."

"Besides, I still have the regular weekly gig. I haven't lost that. So I'm just status quo."

"And speaking of keeping things status quo, I need to have a few words with Haven."

Josh stalks over to confront his nemesis, and I hear a few words of their conversation.

"You come in here to try to steal more clients from me?"

She crosses her arms. "As if I have to steal them."

"You know that's exactly what you're doing."

"Maybe you ought to do a better job holding on to them."

He inches closer, getting up in her space. "You do know there's a reason why you shouldn't be doing this?"

She juts her chin up at him, looking unintimidated by the way he towers over her. "And there's a reason, too, that I enjoy it so damn much."

I'm pretty sure he growls at her next, and her eyes simmer. I'm also pretty sure that in a parallel universe, they'd go off and fuck it out. But that's just a hunch.

I turn to Walker. "Did you feel like you just accidentally tuned into the start of a new TV romance or something?"

"That was some of the best theater I've ever seen. Rivals, eh? I want to hear more, but now, I need to get back out there and spin some tunes. Why don't you get on the floor and dance? Everything in life can be solved with a dance-off."

"I have nobody to dance-off with," I say.

He gestures to the entire floor. "The place is packed. Find a stranger. Dancing clears the mind. Sorts the thoughts. A few dances, and you'll know exactly what you need to do next."

I do move with the crowd for a few songs.

It does clear my head.

I do feel better having seen my friends.

Walker is right. When it comes to work disappointments, you move on, and you don't let them get you down. You brush them off and keep chasing the dream.

By the time I leave the club, I've lightened the load and shed my annoyance. As the thumping subsides in the night air, I check my phone, finding a message from Truly.

Truly: Nailed it like a gymnast hammering pinball machines!

I laugh at the absurd way she's mixed all three analogies. I smile too, because I'm proud of her. Because I want her to have all her dreams come true.

I read the text again. Then one more time. I can't wipe the grin from my face. I was a right idiot to be pissed at her. She's only ever had good intentions. She tried to help Marcus, just as she's been helping me. For as long as I've known her, she's been supportive of my business and my efforts to help Abby. She's been available for a chat, a night out, a workout, and a jujitsu class every time I've needed it. She's been everything I could want in a friend, and I'm lucky to have her as one of mine.

Friends don't only help you through disappointments.

They also cheer you on in good times, like Truly's.

I'm not far away from Gin Joint.

Not far at all.

I make my way to her bar so I can congratulate her in person on nailing it. Along the way, I follow Walker's advice and make a donation to an animal rescue. There. I feel better. When I reach Gin Joint, I don't see Truly behind the counter, so I ask the guy mixing drinks where I can find her.

"She's in her office. Is she expecting you?" he asks.

A jerk would barge in. A gentleman asks. "No. But I have to see her anyway. Do you need to call her first and tell her I'm here?"

He smiles, shaking his head. "Nah. I've seen you around. Go on ahead."

I turn down the hallway, head to the last door, and knock. When she answers, she's like a breath of fresh air, and I want to breathe her in all night long.

Because she smells like so much more than a friend.

"So you nailed it? Just like I knew you would."

Her smile is huge as she ushers me into her office, the door falling shut behind us. She's so giddy that her enthusiasm is practically a new perfume, and it's going to my head.

"Yes! I met with him today, and I went over all my plans. He said it sounded fantastic. He just needs to check with his partners and"—she stops, crosses her fingers—"then we should be good to go."

"And do you have a name for this new establishment?"

"I was thinking of something really on the nose like An English Pub because, hey, then won't I come up quickly on search results?"

"That's what I admire about you—always thinking."

"Always hustling." One corner of her lips curves up, and she shoots me another smile. "Thanks again, Jason. I really couldn't have done it without you."

"I'm not so sure about that. I think you had it in you already. I was just company."

She leans against her neat desk, looks me up and down, and says, "Good company indeed."

Her voice has changed slightly. It's softer and a little bit more seductive. How is that even possible?

"And a great friend too," she adds.

Is that a reminder to herself? But I can't read in her tone whether she's underscoring the word as a barrier or stating the simple truth: we are great friends. The way we've interacted this week affirms it. "We're doing pretty well at this friendship thing, aren't we?" I ask.

"We're rock stars at it."

"No one is as good as we are at getting right back into the friend zone," I say, and it feels like it could be true enough until she touches my arm, setting off sparks. Heat rolls through me, fanning the flames of my desire for her, stoking the fire into a blaze.

"Jason, I really did need you for this. You might think you were just company, but I couldn't have done this without your help. You have such a fine eye and a nose for details. That made all the difference in the world."

My heart thumps a little harder, a little more insistently. I wish I didn't like her compliments so much. I wish I could take them on a surface level. But there's nothing surface about what I'm feeling for her, and I don't want to sling quips and dirty words right now.

"We helped each other," I say. "There's no one else I could have asked."

"It's the same for me. You're the only one with the

insight I needed. And it was a lot of fun to scour pubs together."

"It was incredibly cool. And I loved spending all that time with you," I say, choosing the bare truth.

Because here it is: I don't want to be in the friend zone. I want to be in *her* zone.

Her eyes widen. I see hope in them, and I want to believe she feels the same way I do, that this extra time we've spent together in the last few weeks has done to her what it's done to me.

She runs her hand up my arm. "I loved spending all that time with you."

I'm not entirely sure what is happening here. But we're swept up in a storm of compliments. A sea of confessions. And in the eye of this storm, there is no more room for innuendo or flirting. We're both standing here saying only what's true. And what's true is that I want her to have everything she desires. "I'm happy for you, Truly. I want all your dreams to come true."

"I want yours to as well."

I take another drink of truth serum. "Going to Chip's wedding with you . . . it never felt like you were a fake date."

Her voice is breathy. "It never felt fake to me either."

Tonight doesn't feel like the baseball game, the last pub visit, or the jujitsu class. This doesn't feel like anything else we've done before. Maybe I simply had to clear my head of all the noise that was in it to arrive in this new zone. This is the zone I want to be in.

I wrap a hand around her waist, running my thumb

along her hip, making her shudder. "You smell amazing."

"What do I smell like? I don't really wear any perfume."

I lift my chin, drawing a deep breath of her gorgeous scent. "I know you don't wear perfume. Your scent is in my head. It's in my brain. I can't get it out. It drives me wild. You smell like fresh air."

She laughs. "I suppose there are worse things to smell like."

"There's nothing better to smell like. And the funny thing is, I thought I was immune to it."

I move closer, lift my hand, and finger a strand of her hair. Her breath catches. "How is one immune to air?" she asks.

I shake my head. "Don't know. I'm certainly not."

She nibbles on her lip and meets my gaze, her eyes soft and vulnerable. "I don't want you to be immune to me."

"Don't you worry about that. I think I've lost all resistance."

"Have you now?"

"Pretty sure." I'm damn well certain this is the zone I want to be in. The contact zone.

She lifts her hand, reaches for my collar, and brushes her fingertips over it. "I love being friends with you. And I love all the other things in our lives. I don't know how to make sense of what's happening or what I'd do about it if I did. But right now, I need you to kiss me. Because you can't just stand here in my office looking like this and talking like this and saying these things."

I flash her a naughty grin. "I can't?"

Shaking her head, she jerks my collar and tugs me close, her forehead pressed to mine. "You can't. Because I want you too much. And it's not like the other times, Jason. I can't pretend we're just friends after everything that's happened. Kiss me now."

I cup her cheek and claim her lips. I crush her mouth in a searing kiss that goes straight to my head, that makes my mind spin deliriously in a Truly-induced haze. I kiss her like it's a living hell not to have my mouth on her, all over her, everywhere.

Her hands tangle in my hair, and she pulls me even closer, kisses back just as greedily. Her sighs and murmurs wind me tighter, send me higher. We kiss so hard our teeth click. We kiss so fiercely that we bite. I grab at her shirt, her skirt, wanting to tear off her clothes.

"Do you have to go back out there?" I ask.

"I do. In like five minutes." Her voice is breathy, desperate.

"Five minutes? We haven't got a second to lose. Let me bury my face in your pretty little . . . *summer* . . . so I can make you come on my tongue."

Laughing, she scoots back on her desk and opens her legs.

Fuckkkkk. "Seems you like that idea."

She grabs my chin, meets my gaze. "Your mouth is insanely talented, and I've missed it. Go down on my . . . *lily*." She chuckles.

"I'm going to, but I can't fucking say *summer*, *lily*, or

silver again, so I'm just going to eat your fantastic pussy like it's dessert."

"Do it now." She hikes up her skirt, a blatant invitation.

I park myself in her desk chair, slide my hands up the smooth skin of her thighs, and yank the lace of her knickers to the side.

I groan at the sight of her wetness. She practically shimmers with desire as she hooks her shoes against the edge of the desk. Fucking perfect. I lick one delicious line up her center. My eyes roll into the back of my head from the intoxicating taste of her. I'm burning everywhere from one lick, one touch, one kiss.

She is too, judging from the way she grabs my hair, curling her hands around my skull and whispering, "Do it fast. You know it won't take me long."

I smile against her heat, moving my face back and forth, letting her feel my stubble. "I love your confidence in me."

"It's because you have an impeccable track record."

"Far be it from me to break it, then."

I return to exactly where I want to be—feasting on her, tasting her, flicking my tongue, kissing her hard, devouring her.

I've only done this to her once before, but I've missed it immensely. And I remember exactly how my woman likes it. She likes to be consumed, with hungry kisses and a lot of penetration. I bring my fingers between her legs and slide two inside. She bucks against me, thrusting and rocking and moaning and groaning, and I'm in absolute heaven with her, eating her out on her desk. This powerful, sensual, strong woman who all but told me we're not simply a good fuck anymore. That we're *something more* too. I don't know what that's going to be. All I know is I need to send her over the edge right now.

She rocks faster, moans louder.

So good.

Oh my God.

Just like that.

I'm close, so close, keep going.

Yes, yes, yes. I'm there. Oh, God. Oh, God. Oh, God.

She detonates, coming on my lips like the over-achiever she is in the having orgasms department. This woman can climax like a rock star.

When she comes down, I help straighten her up, sorting her skirt and her knickers. She gazes at me with glossy, hazy eyes and whispers, "I don't think we're in the friend zone anymore, Toto."

37

"So, yeah. I have to agree. There was nothing particularly friendly about that," I say.

"I don't feel friendly at all." She grabs my face and plants a searing kiss on my lips, more intoxicating because I know she tastes herself on me. Because she has the same appetite I do, the same intensity.

When she pulls back, she slides her hand along the front of my pants. "I want you. Want to taste you. Want to have you."

"I'd be amenable to that as well," I say, groaning in frustration, since I know it can't happen now.

"I wish I didn't have to get back out there. But I want you to know I'm going to be thinking about you." She squeezes, sending a fresh wave of heat rolling down my spine. "But not just this. All of you."

"So, not just the sex parts of me, which obviously I want you fantasizing about ninety-nine percent of the time. But also the other parts?"

She laughs. "Yes, the other parts."

"They're very happy with one percent."

"Might be higher than that." Letting go, she smooths a hand over her skirt then meets my gaze. "So, I know we should probably figure out what this is, but there's a part of me that also doesn't want to. At least, not yet. Not tonight."

"I know what you mean. It's all sorts of unexpected. And yet, not."

"Exactly. I didn't even think I'd see you tonight, but then you showed up, and look at us. We can't stay away from each other, can we?"

Proving her point, I thread my fingers through her hair, savoring the feel of the soft waterfall of silk on my fingers. "It seems we can't entirely."

She leans into me, and ever so briefly, I embrace her, savoring the tender, but too short moment.

When she pulls back, she presses her hands to my chest. "The only thing I know is we're pretty good at sleeping together and staying friends. Don't you think?"

"We're aces."

"Maybe we should try sleeping together again and staying friends? Till we get the whole 'sleeping together' out of our system?"

I flinch for a second then rein in my surprise. I don't want to be friends with benefits. I want her in my system, not out of it. I want so much more of her. But I also know now isn't the time to have this conversation. She's already pushing the edges of her small window of time. "Sleep together, then go back into the zone?"

"Sure?" She sounds like she's trying to convince herself. "What do you think?"

"Let's make a go of it."

I'll take what I can get for now. I'll accept her gracious offer because I can't think about anything except her now. She's in the front of my mind, and she's rapidly claiming a stake in my heart.

I'll sort out the rest later.

For now, I'm going to walk home and enjoy the night air with the taste of her still on my lips.

38

From the pages of Truly's Drink Recipe Book

The Get-Him-Out-of-My-System Cocktail:
Gin
Pineapple Juice

Sometimes you break not just the rules, but *your* rules.

You could say it's because you can't resist.

But honestly, that's not the answer.

You're an adult. You make choices. You choose to relinquish resistance.

You let it fall through your fingers like grains of sand.

You don't care where the sand winds up. You want what you want.

Even though it's so much more than want now.

It's deeper, more intense, and scarier too.

This feeling in your chest? It's making you rethink everything. And when you feel this way, you need a little gin and some pineapple juice.

It tastes strong and decadent too, like all your desires. Like your dangerous and delicious choices.

Go fill a bowl of popcorn and have a snack with your cocktail.

Yes, a whole bowl.

After all, you can't eat just one handful. And it's not because you can't resist.

It's because you're choosing something else.

And because you know this drink name is a lie. You don't want him out of your system. You want him in it.

You just don't know how to get that without having the whole friendship burn to the ground.

39

Sully struts into the coffee shop, pointing to his trainers. "Check them out."

"You took the VaporMax out for a walk?" Troy asks, shooting an incredulous look at his fellow groomsman before smacking his forehead in exasperation. *"Lord, what fools these mortals be."*

"First off, no, I did not take my shoes out for a walk in New York City. Do I look stupid?" Sully asks.

I hold up a stop-sign hand. "Don't answer that, Troy."

"What? I don't think he looks stupid. But I do contend wearing expensive shoes in New York City is the height of foolishness," he says, answering anyway.

Sully jumps in again. "Second, I *know* that's from *A Midsummer Night's Dream.*"

The coffee cup nearly slips from Troy's palm. "Wha . . .?"

I snap my gaze to the sneakerhead who plops down

in a leather chair, crossing one leg over the other, his shoes on full display.

"You know where that's from?" I ask.

Sully scoffs. "I do indeed. Because I knew he was going to call me a fool. I knew he was going to quote Shakespeare to make his point. So I googled Shakespearean quotes on foolishness before I arrived. I was ready."

"Damn. You are an impressive fella. I have no choice but to high-five you." I hold up a palm, and Sully smacks back.

"You did that? You went to that level of prep to get my goat?" Troy asks, his jaw agape.

Sully nods, takes a long pull of some kind of coffee drink, and exhales exaggeratedly. "I gamed it. Took my chances when I researched the quotes. I figured it'd be that one or *The fool doth think he is wise, but the wise man knows himself to be a fool.* That's from—"

"*As You Like it,*" Troy and Sully name the play in unison.

"But see," Sully continues, clearly enjoying his moment in the sun. "I went with the *A Midsummer Night's Dream* one because I figured Troy would go with the simpler quote. The shorter one. Troy is all about brevity. And *brevity is the soul of wit.*"

Troy's eyes pop.

Sully slams his hand on an imaginary buzzer. "And that's from *Hamlet,* boys."

"I knew that, and I also know this." Troy stands, bows, and declares, "We're not worthy."

Sully pats his head. "And you better know that's from *Wayne's World*."

"Of course," we both say together.

"I'd have to turn in my man card if I didn't know that," Troy says.

Sully takes another drink. "Also, to answer your question, oh ye of little faith, I carried my shoes in a bag, and I put them on at the door to show you clowns."

"Aww, that's sweet that you're giving us a special viewing of your shoes," I say.

"All right, gentlemen, let's get down to business," Troy says, rubbing his palms.

Briefly, I'm taken aback because I usually lead these meetings, since I'm the boss. But Troy jumps into the deep end. "Tonight, you want us on our best behavior, you want us in our suits, and if anyone asks, we work in media production—keep it plain and simple. But wait. Why can't I be a model like Enzo? I look like a model, don't you think?" Troy gestures to his jawline.

Sully shakes his head. "Have you seen Enzo? Dude, if you think you can model next to him, then I can dunk like Michael when I wear these shoes."

"Fair point."

"Maybe I could be like a Sears catalog model," Troy offers.

"Now you're talking realism," Sully says. "Except Sears is defunct."

"And another dream dies," Troy says.

We resume the rundown, reviewing the plan for tonight's cocktail party, which is taking the place of a rehearsal dinner. When we're done, I head home to get ready, and at seven fifteen, my phone rings with Truly's name blasting across it. Odd. I didn't expect her to arrive till seven thirty. "Hey, minx."

"I'm early. Want to let me in so I can finish what you didn't let me start last night?"

40

She eyes me from head to toe. "You in that suit. That sexy tailored suit. Yes. That's what I want."

I slide my hand down the wine-red tie. "You want to suck my cock while I'm in this suit?"

She gazes at me like a lioness ready to pounce. "I absolutely do."

I undo my belt, taking my sweet time, loving that she came to play. I want to give her everything she wants, in and out of the bedroom. And in the bedroom, she likes the dirty talk. "Then far be it from me to deny you. Do it now. Suck me hard and good, just the way I like it."

"As if I'd do it any other way." She points to my couch. "Sit. Take out that cock. I know you're hard already."

"I was hard the second I saw your name on my phone." I sit, unzipping my trousers, then pushing down my briefs. "Get on the floor. I want you on your knees."

She licks her lips, hikes up her black dress, and

drops between my legs. No foreplay. No kissing. No need for that. I offer her my cock, and she takes it, dipping her mouth to my length, swirling her tongue across the head.

I groan, electricity crackling over my skin from that first touch of her miraculous tongue. She licks the underside then back up, her fist wrapping tightly around the base.

"Don't tease me. Just suck it."

She shoots me a *settle down* look. "So impatient. Maybe I want to lavish attention all over your dick."

She hums as she wraps her lips around the head, and I nearly lose my mind. A jolt of lust surges down my body as I stare at her. My Truly, the woman I'm desperate for, has my dick between her glossy lips and is teasing the fuck out of me.

"Maybe I want to come all over those pretty red lips," I say, since two can play at this. Because the tease, the way we tango, is part of who we are, how we connect, in the bedroom and out.

"I bet you'd like to come all over me," she whispers naughtily, tugging at the neckline of her black dress, pulling it all the way down, then back up, giving me a tantalizing peek at her breasts. I'm aching for her. She's only been in my place for a few minutes, and she's already torturing me in the most exquisite way, as she grips tighter and squeezes the base, sucking deliciously on the tip.

"You're killing me," I groan as my skin sizzles.

She lets go. "Would you rather I stop?"

My eyes widen, and I breathe out hard, grabbing her face, meeting that naughty, naughty gaze. "Please," I ask, because I'm not above begging.

"Please what? Please stop?"

"Don't stop. Don't you dare stop for another second. I want to fuck your perfect mouth. I need to come between these sexy, decadent lips so damn soon."

Her smile spreads, slow and dirty, as she answers me by taking me in and drawing me deep. My pulse throbs everywhere. Pleasure careens through my body. My fingers curl around her skull, moving her head, finding a rhythm.

She looks magnificent, such a dirty beauty, such a gorgeous, seductive woman. She knows what she wants. She radiates sexual confidence, and it turns me on more than anything ever has. She's a woman who knows her own mind and her body. She gives and she takes, and she takes and she gives. And right now, she's giving me the best blow job of my life.

I'm burning up with desire for her, watching her lips slide up and down, feeling her tongue flick over my shaft. It's a blow job, but fuck, it feels like so much more. It feels like the most intense pleasure given by the person—the only person—I want to give it to me.

I thrust up into her mouth, starting to lose myself to these wicked sensations.

But I don't want to get lost in her mouth. I want to get lost in her.

"I need to get inside you. I need to fuck you right now."

She lets go, gazes up with hooded eyes, and nods. "Yes, you do. Because I will be a desperate wreck all night if you don't."

I take her hand, pull her up, and take her to the back of the couch. "Bend over. Let me see that beautiful ass of yours."

She pulls up her dress to her waist, and I yank down her knickers, a rumble working its way up my chest at the sight of her boot-camped booty. "Such a perfect ass." I smack her cheek, and she yelps, then wiggles, asking for more.

I give it to her, swatting the other cheek before I reach for my wallet and roll on a condom. I rub my cock against her heat, and I slide inside, shuddering from the sheer intensity.

"I want to spend all night making you feel good," I groan, bending my chest over her back, gripping her hair. "But we have to go soon. So I'm going to fuck you hard and fast. But know this—I've never wanted anyone this much, this intensely."

"I want you too. So much."

"And even when I'm fucking you like the clock is ticking, you've got to know I don't want it to end."

She turns her face, her blue eyes fierce as she meets my gaze. "I don't want it to end either."

Maybe we're both saying other things, meaning other things. But now's not the time to figure that out. Now is the time for hot, dirty fucking.

That's what I do, pumping into her, filling her. Thrusting hard, deep. Gripping her.

She moans and groans, pants and cries out, and our noises mingle. Sliding a hand between her legs, I touch her where she wants me most.

She trembles beautifully beneath me, her back arching, her hands clasping the furniture as if she's holding on for life. "You like it when I do all the work," I murmur.

"Love it, fucking love it."

"So do I. Love it this way with you. Love it every way with you."

Words cease, and grunts and growls take over. Slaps of flesh. Bodies pressing together.

Until she cries out, incoherent as she flies into blissful oblivion.

It doesn't take me long to follow her over the cliff as I come hard inside her, loving everything, absolutely everything, about the way she makes me feel.

I wrap my arms around her, unable to resist kissing her. I brush my lips to her cheeks, against her hair and the shell of her ear. "You're spectacular."

"And you're going to look less than spectacular in that suit if we don't get out of here soon."

We clean up quickly, straightening dress and suit, hair and lipstick. Then we leave, and in the elevator of my building, I take her hand.

That's all.

And it feels all too right.

So right that it occurs to me—for the first time in ages, I'm not thinking about my lack of interest in relationships. I'm not considering how to avoid entanglements. I'm definitely not dwelling on how to keep someone at a distance. I'm thinking about how I want her all the way in.

And I don't know how to get her there.

41

I'm rarely at a loss for words. I traffic in them, I juggle them, and I spin them into different combinations, whether with my mouth or my pen. But tonight, I'm not certain I remember how to make the shape of them on my tongue.

Words evade me as we catch a Lyft to the swank cocktail party in a ballroom at the Luxe Hotel. Maybe that's because there are too many words jostling around my mind, squeezing hard against my heart.

Perhaps that's the issue.

Words are taking over in a mad alphabet soup. Words I never intended to attach to myself. To my emotions. And as for those pesky things—didn't my emotions get the memo that I banished them long ago?

I've been following a stoic plan for ages, marching forward, and part of that plan was avoiding this kind of wild rampage in my heart.

Too late.

I feel it. I feel it everywhere.

The last time I felt anything remotely close to this, I was blindsided by my ex.

But then, as Chip said, heartbreak doesn't have to break you. It can be the best thing that ever happens to you.

Looking at Truly on the way to the party, all I can think is he's so damn right, because the words that tango on my lips feel like they're comprised of four letters, and those are the most dangerous words of all.

Falling for Truly means falling for the one person who'd wildly complicate my life.

And yet . . . I don't want to turn away from whatever is brewing between us.

When we reach the hotel and head into the elevator, I locate words again. I face her, take both her hands in mine, link our fingers, and meet her gaze. "I know we said we'd figure this out. I know we said we'd get this out of our system, but I really can't foresee a world where you're out of *my* system."

For a second, I hold my breath, hoping I haven't scared away the woman who values her space, the woman who's already beholden—to Gin Joint.

But the look in her eyes nearly knocks me to my knees. It says everything. That I'm not alone. That she's feeling all of this too.

Maybe this is what happens when two workaholics meet their match.

She strokes her thumb across my jaw, making me shudder with desire and longing for her. She inches her face closer to mine and whispers, "I don't want to live in a world where you're out of my system. What are we going to do about that?"

"I don't have a clue. But let's try to figure it out soon, yeah?"

She smiles and whispers "Yes" against my lips. A yes that thrums through my whole body and beats in my heart.

Once inside, I shake off all these new sensations, because it's time to focus on business and being here for the man of the hour. Enzo moved to the States mere months ago and hardly knows anyone, so my job is to be his wingman in a world where his woman knows everyone.

As Valerie works the room, Enzo leans effortlessly against the bar, surveying the glittering crowd in the chandelier-encrusted ballroom. "Ah, when I was growing up, a poor boy in Madrid, I never imagined this might be my life."

I raise a glass. "It's a good life."

"I have a solid job, the love of a fantastic woman, and I'm starting to make new friends in a new town."

"I'd say your job is more than solid, mate. It's pretty damn secure."

He flashes that grin, and somewhere, someone with a camera snaps it. "But is it though? Is any job truly secure? Is yours secure?"

"You got me there. My work is anything but secure," I answer.

He raises his champagne glass. "To insecurity in work."

I clink my glass to his, since nothing feels truer than the utter lack of reliability I'm experiencing on the business front. His comment is a reminder that I haven't heard a word from Ryder, and he usually books me by the end of one week for the next one. My shoulders tighten in worry. Even if I didn't win the full-time gig, I hope I'm not losing the part-time one on his show.

But tonight I'm here for Enzo, not me.

Enzo glances toward Truly, who's chatting with Troy and Sully. "But perhaps there is no insecurity in love?"

I shoot him a look. "What do you mean?"

"You're funny. Maybe you think it's not obvious."

"What's not obvious?"

"She's more than your date."

I could deny it. I could lie. But I don't want to pretend with this. "Let's hope so."

Valerie marches over, raises a glass of champagne, and offers a toast to us. "To my kind and thoughtful husband-to-be and his very charming best man. Now, what is it that you men were discussing? Sports cars, stealth bombers, aftershave, and other exceedingly masculine things?"

Enzo smiles. "I was simply telling him that I think he needs to sort out his feelings for a certain lady."

"You're kind to worry about my romantic affairs, but I swear I'm fine. Let's focus on this fantastic union," I say deflecting, deflecting, and then deflecting some more.

Valerie swings her gaze around to Truly then back to me. "Do you know what I've learned about men?"

"What have you learned, my love?" Enzo asks.

She points to his eyes, then to mine. "I've learned that it's all in the eyes. That's how you read them. That's how you can tell. When I work on deals, I always look a person in the eyes. They never lie. Yours never did," she says to Enzo. Then to me, "And when I look at yours, and I see the way you gaze at that woman, all your truths are self-evident. Inescapable."

"Maybe they are," I muse.

Enzo nudges her. "Just as we predicted."

"We did," she says. "We can always tell when love is blooming."

"Good skill," I remark, because what else is there to say? She's right. For me, at least.

Enzo catches someone's eye and points to a dapper man in a suit. "I must go talk to Carlos about a painting."

"Oh yes, the one that reminds us of an Edward Hopper. Get it for us."

He makes a growling sound at her, as if this art acquisition is part of their foreplay. "Consider it done."

He heads off, and Valerie cocks her head, her brown eyes locked with mine. "Now, tell me stuff. I want to know more about you. I'm so fascinated by your job. I absolutely love hearing about all sorts of new professions."

But now isn't the time to spill the details that clients don't need to know. "There's not really much to tell. It's a simple job," I say, lying through my teeth, because it's completely complicated. "You find me, you hire me, I do a job." I subscribe to the less-is-more approach.

"Yes, I know that. I hired you. Because I wanted more groomsmen. Because Enzo doesn't know many people here in New York yet. But I'm not interested in *my* story. I'm interested in yours. Tell me how you came to be in this field, because I doubt you were trying to imitate Kevin Hart from that film."

I push out a laugh. "You're correct. I started before that movie came out. I can write the hell out of a best man's speech. That's how I got started."

But that's not enough for Valerie. She asks where I'm from, and since that's innocuous enough, I tell her just outside of London. We chat about the neighborhoods in that city, also a safe topic.

"London is one of my favorite cities. I find it so much more civilized to attend the theater in London."

"I can't say I disagree. The relative lack of ticket scalpers does help the civility there."

"In general, you can't beat the politeness in England. I do enjoy good manners."

I chuckle. "Manners are pretty cool."

She narrows her eyes as if studying me. "There's something about you that feels so familiar."

A doubt of worry shoots down my spine. Was it my manners comment? That can't possibly be enough to give anything away. Surely I can't be the only writer/blogger/podcaster/media expert who gives a damn about manners. I've worked hard to keep my worlds separate—fake names on this side, no photos on the other. I work in a business where privacy and discretion are critical. "I'm sure I sound familiar because, well, I probably just sound like Daniel Craig," I say, doing my best to keep the answer light and airy.

She shakes her finger at me, a sly smile sneaking across her face as she gestures to her ear. "But I swear I can hear something else in your voice. Something in the way you speak, in your command of words and the things you say about cities and life, and men and women."

My muscles tighten, and I weigh my best options. Run and hide behind the bar for the rest of the night and hope she won't find me, or deny, deny, deny.

"After a while, all Englishmen sound the same, I suspect."

She snaps her fingers. "I know. Did I meet you at Ryder Lockhart's—"

I go cold everywhere. Ice freezes in my veins. Walker's warning rings loud and terrifyingly close. *Someday, you're going to be waxing eloquent on the radio about how to land a promotion, and when you leave, the guy down the hall will remember the toast you gave at some wedding as Jay the best man, or Jackson or Jackoff.*

Or the reverse, I'm learning.

"His ping-pong match. He's a business associate of mine. Weren't you there? I swear I saw you there."

I breathe again, grateful to tell the whole truth when I say, "You should see my ping-pong game. It's total rubbish. Must have been someone else."

She drums her fingers against the bar. "Perhaps."

But the fact that she's friends with him underscores

the bigger issue. I need to move on my exit plan, and I need to move fast.

* * *

I can't shake the feeling that planets are on a collision course tonight. Even as I chat with Truly, Enzo, and other guests at the party, I can't completely let go of that encounter.

Troy seems to sense my unease, and he pulls me aside. "You're distracted. What's going on? Whatever it is, you can't let it get to you right now. It's showtime."

He's right. Damn it. He's absolutely right. I'm letting this worry knock me off my game. "It's nothing."

"No, it's something. Will talking about it help?"

"I actually don't want to talk about it."

"Sometimes things are better when you talk about them."

I drag a hand through my hair, then serve it up in a whisper. "I think Enzo's fiancée is starting to draw the connections. I think she knows what I do in my other job."

"Is that such a bad thing?"

"I want to keep everything separate."

"Why?"

"How would it look? My work depends on me being credible and trustworthy. If someone like Ryder finds out I'm a paid friend, how would that look?"

"Like you're a man making a living. Like you're figuring out how to chase your dreams and pay your bills. Isn't that what your schtick is all about? Helping men be the best?"

"Yes, but . . ."

He clasps my shoulder. "You need to remember you're not dealing drugs, you're not running illegal pit bull fights, and you're not sex trafficking. You're helping people have the wedding of their dreams. I feel like that's exactly what a modern gentleman would do. Now, if you'll excuse me, I need to go play that role, and you should let this all go."

He weaves his way back into the crowd, saying hi, making conversation, and playing the part to a T. Perhaps I've trained him better than I thought.

* * *

I make my way back to Truly, deciding to follow Troy's advice. What's the worst that could happen? What is Valerie going to do? Out me before her entire wedding? Declare for everyone here that Jay the best man is actually Jason Reynolds, the Modern Gentleman? What good would that do?

Later, I raise a glass, give a toast, and say a brief speech about Enzo, ending it with "And what is most lovely of all is to see two people who support each other, who care deeply for each other, and who have shared passions. That's what I see when I look at Enzo and Valerie."

As I lock eyes with Truly, my heart seems to expand beyond the space allotted in my chest. The way she looks at me, the way I see so much of my future in her eyes, is all I need to shed whatever remaining worries are setting up camp. Everything is going to be fine. How could anything be less than fine when my woman looks at me like she feels the same damn way?

When the event is over, I take her hand, bring her close, and say, "Come home with me tonight."

"I'm already there."

* * *

On the way home we have the safety talk. She tells me she's on the pill, and I want to kiss the sky. I'm going to take my time with her tonight, to savor every *bare* inch of her.

At my apartment, we're not fevered and frenzied. We don't strip in a mad rush, and I don't bend her over the couch. I put on music, bring her to my bed, and undress her slowly, then lay her out before me. After I take off my clothes, she pulls me to her, whispering, "Get in my system. Because that's where you are."

She's not saying she's falling for me. But I know this woman—she won't jump first. I have to.

I'm falling for her. And if there's one thing I've learned in both my jobs, it's that words matter greatly. I run the backs of my fingers across her cheek. "Do you know something, my naughty little minx?"

"What is it?"

"I'm crazy for you."

Her smile is magnetic. "That's what I meant to say too. I'm pretty crazy for you."

"I don't know what this means for tomorrow, but

right now, I don't want to figure out anything except what it feels like to make love to you. I already know what it's like to fuck you, but I want to know what this is like too."

"So do I."

As she pulls me close, brings me inside her, I have the answer.

It's everything.

It's everything I thought I could avoid.

It's everything I desperately want.

We move as one, our bodies curled together, our skin hot. Her breathing intensifies, and she arches against me, her back bowing spectacularly. I have no words. My throat is arid; my chest is a furnace. When her hands tangle in my hair and she shudders, I'm positive this is the most beautiful sight I've ever seen.

She's the most beautiful.

Her whimpers and murmurs turn into cries as she tumbles over the edge, and I'm right there with her.

After, as we lay spent and sated, I'm sure I've never been this happy, and I'm just as certain we're going to have to figure out incredibly soon what we're doing next.

Like in the morning, when we leave to grab a quick breakfast before my softball practice and see a familiar face outside my building.

42

"Fancy meeting you here."

It's Nick.

He's with his daughter, and he's leveling a curious and completely knowing stare my way.

Truly stops in her tracks, flinching, then recovers to smile at the tiny redhead by Nick's side. "Hey, you!"

"Truly! We're going to the dog rescue after softball!"

Truly offers up a hand to high-five Skye, sliding perfectly into kid mode. "And you're going to get Jason the dog today?"

"I hope so. Look at him. Daddy, show Jason to Truly. I mean, please. Please show Jason the dog to Truly."

Nick grabs his phone and slides his thumb across the screen, sharing a picture of a Chihuahua min-pin mix. "Pretty adorable, right? In spite of the name."

"Completely adorable. Also, that's an awesome name," I second. My voice barely sounds like my own because Nick's eyes return to me and he's staring like he has something to say. He turns to his daughter, fishing in his pocket for something then handing her earbuds. "Hey, sweetie. I want you to listen to that new song you like so much. Can you do that right now?"

"Yes! Double yes!" She pops the earbuds in and starts bopping.

Nick looks to me then to Truly, then shakes his head knowingly. "How's the friend zone working out for you guys?"

Truly shrugs sheepishly. "Not real well, it seems."

Nick laughs. "Let me give you guys a piece of unsolicited advice. You need to deal with this head-on. I know you didn't ask. But I've been there, done that, on both counts. Falling for a friend and falling for my best friend's sister. And hey, look at the result." He ruffles his daughter's hair as she dances. "And don't forget my son either. He and Harper popped into the bakery around the corner."

"I don't think we're going to start popping out babies," Truly jumps in, quickly squashing that notion. "Or popping into bakeries around the corner with them, for that matter."

"That's not the point. The point is, if I run into you here on the way to softball practice—and incidentally, we weren't even stopping at your building—what happens when Malone does the same?"

The image he paints is unappealing. I don't want to blindside my friend like that.

"Just tell the guy. Also, for the record, everyone has known for the longest time that the two of you have this ridiculous chemistry."

I blink. "Everyone?"

He rolls his eyes. "Every single one. As in, all of your friends, as in everyone you've ever encountered, as in all of New York. In fact, I'd be willing to bet Malone won't be the least bit surprised."

"Seriously?" Truly asks.

"Seriously. You guys give off that whole *we hate each other, yet we can't stop flirting* vibe, and you've given that off since the dawn of time."

A new voice cuts in. "It *is* kind of wafting off you." That's Harper, who's arrived with Carson out of thin air, it seems, a bakery bag in her hand. I swear the woman can apparate. "Like, it's so strong you could bottle it, sell it, and make some serious jack."

Truly jerks her gaze toward Harper. "How did you do that? Just figure out exactly what we were talking about?"

Harper taps her temple. "Women's intuition."

"The force runs strong in this one," Nick says.

Harper gestures wildly to us, the bag flapping around. "Plus, hello. Look at the two of you. I mean, really. It doesn't actually take any intuition. We've had a pool betting on when it would happen." She leans in to whisper to her husband. "I won. Pay up, sweetie pie. Pay up."

Nick scoffs but pretends to hand over some money to his wife, who then mimes pocketing it.

"He bet you two would become a couple a year ago," Harper continues. "I said you were both too stubborn, so I predicted, hmm, right around now as the starting point. But does this mean you've finally, officially put us all out of the misery of watching you behave like, well, cats who chase each other into corners but then snuggle up at night?"

"I like cats. Can we get a cat too? I want to name our cat Calvin and Hobbes," Carson chimes in. "And Malone can give him his shots."

"We will definitely consider a kitty cat. But can he be Calvin and Hobbes McDoodle? Because that's a fun name," Harper says.

"That's a super-fun name," Carson says.

"Speaking of Malone," Harper says, shooting Truly and me one of those purposeful looks that women shoot from their eyes like laser beams. "You know what to do, and like I said the other week, he probably suspects it anyway. He's kind of smart like that, especially when it comes to, ahem, cat behavior."

I heave a sigh. "He is. And message received. You guys are probably right."

"Of course we're right," Nick says. "But listen, are you coming to softball practice? Because we're on our way to the park. My woman and my kids are going to watch me hit home runs because I'm awesome like that."

"And humble too," Harper adds, squeezing his arm.

"Yes, I'll be there shortly," I say.

They take off, daughter holding her father's hand, son holding mom's, while they stroll up the streets of New York on a summer day.

I turn to Truly, the Saturday morning crowds scurrying by. "He's right."

"I know."

"Why don't we try to talk to your brother later today? I know we haven't entirely sorted out what this is, but I also think we both know it's not stopping, and we ought to be honest with him."

"Because of that whole 'crazy for you' thing?"

I smile. "Yes, because of that little part. I'll invite him to lunch. And we'll go together."

But later that morning after we parted, a message from Truly arrives, asking me to meet her first.

43

From: Darren Whitcomb
To: Truly Goodman
Re: Your Proposal

Dear Ms. Goodman,

Thank you so much for the thoughtful and well-researched presentation. It's clear you devoted a lot of time and insight to your proposal. I wholeheartedly believe your new pub concept will be a tremendous success.
That said, my partners aren't ready to move forward yet, but we'll be in touch down the road. Thank you again, and we wish you success in all your endeavors.

All the best,
Darren

* * *

From: MixologistExtraordinaire at gmail
To: MixologistExtraordinaire at gmail
Re: Disappointments

Dear Truly "Don't Let This Get You Down" Goodman,

This is the e-mail I will save. This is what I want to remember. How it feels to try something different.

Because today goes like this:

After I cry pathetic rainfalls of tears that I collect in buckets of misery, I consider calling my brother. Then Charlotte.

They've always been my people. They're the ones I'd turn to.

*But it's a Sunday morning, and Charlotte is with her kids and hubby. My brother is likely busy with Sloane.
I wipe my tears, wash my face, and draw a deep breath.*

I review the facts.

So what if I wanted to do a Parisian-themed place more than an English one? So what if he doesn't want either the English pub or the Paris-type bar? So what? So fucking what?

He's not the key to my happiness.

I will do what I've always done. Solve the problem. Turn down another avenue.

But maybe I don't have to do it alone. Maybe, just maybe, there's someone who understands me who I can turn to now.

Yes, I think there is. Time to do things differently.

Xoxo
Truly

44

After softball practice, Malone tells me he'll meet up with me in thirty minutes, after he runs a quick errand with Sloane. His fiancée waves goodbye and says she'll see me again soon.

I leave Central Park and head to the diner, prepping along the way, as I do. Walking and thinking, running and thinking, practicing what to say. It's like a best man's speech. You put your best foot forward. Be self-deprecating, but also don't take yourself too seriously. Be honest, but also fun.

I can do this. I can talk to my friend and sort out my feelings for his sister.

I'll just say something like, *I'm crazy for your sister. I'll treat her well. We'll make it work.* That's really all there is to it. With my plan ready, I check my phone to make sure there aren't any last-minute issues with tonight's wedding.

And nope, all is well.

Perhaps this is the winding down, the beginning of

the exit plan.

I'll finish out this wedding, serve as the groomsman for one of Josh's skateboarding clients in a couple of weeks, then do one last job that came in a couple of days ago. With that, I should have almost everything I need for Abby. Then, I can devote all my energy to growing the Modern Gentleman.

I spot a message on my phone from Walker that he'll be at the wedding tonight. That's a surprise.

Walker: The DJ is sick, so I got the sub call. That's why I say you should never eat sushi the night before a gig. Bad fish. It's always the fish.

Jason: "Fish" is a suitable answer for whenever someone asks what went wrong.

Walker: True that. When I see you tonight, should I act like I don't know you? :)

Jason: Just act like someone who refuses to play Coldplay, and we'll be all good.

Walker: Check. If you hear their music, consider it a sign of the impending apocalypse.

Jason: Duly noted.

After I send that, a text from Josh pops onto on my screen.

Josh: Hitting the gym this afternoon. Want to meet up? Even though I know it'll be hard for you to keep up with me. Consider this my charitable act. Walker would be so proud of me.

Jason: Wow. How utterly noble of you. And just for that, I will kick your ass on whatever machine you're riding.

Josh: Sorry for the slow reply . . . I was swept up in a fit of laughter from your last note.

Jason: Did you forget? Division 1 here.

Josh: Did you forget? Competitive bastard here, like you've never seen before.

Jason: See you in a couple of hours, asshole.

Josh: See ya, dickhead.

God, I love my friends. They're such great assholes, and I fucking adore them for it.

I'm about to close my phone when a new e-mail icon pops up. It's from Ryder. With a burst of hope—maybe it's good news about more appearances—I click it open.

Hey. Just want to let you know I don't actually need you this week. In fact, I'm not sure I'm going to need you on Mondays anymore going forward. Lots of things in play here. I can't share much info right now. We'll talk soon.

I reach for the street sign, grabbing hold of the pole.

I can't walk straight.

I can't process this shit sandwich of news.

He won't need me anymore? He won't need me at all?

Forget running in place. This isn't even back to square one. This is take-all-the-steps-in-the-infernal-world-back-to-the-swamp-you-came-from news. Do not collect two hundred dollars, do not pass go. Sit in the godforsaken corner like a bad boy.

This is the most important gig I've had, and losing it tastes like eating bacon. Like greasy, undercooked pig fat. Disappointment rages inside me, ripping through my body like a virus, infecting my brain, my heart, and every part of me.

As I cross the street, I swallow past the acid in my throat. Is this Valerie's doing? Did she rat me out?

That can't be. Yet she is a powerful, strategic woman.

Or is this something else? The inevitability of failure? Perhaps I was never going to get the gig anyway. Maybe it was always going to go to someone else, to Marcus, somebody who sounds just like me who followed my damn advice.

My jaw clenches, and I want to write back and say, *WHY???????*

But I'm not going to beg. That's exactly what I advise the men who listen to me to never do—*never beg for a thing*.

The only acceptable begging is to the gods of baseball, football, hockey, or whatever your respective sport is. Only then may you beg for a victory.

Otherwise, I say never beg a woman. Never beg an employer. And always bow out gracefully.

I reply to Ryder.

I appreciate the heads-up. It has been an absolute pleasure working with you. I hope our paths cross again. All the best, Jason

I send it even as anger lashes at me. While I walk the rest of the way to the diner, I try to pinpoint what went wrong.

When I pass a dry cleaner that also cobbles shoes, tailors dresses, and sells craft soda—but adorns its window now with a GOING OUT OF BUSINESS sign—the answer becomes clear. I'm doing too many things. I'm juggling too many plates. I'm ignoring my own tips—I always advise my readers to pace themselves, to pursue balance, to make sure they aren't spread too thin.

Like me.

I'm distracted, and it's affecting all my work. It affected me last night when I let that "manners" comment slip in front of Valerie. Troy even noticed that I wasn't at the top of my game, and that's a problem. I have another wedding to do tonight, then a handful more, as well as some speeches to write.

I need to finish out the commitment I made to my sister, so when Truly sends me her note, I'm pretty sure what I need to do when I see her too.

As hard as it may be, and as much as it'll hurt.

I brace myself for the pain. But no pain, no gain. Grit your teeth and suck it up like a man.

45

She's waiting for me inside a booth, her eyes the darkest shade of midnight blue I've ever seen, but there's a softness in them too. That vulnerability she shares with me.

I can't let it draw me in. Can't let it distract me more than it already has.

"Hey," she says, and the sweetness in her tone nearly does me in. I don't want sweetness right now. Don't deserve it, can't give it, and haven't a clue what to do with it. I'm a snake, coiled tight, ready to strike at the next thing that shakes my world.

I don't kiss her hello. I'll cave if I touch her. I'll haul her in for a searing kiss to blot out the misery churning in my gut.

"Hi." It comes out tight, clipped.

The second I sit, she blurts out, "The investment deal fell through."

I blink in surprise. "It did? Why?"

She takes a fueling breath. "The partners weren't in love with my concept, I guess. I can't figure out why.

His e-mail was so . . . bland. It was a *thanks, but no thanks*. And I thought I'd done a great job with the pitch." She takes a long breath, then holds up her palms, giving a *what can you do* smile. "That's how it goes. It happens. Right?"

I blow out a long sigh of frustration, and I'm pretty sure good manners dictate that I ask her how she's feeling about it, what she wants to do next, but misery loves company, so I serve up my side dish. "I'm in the same boat. My guest spot is gone. Ryder doesn't need me anymore."

Her expression transforms in a heartbeat. The sadness vanishes. She's Fierce Truly now, her eyes narrowed. "Are you serious?"

"Unfortunately, I am."

"That's ridiculous. You're the best thing to happen to that show." And now she's Defender Truly, and that's damn tempting too.

Except temptation put me here, and I'd be wise to remember that. "I appreciate that, but he doesn't see it that way."

"He's wrong." She stabs the table with her finger. "Dead wrong. You know that, right?"

"No, I don't know that." I slump back in the booth, dragging a hand through my hair.

"You should, because you're terrific."

"Thanks, but it doesn't really matter, does it?" I ask, more briskly than I'd like. "And I think what stings the most is I knew I wasn't getting the full-time gig. I was fine with that, accepted it. But I thought this one was safe. Turns out that's not the case. Guess I was wrong on that count too."

"There will be other opportunities, Jason." She sets her hands on the table, then makes a move like she's going to reach for mine. But I don't know what to do with kindness right now. I don't know that I can handle it.

I keep my hands in my lap.

"Maybe," I mutter.

"There will be. But I know you wanted this one, I know you were counting on it. I'm sorry." She sets her hands in her lap, smiling sympathetically, and I hate that. But I also love it. I love it a lot—the way she cares, the way she wants to make me feel better. For a few seconds, I nearly cave. Because it's comforting to have someone who understands.

I could join her on her side of the booth, kiss her hard, kiss away all my frustration. Hell, I bet we could fuck it away, and I'd be fine.

But the trouble is, I'd be in the same position after a roll in the hay. Besotted with her, instead of work. And I'm pretty damn sure that's part of the problem.

Rather, that *is* the problem.

I swallow harshly, scrubbing my hand across the back of my neck. "I'm not at the top of my game. That's the trouble." I take a deep breath, steeling myself for the inevitable. "I think that falling in love is absolutely fucking distracting and ruining everything we've built."

"What?" She flinches, shirking back like my statement didn't compute.

But it makes as much sense as two plus two. This is easy math, even if I don't like the answer.

"This seems proof of it, don't you think? Love, feelings, all that stuff—it's utterly distracting. It's causing both of us to lose sight of our goals."

She's a mixologist—she ought to know. Add love to the cocktail mix of good sex, and what do you get? A drink that makes you lose your mind.

I've seen what love leads to. Seen how it makes you a fool. Witnessed how a man can end up with nothing when he chases it.

"It can be distracting, but it can also maybe be something . . ." Her voice rises like she's waiting for me to fill in the answer. Hoping for me to color it in.

There's no room in me for vulnerability. Emotions have been my foe, and letting them become a bedfellow was what brought me to the place where my business is falling apart.

She's still looking, waiting for a word to fill in the blank, and so I give it to her. "Something like a problem. That's what you were saying? It can be a massive boulder careening toward you, ready to crush you. You take your eye off of responsibilities. Off the prize. You start making mistakes. Don't you see it? Obviously, it's happening to both of us. You and your deal, me and my job."

She's silent for several long beats.

"Right?" I push.

She purses her lips.

"I mean, what else could it be?"

A long breath, and at last she answers, her voice

crisp. "You're right. We were crazy to think anything else. We should do what we've always done—be friends."

Relief surges through me. "Exactly. That's what I'm saying. Before we muck that up too. We still have time to go back. And it'll all be fine. I can focus on business; you can focus on business. That's what we both wanted to do all along."

She offers a smile, then says, "I agree."

Yes, she sees the wisdom of it. She's a smart woman —I knew she would.

She laughs and waves like she's dismissing the madness of the last few nights. "You're so right. Love. Pssh. What is that? Silly distraction."

"Thank you. I knew you'd feel the same way. Two workaholics, right?" I say with a wry grin.

She nods savagely, biting out a response. "Absolutely."

"So, listen. I'll finish paying off my sister's school. Wrap up my best man jobs, devote more time to the Modern Gentleman. And you can go full speed ahead with finding another investor for the pub. Once we get all that sorted, we'll see where we are. How's that sound? Because it sounds fucking brilliant to me."

She smiles so big and broadly, I bet it hurts. "Yes, that's obviously the way to go."

I breathe a massive sigh. "I'm so glad we're in agreement."

"Me too."

The bell above the door rings, and when I jerk my gaze in that direction, Malone's walking in.

"What should we tell him?"

"The truth. Since we're not together, it shouldn't be a big deal."

"Exactly. No big deal whatsoever."

"What's wrong with the two of you? You look like someone told you that you have to eat bacon for the rest of your lives."

Truly gives a forced laugh. "That does seem like quite a jail sentence."

He smiles and studies us curiously. "I feel like I should order bacon just to drive you crazy."

"I'm not ready for that kind of punishment," I quip, feeling pretty good about how Truly and I just worked that out like adults. And about how now we can have lunch with her brother. Like adults. And we can all make jokes. Like adults.

Malone glances at me then at his twin. "All right. I'm ready for your confession. You guys asked for this meeting. Let me guess—you're finally going to tell me you're into each other. I'm shocked. Absolutely shocked."

Wow. Nick called that one. From ten miles away. Still, that's not what this lunch is about.

"Yes, that's what I want to tell you," I say, keeping it professional and straightforward. "Truly and I were involved briefly, but we're not going to be involved anymore. We're staying friends. We both agreed to it. It'll be great."

"It was mutual," Truly chimes in, cool, calm, and rational. More proof that this decision is the right one. "We had a thing. It happened a couple of times. But we're just not at the place in our careers where we can date each other. We're still good friends, and we wanted to assure you of that, because we don't expect any weirdness."

My God, she sounds so on top of this. She's a brilliant businesswoman, unperturbed by blips.

"If you're back on the friendship train, why are you telling me retroactively?"

I jump in. "We wanted to be up front because we were involved behind your back for a little bit."

Malone snickers. "You make it sound like I'm the wronged spouse. I'm your friend, dickhead. Not your wife."

Truly reaches out her hand and clasps her brother's. "You and I had an agreement. We had a pact, and I don't want to do anything to ruin your friendship with Jason, so we wanted to be straightforward, even though we're not together. And we're completely fine not being together."

Malone holds up his hands to slow this conversational train. "Wait. Are you two breaking up because you think it bothers me? Because it doesn't, and I would also never tell either one of you not to be involved with each other. Not my place, not my role."

Truly is intense when she answers. "I'm telling you because after what happened with Sarah, we made a deal that friends were off-limits."

He sighs, his voice softening. "Truly, we made that

deal when we were twenty-one or twenty-two. We're thirty-five now. And Sarah was a lunatic, if you ask me. I know it hurt to lose her, and I'm not belittling that, but I don't want some pact we made well over a decade ago to keep you from happiness."

"I'm happy. I swear. So happy. So totally happy. Work makes me happy. It's all good. Who has time for relationships anyway?" she says, laughing, underscoring my point—she's on the same page, and she's obviously ecstatic. Hell, she said she was happy four times.

Malone raises his hand. "I do. A lot of people do."

She pats his shoulder. "And that's great. But we're in a different spot. The timing simply isn't right."

"The timing is rubbish," I second, because how can he not get it? We're doing the right thing here—being honest, being up front, and letting go of something that's too distracting.

He leans back in the booth. "Let me see if I have this straight. You like each other. You've been involved, like we all thought you would be. But you're not going to be involved with each other anymore because of"—he coughs like he can't quite believe what we're saying—"*timing?*"

But speaking of timing, I have work to do, so I cut in. "Listen, I'm glad you're not pissed. You are truly a prince among men. But the reality is, Truly and I are fine with this decision. We both agreed to concentrate on growing our businesses."

Malone nods like he has a surplus of them to dish out. "Right. Yeah. Growing your business is definitely the most important thing in life."

I arch an eyebrow. "Do I detect a note of sarcasm?"

"You should detect about fifty thousand notes of sarcasm. Because the two of you are idiots if that's the reason you're not together."

I jerk my gaze to him, staring sharply. "You want us to be involved?"

"If you like each other, you should be together. It's really that simple. I'm not the barrier you might have thought I was. I'm also absolutely not surprised you're in love. The two of you have acted like a couple for the longest time, and it has never bothered me. In fact, I'm surprised it didn't happen sooner." He points to me, then to his sister. "But what does surprise me is how you're both so goddamn stubborn and ridiculous. I can't believe you're claiming that *timing* is the reason you're splitting up."

Truly lifts her chin, clearing her throat. "It makes perfect sense for Jason. For me too. And right now, what makes perfect sense is enjoying a chicken sandwich and french fries. Let's do that."

With that slice of the knife, Truly ends the conversation.

When the check arrives, Malone lunges for it then says, "What I'd most like to do is bang your heads together, but all that would come out is hot air and a bunch of canned responses about work, work, work. So instead I'll leave you with this: hope you enjoy curling up with your job tonight."

When we're through, I'm so damn relieved to get the hell out of there, because he just doesn't get it.

46

From the pages of Truly's Drink Recipe Book

Get Your Ass Back in The Saddle:
One Shot of Tequila

Let's say you lost out on a chance that was important to you.

Maybe you wanted something so badly, and it felt so right, but then you let it slip through your fingers.

But you had to.

You had your reasons. After all, you weren't going to beg him to stick around. He clearly wanted out. And you know what that's like. Hell, that's why your last relationship ended. Over work. It would be unladylike to beg him to stay when you would have laughed in the face of a guy who did that to you. Letting him go gracefully is the right thing to do.

This way, you stay friends.

This way, he won't know how much it hurt.

That's why it's time for a straight-up shot of gin.

But fuck gin.

The truth is this: you need a shot of tequila. You need something that burns.

Take one shot of tequila.

It will burn the ache away.

Chase it with the fire in your belly, and then get your ass to work.

* * *

Charlotte: Tell me everything.

Truly: I wanted to lean on Jason's shoulder. He made it clear that shoulder was off-limits.

Charlotte: Grrrr.

Truly: He believes falling in love distracted him, and I'm not going to sit there and try to convince him otherwise. I wasn't going to make a fool of myself and say *no you idiot, that makes no sense.* Instead, I said it sounded . . . brilliant

Charlotte: Let me make sure I have this right. Mister Modern Gentleman somehow finessed a breakup to make it seem mutual?

Truly: I suppose he did. Clever guy. But what was I going to do? It was clear he wasn't ready. So I went along with it and said I agreed, and that's what we told Malone too.

Charlotte: So you two made it seem like you preemptively broke up so you wouldn't lose your focus even though your brother is and was totally fine with you two being the couple we all had bets you'd become?

Truly: And you all lost, I guess. Turns out we're not a couple at all.

Charlotte: I'm sorry, sweetie.

Truly: It'll be fine. Men, right?

Charlotte: I swear. They don't always see what's in front of them. And it sounds like he's spiraling. His words. I've read his columns on it. He actually has given really good advice to men when they spiral, and yet, the ding dong is spiraling. He's feeding this storm inside him.

Truly: Sounds like he might be, but it doesn't matter now. Maybe it's for the best. I can use this time to recalibrate. Figure out if I want to find a new investor, or something else.

Charlotte: So glad you're diving right back into work and more work and h*ey, let's have another serving of work.*

Truly: What should I be doing? I have responsibilities to Gin Joint. I have employees to take care of. And I need to zero in on my expansion plans.

Charlotte: You already run an incredibly successful establishment. Hell, we both run incredibly successful bars. We are kick-ass businesswomen in New York City. So what if you don't expand? You have a great place in front of you.

Truly: But I lined up my people. I had employees in place. I have a gal who was going to help run the new pub.

Charlotte: Promote her to manager at Gin Joint. Maybe you could work less then.

Truly: I don't work *that* much!

Charlotte: How do you say that with a straight face? It's a Saturday afternoon and you're at work. Am I right?

Truly: Saturday is my busiest time. It's normal to work on a Saturday.

Charlotte: Yes. But you *also* worked Sunday, Monday, Tuesday, Wednesday, Thursday, Friday, and Saturday. *All day.* I bet you work Saturday night too.

Truly: Which reminds me. I still have to go to the stupid wedding with him tonight.

Charlotte: Good thing you're at work then. You definitely need a shot.

47

Sometimes you need comic relief.

I find it at the gym that afternoon.

Josh is cycling on a stationary bike like he's trying to win the Tour de France. What kills me is how he looks.

I walk straight over to his bike and wave a hand in front of his face, since he's staring at ESPN like he wants to rip off the screen with his bare teeth. I glance over at the television captions—something or other about an NFL rookie who signed with Dallas.

Let me guess—not Josh's client.

But I don't need to stir the grizzly bear.

Instead, I point to the Bluetooth device dangling from his ear.

He looks to me. "What? What's going on?"

"You really don't know?"

He looks at me, still cycling, still panting, still not giving a shit that he looks like a total idiot.

"You have your earring on. Your Bluetooth, dickhead."

He reaches up and laughs self-deprecatingly as he tucks the device in his shorts pocket. "Oh. Guess I forgot to take it off."

"You realize you look like a complete twat like that?"

"Hey, I don't look like a twat. I look like a dipshit."

"No, you look like a total tool. That better?"

He offers me a fist. "Knock me, brother. You're getting the lingo down properly now."

"You're so American."

"You're so British."

"All right, so you've taken that dumb Bluetooth off," I say as I hop on the bike next to him and begin a warm-up cycle.

"Yeah, but I was talking to a client before, when I was climbing a hill. That's why I had it on."

"I'm sure your client enjoyed when you were talking to him and panting."

"They're athletes. They're always working out when I'm talking to them." He narrows his eyes and raises his chin in a question. "So what's going on? You're not your usual happy self."

"Am I usually happy?"

"You're like the happiest *lad* around. You're always a barrel of sunshine or a bollock of dogs or a bushel of cats' pajamas, or whatever it is that you say," he says, deliberately botching sayings he knows well.

I sigh and decide to tell him what went down today. When I'm done, I add, "So that's the whole pathetic story."

"I told you, you can't let work get you down. You can't let work dictate your life."

"Says the man who wears his Bluetooth at the gym."

"I was taking a call. And I had to because this is a cutthroat business. Sharks are swimming everywhere, and I need to protect my clients. I have to talk to them whenever they need me."

I arch a brow. "You're proving my point exactly. You're constantly on. You don't have an off mode. I have to be the same."

"No. I'm telling you that sometimes you have to let things go."

"Why do I? Do you let things go? I don't think you do."

He stabs a finger against his chest. "I'm as single as the day is long. Different boat, my friend. No one gets hurt when I work all hours. But you? You do. You love this woman, right?"

"Did I say I loved her?"

He rolls his eyes. "You're such an asshole. You don't have to say you love her. You don't have to use the word *love* for it to be apparent. The way you told that story, it was stupidly obvious that you're madly in love with her."

"'Madly in love with her'?" I parrot, because there's a hard shell over my heart right now, and I don't even know how to crack it.

Josh slows his pace and stares hard at me. "Yes. Madly in love, Jason. I don't know about you, but if I felt the way you seem to feel, I'd like to think I wouldn't let work stand in the way. Just food for thought." He presses a button to end his workout. "And on that note, I have a meeting about the shortstop I'm trying to win."

"So you're not letting work stand in the way, right?"

He moves to the front of my bike and parks his hands on the handlebars. "I'm not in love with the shortstop, dickhead."

"Love you too, asshole."

* * *

When I return to my apartment, I Skype the one person who'll understand. Abby answers on the first ring with a yawn. "It's practically eleven p.m. Why are you calling me now?"

"Because I love you."

"I love you too. But you never call this late unless something's on your mind. Spill."

I flop onto my couch, my arm hanging off the side. "I've got to go to another wedding tonight. And it's going to fucking suck."

"Why is it going to suck?"

I grit my teeth then fume. "Because evidently I have feelings for Truly, but I can't be with her, and yet I have to be with her at a wedding tonight. Doesn't that just take the piss out of everything?"

She laughs. "That takes the piss out of literally everything."

"I thought it was going to be easy until my friend Josh reminded me of one annoying fact."

"What did he remind you?"

"Turns out I'm actually in love with her."

She smiles from across the ocean. "Aww. Love is

awesome. Studies show hearts are healthier when you're in love, so it's good medicine too."

"Ah, so that's what you're learning in medical school."

"Pretty useful, wouldn't you say? But why is being in love hard? I thought the issue was you being best mates with her brother?"

"Who knew? Apparently the bastard is fine with it."

She pumps her fist. "Yay. That's awesome!"

"No, it's not. It's awful. Because there's no time for love. Love is distracting, and nothing is working. Therefore, I'm pissed and annoyed, and I hate everything."

She stifles a laugh. "Poor you. But are you annoyed because of work or because you're in love with her?"

I sit up, dragging a hand through my hair. "Because I'm trying to meet these bills. I'm trying to make things happen," I say, letting too much slip.

She narrows her eyes. "Wait. Hold on. We had a deal. You were paying for my school, but not if it drove you mad. And clearly, you're going mad. Barking mad, as Ron Weasley would say."

"He's a twat."

"Don't be harshing on my Weasley."

"Weasley is a twat, like me. Both of us are penniless twats."

"Wow. This is a whole new level of moping. Also, for the record, I'll take out a loan for the rest of med school. I never wanted you to pay for it if it was going to make you miserable and work twenty-four seven, you daft idiot."

"Daft idiot?"

"Oh, excuse me, like you've never heard me call you that before?"

"No, I think you should've called me a daft prick though," I say, and then a laugh I didn't expect bursts from my chest. Because holy fuck. That's exactly how I'm behaving. I'm behaving worse than the night I went to Walker's club.

"I should get ready for the wedding. I have to see Truly tonight, and I need to be one hundred percent focused on my client. Perhaps I should take up yoga in the next few minutes to get her out of my mind."

"Or maybe don't?"

"Don't take up yoga?"

"Don't worry about getting her out of your mind, because that's not where she is. She's in your heart. And you're so damn focused on work. You say it's because of me and school and bills, and that's true to some extent, but I swear, I can find a way to cover them. Or take out loans and still be just fine. Please don't let me be the person who stands in your way." She takes a beat, takes a breath. "But I don't think I'm actually the reason."

"What? Are you kidding? I made you a promise, and I'm not breaking it."

She groans and moves even closer to the screen. "You're not listening, Jason. I'm not talking about money. I'm talking about that heart of yours. You locked it in a cage after Claire left. It's made you afraid. You're afraid that you're going to lose out, that you're going to have to reinvent yourself like you did after Claire left.

But things will always change. That's life." She clears her throat and dives back into it. "No matter what happens with Truly, you're going to have to figure out what to do with work and where the Modern Gentleman goes next. Don't you see my point?"

"I'm not sure I do." But for the first time all day, I start to shuck off my hard edge, my anger, my frustration. Because I want to understand my sister and what she's telling me. Maybe, just maybe, I want to find a way to the other side of this terrible mess. "Try to help me see it."

She softens further, taking a lower, kinder tone. "The question is, do you want to sort out all these work issues on your own? Or do you want to sort them out with somebody who loves you and supports you, and probably wants to be there for you as you navigate your way through?"

And like that, today becomes crystal clear.

Thanks to my friends and my sister.

I am indeed a daft idiot.

I'm spiraling.

I'm letting work get in the way of love. I'm letting old wounds reopen. I'm forgetting every piece of advice I've ever shared.

I lost one bit on one show, but I was doing fine before. I can't lose sight of all the other opportunities out there. Hell, I'll be my own Ryder if no one wants me on their program.

But I'm not concentrating on what matters.

What matters is Truly.

I might have lost the job, but I'm not going to lose the woman.

That's the advice that every man should follow, and I'm going to do so to the letter tonight.

48

The thing about getting your shit together is it doesn't always work like it does in the movies. Just because you figure out how to remove your skull from your ass doesn't mean you can cut across Midtown traffic like you're the star of the show.

Nor does it mean the woman will answer the phone.

I keep calling Truly to see if I can meet her ahead of Enzo's ceremony, but I reach voicemail every time. I hope she's not abandoning me before the wedding, but if she does, I deserve it.

I get dressed quickly, putting on my tux and knotting the bow tie, and catch a cab to the hotel where the happy couple will exchange vows in a flower-festooned ballroom. I search for Truly in the lobby, down the hall, and around the corner.

I don't see her, and a knot of worry tightens in me.

I poke my head into the ballroom, scanning the seats. She's not here early. I'm dying to wait on the front steps for her, but I can't spend any more time on this mission just now.

Because here's the other thing: commitments matter. A man should keep his promises. I need to stick to mine, so I put my phone away, join the groom, and head to the front of the room.

Wondering where Truly is when she hasn't appeared by the time the ceremony begins, I take my place by Enzo's side as he promises to love Valerie for the rest of their lives. As he kisses her, I'm struck by a certainty—*he will.* I have no doubt, just like I don't doubt Chip's love, or Gavin's, for that matter.

The men I've stood for might have needed help in the friend department, but not in the love department. They've all seemed true to their hearts, and looking back, I've learned something from each of them.

Find a woman you want to spend each day with. Find someone who shares your passion. And give the woman what she wants.

What does Truly want?

As I flash back to the diner, the way she looked when I arrived, how she wanted to share her thoughts with me, I could smack myself. She came to the diner to *talk* to me about her news, and I made it all about me, me, me. And even when I did, she defended me. She told me *The Consummate Wingman* had been lucky to have me. And when I said love was distracting, she didn't answer with a yes.

She answered with *It can be distracting, but it can also maybe be something . . .*

Something wonderful. Maybe that was what she was going to say before I cut her off.

When I spot her at last in the back row, wiping her eye as Enzo and Valerie slide on rings, I can't wait to tell her that I agree.

I mouth, *"Wait for me."*

She gives a quick, crisp nod that does nothing to ease my mind. But that's not the point. I don't get to have my mind eased. I need to ease hers.

I wait till Enzo kisses his bride.

I wait till they're declared man and wife.

I wait till they walk down the aisle into their happily ever after.

Then I steal time.

I practically run past the rows of people, stopping inches from her. "I was a daft prick today. You should bang my head against the wall."

"Is that so?" she asks, careful and measured.

"Bricks would fall out of it if you banged it hard enough. Or even pigs, because I was stupid and pigheaded."

She raises an eyebrow. "There are pigs in your head?"

"There must be, or what other excuse is there for how I behaved? But I know this: when a man has made a mistake, he should own up to it. And I want to own up to mine."

She's deliberate, taking her time as she asks, "What mistakes do you think you made?"

"Oh, the list is a mile long. But let's start at the top. How about the time I said falling in love is absolutely fucking distracting and ruined everything we've built? That was a horrible mistake. Because love hasn't ruined a damn thing. In fact, I think it's made everything better." I lock eyes with her, waiting, hoping. Hers seem to sparkle a little more than a moment before.

"What do you think?" I press.

"I do think love can make everything better," she says, still careful in her tone.

"And another mistake is when you said, *Love can be distracting, but it can also maybe be something*, and I answered it all wrong. Completely wrong."

A smile plays across her lips. "Would you like a do-over on that answer?"

"Yes." I cup her cheek, and she lets me. She doesn't turn away, even as a woman slides past us to walk out of the aisle and out to the foyer where waitstaff serve sushi appetizers. "Love is distracting, but it's also something wonderful."

She seems to fight off a smile—a huge, winning grin. "It is wonderful."

I thread my hand through her hair, so damn grateful to touch her again. "I need you. I want you. I love you, Truly, and I love you in a way that terrifies me and thrills me too. And I think that scared me more than anything. I thought I'd protected my heart from hurt, but I can't keep it safe from you. And here's the thing—I don't want to."

She sets her hand on my chest. "I'll keep it safe for you."

This woman. My God. My heart thunders in my chest, beating madly with this barrage of emotions. And with emotions come words. "I want to give you everything you want, and everything you need. If that investor can't realize what he has in front of him, then let me be the one you lean on. Let me be the one you talk to. Let me be the one who helps you figure out what to do next."

"You'd do that? You want that? Are you sure?"

My answer is straight from the heart. "I should have done that earlier today. I know now that's what you were looking for, and I want to be the one who supports you. Will you let me?"

She melts against me. "I thought you'd never ask."

I press my forehead to hers as I learn something new. Sometimes you do need to beg when it comes to asking the woman you love to have you again. But beg like a gentleman. "Then will you *please* take me back?"

She laughs, and her laughter turns to happy tears. "I don't want to curl up at the end of the day with work. I want to curl up with you. And we can help each other when work doesn't go our way. You're the one I want to depend on, because I'm in love with you."

My heart soars—out of the hotel, up to the stratosphere, far, far away from me. I no longer have any control of it. Maybe I never did. Maybe it's simply time to let go of my fears, the true shackles that were holding me back. To let go and love again.

Or really, to love in a whole new way.

Because this is real love. The forever kind.

"I can't believe I was stupid enough to almost let you get away." I haul her in for a kiss.

When I break it, she says, "Simple solution: don't let me get away again."

"I can do that. I can definitely do that." I take her hand, and we head into the reception where I give a kick-ass toast.

Valerie thanks me with such earnestness that I scrap any notion that she sabotaged me. The job simply didn't happen, end of story. There will be others.

But love? As I've learned from the men who've hired me, you don't let that slip away.

In fact, you don't let it get away even if Coldplay is playing.

I groan when Walker puts on a tune from the band that kills eardrums. "*Is it Armageddon?*" I mouth to him.

He shrugs impishly.

At the head table, Enzo's eyes light up. "I love Coldplay. They are big in Madrid."

"Oh, Enzo, I'm going to have to introduce you to U2 and Panic! at the Disco and Arcade Fire," Valerie says.

I turn to her. "You like all those bands?"

"That surprises you?"

"Actually, no. You have excellent taste."

She runs a hand down her husband's arm. "I do indeed."

He winks. "She has the best taste. But then again, so do I."

"We both have impeccable taste, my love."

He stands and offers her his hand. "Then come with me and make me look good on the dance floor."

"I believe it's the other way around." She joins him, and they sway.

Truly reaches for my hand, mischief in her eyes. "Dance with me, you Coldplay hater."

"Seriously? You do know it's a deep and powerful loathing?"

"I know. I definitely know. Don't forget, I know a lot about you, and I still like you."

"Let's keep it that way."

"Then let's dance."

"Well, I'm not going to make the mistake of turning you down." I take her to the dance floor for a spin, and somehow I survive the song. That makes me realize something important. "I must really dig you if I can dance to this song with you."

She clasps my cheek and plants a kiss on my lips.

Yes, I can tolerate Coldplay a hell of a lot like this.

A little later, I head over to the deejay stand, leaning against it, surveying the vestiges of the reception.

Walker lifts his brow. "I see you're starting to get your act together."

"Am I now?"

He strokes his chin, a thoughtful expression on his face. "Let's see. First time I've seen you at a wedding where you look legitimately one hundred percent happy."

"Are you saying I've been a grumpy bugger at other ceremonies?"

He shakes his head as he packs up his gear. "Not at all. But there's a difference between the charm you serve up as a best man for hire and the way you are when you're with Truly."

"You've been studying me? I suppose that's understandable. I am fascinating."

"Human nature is fascinating. You happen to occupy an interesting niche of it."

I pat his speaker. "And your niche? Are you simply a fill-in deejay now?"

He flashes a satisfied smile. "Just filling in for a buddy. But I'm no longer taking any new gigs. And I do believe I've achieved nirvana."

"Is that so?"

"Yeah. That is so. I'm doing what I want. Took me a while to get here, but I'm here. I'm happy to help out a friend now and then, but for the most part, I'm on the other side."

"You've made it. You've caught your dreams. Like that Thoreau quote: *Go confidently in the direction of your dreams. Live the life you've imagined.*"

"You'll get there too. Just don't take too long to press go."

"I've been formulating a plan all night. Mulling over options. I have an exit strategy, and I'm pretty sure I'm going to put it in motion tonight. I don't have a safety net, but I don't care. It's time to move on."

He holds up a fist to knock. "You're doing it? Going after what you really want?"

I knock back. "I've decided. I'm going all in on the Modern Gentleman. No more half this, half that. I can't keep playing both angles. I'll be letting this go." I sweep my arms wide to encompass the ballroom.

"Dive in. The water's warm when you follow your dreams." He mimes swimming. Through tropical seas, I suspect. "Also, kudos to you for having the balls to jump without a safety net."

"Wish me luck."

"To all the safe landings. Now how about telling me the details?"

I begin to share my plan when a sexy, smoky voice whispers, "Jason."

I jerk my head in a matchstick response. What the hell? I'm not Jason tonight. I'm Jay.

But it's Valerie beside me, beckoning for me to join her at her table.

For a moment, fear crawls up my spine and slinks under my collar. But just as quickly, I say no to it. I'm not afraid of my worlds colliding anymore. I have Truly, and whatever happens with work, I'll sort it out.

I follow Valerie and sit next to her.

She smiles like she has a secret. "I remembered you."

"Is that so?"

"It came to me in a rush in the middle of the night, and I've been wanting to talk to you. I popped out of bed, hopped onto the laptop, and looked you up. I'd heard you on my friend Ryder's show. And I went and listened to several of your podcasts. And read all your blogs."

"In the middle of the night?"

"I don't need much sleep. My brain is always whirring. And when I read them, and I heard your voice, everything clicked."

Tonight, I don't even consider hiding under the bar

till the morning. I simply lean back in the chair, cross my leg at the ankle—no manspreading here—and I wait. "And what clicked?"

Her brown eyes seem to twinkle. Her lips curve in a devilish grin. "As you may know, I run a multinational media conglomerate. And in that capacity, I often acquire other companies."

"Sure. That would seem a normal course of business."

"And I've acquired a prominent men's magazine in the United Kingdom. *Gentleman's Style*. Have you heard of it?"

"Of course. It's better than *Esquire*. And *GQ*."

"It is indeed. And I'm going to be expanding it in the United States."

That's quite interesting yet surprising, given the state of print periodicals. "But magazines are a dying breed," I say, since page counts are down, ads are down, and so on.

"Of course. But brands aren't. And the brand name has value. Imagine a *Gentleman's Style* series of books. Handy little gift books sold in the front of stores on tips for men. Or perhaps a revamped website with the type of articles that search engines love. Five Tips on Better Communication. The Top Ten Ways to Impress a Boss."

It sounds fantastic. "I can imagine that perfectly."

She leans closer, clearly enchanted with her new property. "And podcasts, since they're the future. Can you picture a quick-hit podcast on top tips of the day? I can."

"I think I can too."

She taps her finger against her lip. "Do you see where I'm going with this?"

"You're going in the direction of creating a US presence for a popular and well-respected British brand," I say, since I'm pretty sure I have that right.

She sighs as if she just can't believe one wouldn't grasp the concept. "Jason Reynolds, I need a voice, someone with a point of view. I need a front man. I need you."

I blink and sit bolt upright, rubbing my ear. She didn't just say that, did she? "Pardon me?"

She laughs, a deep, throaty sound. "You heard me right. I want you to be the front man. I want you to be the voice—and the face if you'd like—of *Gentleman's Style* in the United States. And don't worry, you can keep up your work on Ryder Lockhart's show."

"Oh, he already let me go."

She shakes her head. "That's not what he told me when I called him today."

"You called him today?" I feel like I'm trapped on another planet, trying to decipher distant radio signals.

"Of course. He's a business associate. I wouldn't poach his talent without talking to him first."

"It's not really poaching at this point."

She raises one eyebrow. "Be that as it may, are you interested in my offer?" She puts forth a number that nearly dislocates my jaw. I'm tempted to ask if it's a joke, but I'm also certain I've advised readers and listeners never to ask that when offered a financial figure more than you ever dreamed of.

"I'm incredibly interested," I reply.

"Then it's yours. I'll have a deal memo sent over tonight."

"Tonight? Aren't you heading out on your honeymoon?"

"Of course I am, but I don't send out the contracts. I have people. And someday, you'll have people. Mark my words—I can always spot talent. As an author friend of mine once said when she discovered the perfect narrator for her books: *You're a gold mine.*"

"Smart author."

"Very smart, and a smart narrator to keep saying yes to her."

"You've got my yes."

"One of my favorite words."

When I say goodbye to the newlyweds, I do feel like I've discovered a gold mine, but it's not only in the job.

It's in the woman I take home with me.

49

"A gold mine? You don't say?" Truly tugs on my bow tie, unknotting it in the elevator to her apartment.

"Evidently. Did you have any idea you were fucking a gold mine?" I slide a hand under her dress as the lift shoots us up to her floor.

"I had no idea. But this changes everything. My boyfriend is made of gold. And apparently makes gold."

I laugh at her designation. "Boyfriend? Is that what I am?"

"You're definitely no longer *just a friend*. And I'm pretty sure we don't say *lover* anymore unless we're at a seventies party."

The elevator stops at her floor, and we exit. "I can't take you to a work event and introduce you as my lover? Or if I did, I'd need a Tom Selleck mustache or to be dressed for disco?"

"Something like that," she says, laughing as we head into her place.

The second the door clicks shut, I pull her against

me, sliding my hands into her hair. "Hey, you naughty minx. Thanks for coming with me tonight."

"Thank you for stalking me before the wedding."

"How did you know I was stalking you?"

She smiles, like a naughty little thing. "I saw all your missed calls."

"Why didn't you pick up, you evil torturess?"

"Because it seemed like the kind of thing I'd rather hear in person. I was right. When the person you love realizes he wants you more than work, it's kind of an awesome thing. I know, because that's how I feel for you."

Her words thrill and electrify me. They remind me that taking this kind of chance, without a safety net, was worth it. She was worth the jump.

I grab her wrist and lead her back to her bedroom, where I strip her out of her clothes and lavish attention on her fantastic body all night long.

In the morning, I wake up to the smell of pancakes. The scent draws me out of bed and into her kitchen, where she's crooning into a spatula about her creation.

"You do know that song turns me on?"

She spins around, her eyes hooded, her voice smoky. "They're hot off the griddle. Come and get 'em."

"I will. But like I said, it turns me on. I want you first."

"Jason, don't you know? With me, you can have everything. You can have love and pancakes. And I'll never serve you bacon."

"That sounds like the perfect way to start every single day."

* * *

After breakfast, and after post-breakfast experiments in other uses for syrup, followed by a long, hot shower, my phone rings. When I see it's Ryder's number, I take the call. But I don't feel desperate. I'm simply curious.

And that's a welcome change.

"Hey, Ryder, how's it going?" I ask as I settle onto the couch while Truly gets dressed.

"Great. Apologies for calling on a Sunday, but sometimes business moves at either the speed of tar, or of the Concorde."

"And never at the speed you want when you want it."

"That's the truth. Listen, I apologize for the cryptic message yesterday. I couldn't say much because of the changes going on here."

"No worries."

"Here's the deal though. We're expanding. And I'm taking on a new role. I'm heading up programming for all of the shows and podcasts, so I'm taking a step back from the day-to-day hosting roles."

"Congrats. Sounds like a good gig."

"It's a great one. We're starting new shows, a couple of food podcasts, some restaurant reviews, and a new beer podcast we picked up. An affable fellow Brit is hosting that one."

I furrow my brow. "Marcus?"

"Yes, that's him. He knows his stuff."

"I thought he was . . ." I trail off, not bothering to finish with *taking my job*. Assume nothing—that's what I tell my guys. But in retrospect, I'd like to laugh at myself. Because that role makes perfect sense for Marcus. There's no one better to host a beer podcast.

"And I'd like you to cohost with me."

For the second time in less than twenty-four hours, my jaw clangs to the floor. "You want me to be your *Consummate Wingman* cohost?"

"Yes. I do. Is that too much work? Can you fit it in with what you'll be doing for Valerie? It won't start for another few weeks. That's why I told you I don't need you this week. I want to work on some formatting changes to accommodate the next setup."

"Yes. Yes. I say yes!"

He laughs. "Well, that was easy."

"And it goes against all my own advice. Don't let on how eager you are. But the cat's out of the bag. I'm eager. I want this. And I'll do a great job."

"Excellent. We'll set up some meetings to brainstorm."

When I hang up, Truly pokes her head out of the bedroom, tugging her wet hair back into a ponytail. "What was that all about?"

I tell her the good news, and she throws her arms around me. "I knew it. I totally knew it."

I look down at her outfit. "Why are you wearing exercise clothes? You just showered."

"I know. I can't very well do Punk Rope with sticky syrup on me. Gross." Her eyes light up. "Hey, why don't you come to class with me? It's near your place, so you can grab some shorts there."

I say yes to her offer too. Obviously. It's what we've always done. It's what I hope we'll always do.

As we head over to the exercise class, I take her hand. "So, I've been thinking about all this good fortune that's fallen my way in the last twenty-four hours."

"Well, you are a gold mine. It makes sense that everyone wants to mine you."

"But what I've been noodling on is my promise to you. How I want to help support your dreams too. I had an idea for you."

She stops, tilts her head, and looks at me curiously. "Go on."

"It's about your bar concept."

50

Truly

That afternoon, I head over to Charlotte's bar, when my phone pings with a text.

It's from my guy.

Jason: Good luck. I can't wait to hear how it goes.

Truly: I can't wait to tell you.

I put my phone away, loving the certainty that he'll be here for me however this goes.

When I reach the Lucky Spot, I walk straight over to my best friend. It's early, so it's not crowded yet.

"Hey, you!"

"I have a brilliant idea."

"I happen to like brilliant ideas. Do tell."

I point to her, then to me. "You. Me. Parisian-themed bar. What do you think?"

She gasps . . . says nothing . . . just stands there, bug-eyed. Finally, she finds words. "That. Sounds. Kick-ass."

I smile. "I know, right? Two awesome women running a brand-new place together. We'd do a great job. Don't you think?"

"We'd do an amazing job."

"And screw investors. I have some money saved."

"I've got plenty saved too."

"And we could take out loans for the rest. I know it'd be incredible, and you once said you wanted to do a Parisian-styled bar."

"I absolutely do."

"Do you think Spencer would be cool with it? I know you guys run this place together, but I kind of just want to do something with us. You and me. Girl power."

"Gee, let me ask him. Hey, handsome," she calls out to her husband at the other end of the bar.

"That's me," he replies.

"Question for you."

He strides over, a curious glint in his green eyes. "Ask away, Snuffleupagus."

"What would you think about Truly and me starting a place all our own? A little Parisian-themed place."

He flashes his winning grin, one of the many things that stole her heart years ago. "I'd say *Vive la France*."

"That's it?" I ask with a laugh.

He shrugs. "Some things in life are easy. I've always

thought the two of you would make a good business combo. And as I like to say, happy wife equals happy life. Sounds like this would make my wife happy."

Charlotte plants a kiss on his lips, and when she breaks it, he adds, "And you can count on me to order the first glass of vino."

My friend turns back to me with a cat-that-ate-the-canary smile and extends a hand. "Hello, new business partner. Nice to meet you."

"Nice to meet you too."

When I see Jason later that night, he gives me the most delicious congratulatory kiss.

It almost makes me forget what I wanted to say to him. "Thank you for the brilliant idea."

He shakes his head. "No. It wasn't my idea. It was yours. It was what you wanted to do all along. All I did was remind you."

"It was more than a reminder, but how about you remind me now of where kisses with you can lead to."

He grins. "I can definitely remind you of that."

And he does, all night long.

51

I take a sip of my Earl Grey, waiting for Troy's answer.

I'm expecting a barrage of questions, since that's his style.

But I only get one. "When can I start?"

"How's today?"

"I'm on it. I already have a plan. I've been writing best man's speeches on the side to prep for this moment. I'll keep Sully as my second-in-command, and I've got another friend ready for my third groomsman, just like you had."

"As I suspect, you're really the best man for the job."

He sits up straighter. "*Some are born great, some achieve greatness, and some have greatness thrust upon them. Twelfth Night.*" He extends a hand. "I will bring honor to the humble profession of best man for hire." Then he raises his arms above his head, shaking his hips. "And this means I can finally quit the pole."

Laughing, I scratch my jaw. "I feel like that's not Shakespeare."

He taps his chest. "That's one hundred percent Troy D'Angelo. By the way, you know that's not my real name, right?"

"It's not?"

"You couldn't see through that?" Adopting an announcer's tone, he says, "And now, taking the stage, the one, the only . . . Troy . . . D'Angelo." He pronounces the last name like "dangle" with an *O* at the end.

"Why, yes. I can definitely see through that now. But that's an image I'd like to unsee."

"Me too, my friend. Me too. And thanks to you, I can be Troy Seewoster. Aspiring playwright and best man for hire extraordinaire."

"Your real last name is Seewoster?"

"Yes."

"Piece of advice, mate. Keep the stage name."

He seems to consider this, then nods. "You're right. Troy D'Angelo I shall remain."

"How would you like to start with Zane Jarratt? He's an X Games skateboarding star who needs an extra groomsman to match the number of bridesmaids. Some of his mates are out of town for the wedding. He's a client of my friend, so Josh hooked me up with him, and I'll pass him along to you instead. But wait. Can you do an Australian accent?"

"Can I do an Australian accent? I am Australian. How did you not know this?" he says in a perfect rendition of an accent from Down Under.

"Are you really?"

He laughs, shaking his head. "I'm from North

Dakota. But have I impressed the man who's always teaching others how to make an impact?"

"You have. You absolutely have." I take another drink of my tea. Yes, my exit plan is working better than I expected.

52

Josh

The bat phone rings.

Even though it's the middle of the night, it wakes me up instantly. This is the emergency line.

"Hey. What's going on?"

"Dude!"

Dragging a hand through my hair, I sit up straight. "What's up, Zane? You okay?"

"I am motherfucking awesome. In fact, I've never been better. I'm hanging with Jako tonight," he says, naming one of his best buds in the business, another skater on his team. He sighs contentedly. "So whassup with you?"

I laugh. "Nothing *was* up, my man. It's three in the morning. Wassup with you?"

"Not much. Just chilling. Munching on some sunflower seeds. Man, if you could get me a lifetime supply of these, I would be the happiest cat ever."

"I'll make a note of that. Also, do me a favor. Call me again in the middle of the night to tell me you're awesome and nothing is going on but snacking."

He snaps his fingers. "Shit, I just remembered why I called. I need your friend."

I furrow my brow, trying to figure out who he means. Then again, I'm always trying to figure out what Zane means. A few too many hits on the joint when he was in high school have made his reaction times less than top-notch when he's outside the skate park. In the skate park? The dude kills it. No clue how that worked out, but I'm glad it did. He's been making bank for both of us for more than a decade.

"Sure. I'll help you out. But help me out first. Which friend?"

"You know. *Let's throw another shrimp on the barbie.* That one."

"Jay. Jay, who's from Sydney," I say, using the fake name Jason set up for this ceremony.

"Yes! You're like Stephen Hawking. How do you do that? Do you do brain exercises? Is that how you're so sharp?"

"Yes. Yes, I do."

"Anyhoo, that's him. He's cool. I like that accent. Ooh. Idea! Can you do a little *g'day, mate* accent when you intro me to Monster Energy Bull Rider Drinks, or whatever that sponsorship is you're getting for me?"

"No. I love you, man, but I'm not pretending to be Australian." I'll go to the ends of the earth for my clients and their deals, but I'm not going to perform like a trick monkey for their amusement.

"Fine, have it your way. But you rock! Never forget that. So, the bad news is I lost Jay's number. And I need it. Because guess what?"

"You want to hear him say *g'day, mate?*"

He cracks up. "No, but I'll add that to the list. Along with *the dingo ate my baby*. But I have to talk to him, because he needs to be my best man now."

"I thought Jako was doing the honors?"

"No, man. I'm at the hospital right now with him. Didn't I tell you that?"

I roll my eyes. "You told me you were *with* Jako. You didn't say you were *at* the hospital. Are you okay? Do you need anything?"

"I do. I need a new best man. I'd ask you to do the speech, but that's not cool. I love you and all, but I gotta have some boundaries. That's what my fiancée keeps telling me. *Boundaries.* Anyway, Jako broke his leg doing a gazelle flip. That's the other bad news. And that means he can't do me the honor of being by my side next weekend. He's so fucking bummed. He wrote a speech too. Well, half of it, and you know how Jako is. He hates writing. He hates words."

"Words can be little devils."

"But no worries. We came up with a plan in the ambulance. He'll FaceTime from the hospital bed in his cast, and Jay will deliver his speech. It's going to be rad. Can you hook me up with Jay-man and he can do the speech?"

"I'm on it. One tip though. Don't call him Jay-man."

"Right. Thanks. Jay-boy it is."

* * *

The next weekend, the wedding goes off without a hitch. Jason's buddy Troy has taken over his business. He has zero problems pretending he's Jay-man or Jay-boy—and brings his guy Sully along to fill in as the extra groomsman—and in his role, Troy delivers the first half of Jako's best man's speech and the second half of what, I presume, he wrote.

It's stellar, and it makes Zane smile like he's won a lifetime supply of sunflower seeds. The wedding is everything my longtime client could want, and that's what matters most to me: happy clients.

After the reception winds down, Zane claps me on the shoulder. "You're the man. You know that, right? I'd be nothing without you."

I'm not saying I want him to think that, but I do like that he does. So I keep my reply simple. "You know I'm always happy to help."

That's my goal: go the extra mile. Then another mile. This business is insanely competitive, and being an agent, a negotiator, a therapist, a sounding board, a dartboard, and a fucking wedding planner, along with an occasional Uber driver, is par for the course. It's how I stay ahead, and I always need to be ten steps ahead, given the way the competition is breathing down my neck.

Zane smacks my chest. "Man, you did more than help. You saved the day. You always save the day. I owe you like ten million presents. Want me to send you a new car? I want to get a new Jeep. I could get two. One for you, one for me."

Laughing, I shake my head. "I'm all good. Also, I hope you like *your* gift. I got you a little something."

His eyes sparkle. "Dude. You did not have to get me a present."

"I know. I wanted to."

I don't have to stick around to know he'll be over the moon when he receives his lifetime supply of a certain snack food. "Anyway, glad it all worked out with the new Jay. And congrats again."

When I leave the wedding and hop into an Uber, my regular line rings. *Private.* Could be anyone—team owner, publicist, potential client.

"Summers here."

"Hey, man. It's Lorenzo."

I sit up straight, a burst of possibility flaring in me. "Lorenzo. How the hell are you?"

"I had two RBIs tonight, and we won, so I'd say I'm fantastic."

"That is definitely fantastic. You've been putting up the numbers all season, man. But tell me something, how's your mom? Last time we talked you said she was having chest pains. How's she doing?"

"She's all better. And hey, thanks for asking about her. That means a lot to me, and it makes me feel even better about what I want to ask you."

"Why's that?"

"Because it shows you care about me. About my family. And that's why I'm hoping you'd want to negotiate a fat new contract with the Yankees for me? Think you'd be up for that?"

Fireworks spark across the whole night sky. "I'd love nothing more."

* * *

A couple days later, Jason joins me for a Yankees game in my box seats.

He surveys the swank setup, complete with catering and plush velvet chairs. "Still slumming it, I see?"

"Yeah. Maybe someday I'll move up to the third baseline."

"I trust business is good?"

"It's excellent. Lorenzo is all mine now."

"Ah, so evil Leather Pants Poacher didn't nab him?"

I scoff. "No way. I'm still the man. And your new biz is taking off?"

"Started some of my new work this week. Maybe I'll even write a piece about etiquette when invited to a fancy suite at a ball game. Like, may I please devour all the mushroom canapés?"

"Do you even know what a canapé is?"

"Does anyone know what a canapé is?"

"No one does. Also, I'm glad you figured out your lady issues and your work issues. Like I said, work isn't everything." I tap my ear. "See? I'm Bluetooth-free today."

"But I bet your mobile ringer is on high."

"Of course it is. Bat line too."

He grabs a carrot from the appetizer plate and crunches into it. "Someday you'll meet a woman who makes you want to turn the bat line off."

"Maybe. For now, I see no reason to end my run as New York's most eligible bachelor. But you've ended yours. How's it going with the lady?"

"Perfect. Totally perfect. She'll be here any minute. She has a crush on the shortstop."

"Who doesn't?"

* * *

During a break in the action later in the game, I step into the hall to take a quick call. When I'm done, I hear the click of shoes.

I turn.

Haven Delilah.

She's walking toward me, and why, oh fucking *why* does she have to look the way she does? That chestnut hair. Those chocolate eyes. That body. She's a total smoke show, and the universe must be having a field day, making my biggest rival the hottest babe I have ever seen.

"You following me, Delilah?"

"Yes, Summers. I was up at the crack of dawn, waiting for you. I've been slinking behind buildings and hiding around corners just to follow you to Yankee Stadium. What a shock to run into a sports agent here."

I ignore her sarcasm. "That's so thoughtful that you

came here to congratulate me on adding Lorenzo to my roster."

She crosses her arms defiantly. She does everything defiantly. It's so fucking sexy it should be illegal. "Congrats. Too bad you didn't get a pitcher though. I've heard they have more long-term value. Oh, but probably none were on the market, since I rep half the bull pen."

"It's okay. I get that you're still licking your wounds. But I guess this makes us even now."

She rolls her eyes as the caterer—earbuds in place—heads down the hall carrying an empty tray.

Haven takes a step closer, getting in my space, and holy shit. I can smell her perfume. Or is it her shampoo? It smells like honey, and it goes to my head. Fucks with my senses. "Still having a hard time letting the past go?"

I swallow roughly as she calls me on my bullshit, right as her insanely seductive smell is drifting through my mind.

She pitches forward, squeaking in surprise as the caterer bumps her with the empty tray. "Oh!"

She stumbles closer. Instinct has me grabbing her arm, steadying her. She lifts her chin. She's inches away. Her face is kissing distance from mine. Her lips are dangerously close. Lips I know so well. Lips I've traced, explored long into the night.

For a moment, all our games, all our anger sizzles away. "You okay?" I ask.

She looks into my eyes, her chocolate-brown irises blazing with some unusual combination of heat and confusion. "Yeah, I'm fine."

She looks down at her arm. The arm I'm holding. She seems to register my hand on her bare skin. She swallows then looks up at me.

Her breath hitches when she meets my eyes. And what's that I see? Is her skin flushing? Holy shit. Haven is still affected by the way I touch her.

Well, this changes everything.

53

Several months later

After I record an episode of *The Consummate Wingman*, I pop into Marie's office. "I've been remiss."

She arches a brow. "I know."

"Forgive me."

"Only if you pay up."

"I always make good on my bets."

She holds out her hand. "I did enjoy the hundred dollars. Almost as much as I enjoyed being right."

"And saying 'I told you so'? Do you enjoy that at all? I can't tell."

She wiggles her fingers impatiently. "I did tell you so. I told you that you two would be more than friends. And then I predicted you'd move in together in less than six months. And you acted all independent."

I have the decency to look sheepish. "What can I say? You were right on that count."

I hand her the winnings on that wager. It's far less painful than waiting longer to cohabitate would have been.

She taps her chin. "Next thing you know, I'll be betting on when she's going to pop out babies."

My eyes widen. "No one is saying anything about babies yet."

"Mark my words. You'll be doing that after you say *I do*."

"I haven't even proposed yet."

She shoots me an amused grin. "Seems we have our next wager."

* * *

"And that's how you dress for the first day on the job," I declare as I finish typing my latest column for *Gentleman's Style*.

"Why don't you write how you undress when you come home from a hard day of work?" Truly calls out from the bedroom.

"Fine. I'll tackle that next." I pretend I'm typing like a madman, making the *clickety-clack* sound of keys. "I don't undress myself. My *lover* does when I walk through the door, and she pounces on me like the hungry, naughty minx that she is."

The hungry, naughty minx herself pops out of the bedroom, showing off sexy jeans and a snug black sweater. "Of course I do. That's one of the bennies of living with you. Also, how do I look?"

"Good enough to eat. Like always."

"Ooh, will you have a slice of my summer later? Maybe take a bite of the lily?"

I stand, stalk over to her, and curl my hand around her head. "No. Like I tell you every single time, I will devour your sweet, delicious pussy."

She shivers against me. "You better. Also, stop talking about dessert, or I'm going to try to jump you at the theater. I'm feeling pretty good after that review we got on that gal's nightclub podcast. Coco."

I am so incredibly proud of Truly. She's a powerful, successful entrepreneur in the city. She runs one of the best-reviewed and most popular nighttime establishments around, and the second-most as well, since she and Charlotte just opened Bisou. It means "kiss" in French, and given the sexy, romantic vibe she and Charlotte crafted for the place, it's fitting. It's also earning rave reviews in all the write-ups.

"Why don't you play the review for me again?"

"Oh stop. Stop. You don't want to hear it for the fiftieth time."

"But I do."

"Fine, if you insist."

She grabs her phone, taps her podcast app, and hits play.

"Bisou, I could kiss you. Or be kissed.

That's how I felt when I entered the gorgeous new establishment. It drips with romance. It radiates sex. It's exactly the kind of place that makes a gal want to throw out all her apps and meet a man in person again. Ambiance, people.

That's what Bisou has, and it has it in every single corner. From the drinks to the music to the decor, I just might try to find a way to live there.

Until then, you'll find me at the bar, kicking a high-heeled shoe back and forth, listening to Edith Piaf, drinking my absinthe."

"Can I just say, I told you so?" I ask.

Truly grins at me. "Yes, you can. Anytime."

"I'm also glad you promoted Gabriella."

"She is a goddess."

"I like it because it means you have more time."

"Time to spend with you," she says.

"You have such good time management skills."

"That is true."

We leave her apartment together for the theater.

Our apartment, I should say, since I've moved in with her.

Everything is fitting these days in our life together.

I Adam Levine'd myself these last few months. My business has taken off, and the launch of the *Gentleman's Style* brand in the United States has been met with terrific audience growth and advertiser dollars. A win-win. Valerie has been pleased, and so have readers and listeners. The work I do for her brand dovetails perfectly with my cohost work with Ryder.

And I almost hate to admit this, but that Marcus bloke? He's become a friend. Every now and then, we go out for a beer. As long as he avoids the odes to hops, we are all good.

I also told him he'd best keep his hands off my sister.

Abby came to visit a few weeks ago, and I was sure Marcus was taken with her when we all went out. Turns out, he's dating Coco, the restaurant and nightclub reviewer. Now, they seem perfect for each other.

And it's a good thing Abby's still single, because boys are trouble, and she has school to finish. Turns out, she took out a loan, sneaky little turkey. But I'm clever too. I paid it off for her two months later, since business has been quite good indeed.

Just focus on that whole tailbone thing, and we'll be good, I'd told her.

Didn't I tell you? I figured out the tailbone is connected to the brachial plexus, she'd said.

Truly and I make our way to the heart of Times Square, ducking down Forty-Fourth Street and through the doors of the St. James Theater. She squeezes my hand. "I can't believe we're finally seeing this show. I've been dying to."

"And I'll admit that I'm pretty damn excited to see Nora onstage. She's worked so hard, and she's wanted this so much."

"She's going to be amazing."

A few minutes later, Sloane and Malone join us, scurrying in to grab seats in the same row. They're followed by Spencer and Charlotte, then Nick and Harper. The gang is all here. We say quick hellos before the lights dim, the music swells, and the curtain rises.

Indiana Jones treks across the South American jungle and into the cave where an idol awaits him. After he grabs it, he races past poisoned arrows, falling stones, and a boulder that zooms, not across stage but downstage toward the apron, appearing as if it's going to careen into the audience before Indy escapes at the last possible second. The lights go dark, and the boulder presumably rises somewhere above us all.

A little later, Nora comes onstage, belting out, "Snakes. Why did it have to be snakes? Oh why, oh why, oh why did it have to be snakes?"

Turns out she was upgraded. She served as the understudy for Marion, and when the actress fell ill, Nora took over. Never underestimate the value of a good understudy.

And somewhere in this city or on its outskirts, Troy is likely giving a speech about some fella he barely knows. In fact, I'm going to see him at a wedding next weekend, and I'm looking forward to catching up.

After the show ends and we greet Nora backstage, giving her flowers she adores and compliments she deserves, we take off for our respective sections of the city.

I slide an arm around Truly's waist. "Want to go to the Luxe Hotel for a little nightcap?"

"Not Gin Joint or Lucky Spot or Bisou?"

"I like the Luxe. It reminds me of a certain night."

She wiggles her eyebrows. "You're just trying to have hotel sex with me, aren't you?"

"Is that such a bad thing?"

"I like hotel sex. I like bedroom sex. I like kitchen sex."

"Reason number five thousand, two hundred, forty-four why you're perfect for me."

When we arrive at the hotel, I hope to convince her of one more: that I know her. That I remember how we started. That I appreciate the little things, the big things —all the things.

We step into the elevator, and I hit the close button immediately so we're all alone.

Just like we were the night before Enzo's wedding. "Do you remember the last time we rode this elevator?"

She smiles magnetically. "I do. I told you I didn't want to live in a world where you're out of my system."

"And I said the same. It was the first time we admitted what was happening. I said, too, that we'd figure out what to do next. Now I have another idea of what to do next."

Her breath catches as I drop to one knee and take her hand. "The last time we were in this elevator, I knew I'd want this with you someday. I knew you were the one. You are . . . the only one for me."

"You're the only one for me," she whispers.

"I could give you a speech about all the things I love about you, but I'd rather show you every day for the rest of our lives why I'm madly in love with you. Will you do me the honor of being my wife?"

She clasps her hand to her mouth and nods as tears streak down her cheeks. "I would be honored to be Mrs. Modern Gentleman."

Laughing, I slide a stunning diamond solitaire onto her finger, rise, and kiss the red lipstick off her lips.

"Mrs. Jason Reynolds works too," I murmur. "And so does Truly Goodman, as long as you're mine."

"Always. I'm always yours."

When we reach the twelfth floor, I take her to a suite, and we enjoy reason number five thousand, two hundred, forty-five.

EPILOGUE

The next weekend

"Dude! You're a rock star. I can't thank you enough." Eddie lumbers over to me on the lawn, clasps my hand, and pumps it up and down.

Admittedly, I was a little surprised to receive an invitation to his wedding, but weddings can be fun. I said yes, especially since Troy is working undercover at this one, albeit in a new capacity. He'll be rapping though, so some things never change.

"I'm not sure what you have to thank me for, but I'm just happy to be invited."

He gapes at me, sweeping his long hair off his forehead. "Are you kidding? If you didn't turn down Randy, I'd never have had a chance to score with such a smart and sexy babe."

He tips his forehead to the bride-to-be, the redhead

from Gavin's wedding who wanted to fuck me and my accent.

She rushes over in her dress, a tight white number that's plastered like a bandage around her body. Guess they aren't doing the whole *don't see the bride before the ceremony* bit either. "Jay Bond," she purrs. "I'm so glad you never gave me your digits. If you had, who knows what would have happened? Instead, I went home with this total babe. And he's all mine now, with all his crazy scars."

He winks at his bride. "I've got some new ones thanks to her."

She smacks his shoulder playfully. "And bite marks. Don't forget the bite marks."

"Bite marks, scratch marks, rope burn, you name it," Eddie says, grabbing her arm and dropping his mouth to her neck, ready to give her a vampire's kiss.

She shoos him away. "Don't mess up my hair before the ceremony!"

He snaps to attention. "You're right. I'll mess it up later."

She drags a finger down his shirt. "You better."

And yes, it seems Eddie indeed found his perfect, unfiltered match. He looks my way. "And thanks for doing me the solid with the Troy hookup. He rocks."

"He does. And I'm thrilled for you and Randy. You guys really are perfect for each other," I quip.

Randy squeezes his arm. "We are. Know what my favorite thing about Eddie is?"

I shake my head, sending a prayer to the gods of polite discourse than I'm not about to hear her top ten naughty nights out with him. "You don't really have to tell me."

"I'm going to anyway."

"No, seriously. You don't."

She smacks my chest. "I do, I do. My favorite thing is he loves to cook me dinner. When I come home from a hard day at work, because managing mutual funds all day is exhausting, the last thing I want to do is cook. But he cooks gourmet meals for me. And that's not all. He also loves to rub my feet. Did I score or what?"

That's thoroughly unexpected—her two favorite things, as well as her job.

"I'd say you did," I say with a smile, filing away this latest bit of data about couples. There is often so much more to a couple than you see. You might think you know one thing about them—they're filthy mouthed, they like pugs, she's the quintessential older woman and he looks like a boy toy, but beneath it all, there's more that makes them tick.

Art and foot rubs, love and patience, heart and soul.

I catch sight of Truly standing under a tree, chatting with Troy. She's making small talk with my former subcontractor, looking effortlessly beautiful as she sweeps a few strands of hair off her cheek, tucking them behind her ear.

Once again, I'm keenly aware of how stunning she is, inside and out. How she's now mine, and I'm so damn grateful my friends and my sister didn't let me walk away from the best thing that ever happened to me. I almost let her slip through my fingers because of business, because I was stubborn, and because I was afraid.

But I have her now, and I plan to keep making her happy every day.

We're one of *those couples* now. We share a passion for work, humor, sarcasm, hobbies, fitness, and of course, we connect in the bedroom. We're connected on so many levels, it's like we were meant to be.

But I suppose that's how you should feel when you fall in mad love with a very good friend.

I head over to join my fiancée, dropping a kiss to her cheek.

After we take our seats and the bride joins the groom at the front of the lawn, Troy, now an internet-ordained minister, clears his throat and proceeds to rap their wedding vows, as only Troy can do.

"Dearly beloved, we are gathered here today in the sight of God to join this man and this woman in holy matrimony. Not to be entered into lightly, holy matrimony should be entered into solemnly and with reverence and honor. If any person here can show just cause why these two people should not be joined in holy matrimony, speak now or forever hold your peace."

I can't think of any reason to speak now.

Also, as Sully would say, the man has skills.

ANOTHER EPILOGUE

Truly

A year later

Soft French music filters through the bar. Antique curios and a collection of old clocks line the shelves. The plush sofas in the lounge that hearken back to Belle Époque era are my favorite kind—full.

As in full of patrons, sipping drinks with names like Mais Oui and C'est La Vie.

Bisou is ours, mine and Charlotte's, and I'm so damn glad the deal with Darren fell through. We did this. We built this, and it's thriving thanks to a couple of savvy businesswomen.

Tonight, though, this savvy businesswoman needs to talk to a friend.

Because when Presley walks in, slumps on a stool, and heaves a sigh, all my friend antennae twitch an alert.

"Let me guess. Guy trouble?"

"How could you tell?" She pretends to sniff her shirt. "Is it a new scent I'm giving off?"

"No, but that would be a fun name for a drink. Note to self: craft a new cocktail named Guy Trouble."

"Yeah, and serve it to me," she says as she drags a hand through her chestnut hair.

I grab a bottle of tequila. "Any drink named Guy Trouble should start with tequila."

"Because tequila burns?"

"It sure does."

"Just like exes."

I arch a curious brow. "Ex as in the most recent ex, or someone else?"

She takes a beat, her jaw tight. "Ex as in way back. All the way back. Remember Hunter?"

I nearly drop the bottle. "Hunter? Hunter as in *the* Hunter?"

She scoff-laughs. "Yep. *The* Hunter."

"That was more than ten years ago. How is he giving you trouble now? You haven't heard a word from him. I thought he was in Nepal or New Zealand or wherever his show takes him."

"He's always somewhere, except now, he's going to be here." She stabs the counter with her finger. "My boss just contracted with him to work on a huge new project. Guess who else is heading up that huge new project?"

"Um, gee. Could it be you?"

She lets her face fall to the bar. "I need a double."

"Double trouble."

"Yes, that's exactly what he is." She lifts her face. "Have I mentioned he's still gorgeous?"

"You don't have to. I see him on billboards."

"You're not helpful."

I waggle the bottle. "Oh, yes, I am. Because I have the tequila. Let's mix up your Guy Trouble and come up with a plan."

After all, I'm on the other side of guy trouble. And if I can help a friend figure out her boy problems, I'm more than happy to do that. Especially since my biggest boy problem these days is how I'm going to fit through the doorway. One baby boy is nearly done baking in my belly, and I can't wait to meet my son someday soon, hopefully before I can no longer reach past my belly to pour drinks.

Jason was all too happy to pay up on that bet with his coworker. After all, a gentleman always makes good on his wagers.

AND ONE MORE EPILOGUE

Truly

The number of things a woman will do to impress a man can be quite extensive.

They border on the ridiculous (waking up twenty minutes early to put on a full face of makeup lest he see you less than perfect) to the insane (claiming you like preseason basketball).

No one enjoys preseason basketball.

Also . . . dog-earing the pages of *Zen and the Art of Motorcycle Maintenance* so it looks like you read it? Or declaring you dig Bret Easton Ellis?

Ladies, we can do better.

That means you shouldn't ever feel pressured to say, "Sure, I'll be happy to watch *Blade Runner* with you."

You never have to pretend you like that film.

Fortunately, I don't have to fake it on any of these, and I'm grateful. When I talk to women at one of my two bars (Bisou and Gin Joint are rocking hard. Yay, woman power!), I tell them the same.

When they ask for advice, because that's just something they all want from the master mixologist pouring their drinks, the main thing I tell women is this: *be yourself.*

After all, don't you want a guy or gal to love you for you?

That's what I have with my man. Jason loves all my quirks, all my insanity, and everything that makes me . . . *me.*

That's the coolest thing. Because when you find the person who's your perfect match, you also find you're not so inclined to spend all hours curled up with a computer or a spreadsheet.

But my husband?

Oh yes. I like spending my nights with him, and my mornings too. Especially when we're making pancakes.

I might be referring to the song.

It might also be a euphemism for something else we do a lot of.

After all, we're still madly in love, and this kind of love is the ultimate instant gratification.

THE END

Eager for Presley's romance? Grab the next book in this series FREE IN KU, the second chance romance **PS It's Always Been You!**

The entire Always Satisfied Series is FREE IN KU!

Satisfaction Guaranteed: Lessons in Seduction/Workplace Romance

Never Have I Ever: Enemies-to-Lovers/Forced Proximity

Instant Gratification: Friends to Lovers/Fake Dating

PS It's Always Been You: Second Chance Romance

Want more of the whole Instant Gratification gang? Sign up here to receive a bonus scene featuring five couples sent straight to your inbox!

BE A LOVELY

Want to be the first to know of sales, new releases, special deals and giveaways? Sign up for my newsletter today!

Want to be part of a fun, feel-good place to talk about books and romance, and get sneak peeks of covers and advance copies of my books? Be a Lovely!

ACKNOWLEDGMENTS

Big thanks to Lauren Clarke, Jen McCoy, Helen Williams, Kim Bias, Virginia, Lynn, Karen, Tiffany, Janice, Stephanie and more for their eyes. Big thanks to Helen for the beautiful cover. Thank you to Kelley and Candi, KP and Jenn. Massive hugs to Laurelin Paige. As always, my readers make everything possible. Songs referenced in this book are in the public domain. The exception is the pancake song. That is written by Andi Arndt. Who is awesome.

MORE BOOKS BY LAUREN

I've written more than 100 books! **All of these titles below are FREE in Kindle Unlimited**!

Double Pucked

A sexy, outrageous MFM hockey romantic comedy!

Puck Yes

A fake marriage, spicy MFM hockey rom com!

Thoroughly Pucked

A brother's best friends +runaway bride, spicy MFM hockey rom com!

The Virgin Society Series

Meet the Virgin Society – great friends who'd do anything for each other. Indulge in these forbidden, emotionally-charged, and wildly sexy age-gap romances!

The RSVP

The Tryst

The Tease

The Dating Games Series

A fun, sexy romantic comedy series about friends in the city and their dating mishaps!

The Virgin Next Door

Two A Day

The Good Guy Challenge

How To Date Series (New and ongoing)

Four great friends. Four chances to learn how to date again. Four standalone romantic comedies full of love, sex and meet-cute shenanigans.

My So-Called Sex Life

Plays Well With Others

The Almost Romantic

The Accidental Dating Experiment (coming in June 2024)

A romantic comedy adventure standalone

A Real Good Bad Thing

Boyfriend Material

Four fabulous heroines. Four outrageous proposals. Four chances at love in this sexy rom-com series!

Asking For a Friend

Sex and Other Shiny Objects

One Night Stand-In

Overnight Service

Big Rock Series

My #1 New York Times Bestselling sexy as sin, irreverent, male-POV romantic comedy!

Big Rock

Mister O

Well Hung

Full Package

Joy Ride

Hard Wood

Happy Endings Series

Romance starts with a bang in this series of standalones following a group of friends seeking and avoiding love!

Come Again

Shut Up and Kiss Me

Kismet

My Single-Versary

Ballers And Babes

Sexy sports romance standalones guaranteed to make you hot!

Most Valuable Playboy

Most Likely to Score

A Wild Card Kiss

Rules of Love Series

Athlete, virgins and weddings!

The Virgin Rule Book

The Virgin Game Plan

The Virgin Replay

The Virgin Scorecard

The Extravagant Series

Bodyguards, billionaires and hoteliers in this sexy, high-stakes series of standalones!

One Night Only

One Exquisite Touch

My One-Week Husband

The Guys Who Got Away Series

Friends in New York City and California fall in love in this fun and hot rom-com series!

Birthday Suit

Dear Sexy Ex-Boyfriend

The What If Guy

Thanks for Last Night

The Dream Guy Next Door

Always Satisfied Series

A group of friends in New York City find love and laughter in this series of sexy standalones!

Satisfaction Guaranteed

Never Have I Ever

Instant Gratification

PS It's Always Been You

The Gift Series

An after dark series of standalones! Explore your fantasies!

The Engagement Gift

The Virgin Gift

The Decadent Gift

The Heartbreakers Series

Three brothers. Three rockers. Three standalone sexy romantic comedies.

Once Upon a Real Good Time

Once Upon a Sure Thing

Once Upon a Wild Fling

Sinful Men

A high-stakes, high-octane, sexy-as-sin romantic suspense series!

My Sinful Nights

My Sinful Desire

My Sinful Longing

My Sinful Love

My Sinful Temptation

From Paris With Love

Swoony, sweeping romances set in Paris!

Wanderlust

Part-Time Lover

One Love Series

A group of friends in New York falls in love one by one in this sexy rom-com series!

The Sexy One

The Hot One

The Knocked Up Plan

Come As You Are

Lucky In Love Series

A small town romance full of heat and blue collar heroes and sexy heroines!

Best Laid Plans

The Feel Good Factor

Nobody Does It Better

Unzipped

No Regrets

An angsty, sexy, emotional, new adult trilogy about one young couple fighting to break free of their pasts!

The Start of Us

The Thrill of It

Every Second With You

The Caught Up in Love Series

A group of friends finds love!

The Pretending Plot

The Dating Proposal

The Second Chance Plan

The Private Rehearsal

Seductive Nights Series

A high heat series full of danger and spice!

Night After Night

After This Night

One More Night

A Wildly Seductive Night

Joy Delivered Duet

A high-heat, wickedly sexy series of standalones that will set your sheets on fire!

Nights With Him

Forbidden Nights

Unbreak My Heart

A standalone second chance emotional roller coaster of a
romance

The Muse

A magical realism romance set in Paris

**Good Love Series of sexy rom-coms co-written with Lili
Valente!**

I also write MM romance under the name L. Blakely!

Hopelessly Bromantic Duet (MM)

Roomies to lovers to enemies to fake boyfriends

Hopelessly Bromantic

Here Comes My Man

Men of Summer Series (MM)

Two baseball players on the same team fall in love in a
forbidden romance spanning five epic years

Scoring With Him

Winning With Him

All In With Him

MM Standalone Novels

A Guy Walks Into My Bar

The Bromance Zone

One Time Only

The Best Men (Co-written with Sarina Bowen)

Winner Takes All Series (MM)

A series of emotionally-charged and irresistibly sexy standalone MM sports romances!

The Boyfriend Comeback

Turn Me On

A Very Filthy Game

Limited Edition Husband

Manhandled

If you want a personalized recommendation, email me at laurenblakelybooks@gmail.com!

CONTACT

I love hearing from readers! You can find me on Twitter at LaurenBlakely3, Instagram at LaurenBlakelyBooks, Facebook at LaurenBlakelyBooks, or online at LaurenBlakely.com. You can also email me at laurenblakelybooks@gmail.com

Made in the USA
Columbia, SC
07 March 2024

32835121R00200